Bronstein's
Children

Bronstein's Children

Jurek Becker

Translated by
Leila Vennewitz

A Helen and Kurt Wolff Book
Harcourt Brace Jovanovich, Publishers
San Diego   New York   London

Copyright © 1986 by Suhrkamp Verlag
English translation copyright © 1988 by
Harcourt Brace Jovanovich, Inc.

Library of Congress Cataloging-in-Publication Data
Becker, Jurek, 1937–
Bronstein's children.
Translation of: Bronsteins Kinder.
"A Helen and Kurt Wolff book."
I. Title.
PT2662.E294B7613   1988   833'.914   88-3314
ISBN 0-15-114350-1

Designed by Kingsley Parker / Design Oasis
Printed in the United States of America

First edition

A B C D E

for Christine

Translator's Acknowledgment

To my husband, William—my deep gratitude for the knowledge, advice, and assistance with which he has accompanied me throughout the work of this translation.

Leila Vennewitz

Bronstein's
Children

A year ago my father suffered the worst imaginable trauma: he died. The event—or we might as well say, the disaster—took place on August 4, 1973, a Saturday. I had seen it coming.

Since then I have been living with Hugo and Rahel Lepschitz, and with their daughter, Martha. They know nothing about the background of events that culminated in my father's death; as far as they are concerned, he simply died of a heart attack. Hugo Lepschitz said at the time that the son of his best friend was as dear to him as one of his own would have been, so they took me into their home. And yet the two men had met scarcely a dozen times in their lives, and if they had even the slightest mutual affection, they concealed it like a buried treasure.

That was a time when you could have done anything with me—taken me in, sent me away, put me to bed—anything but question me. By the time I more or less came to my senses again, our home—Father's and mine—had been broken up, and I was lying on the Lepschitz family's couch being stroked by Martha, with the TV turned on.

For days the weather hasn't let up. What a May! I can feel life returning to me—a prickling in my head, the gray cells stirring. It won't be long now before I can think again. The year of mourning is coming to an end. If I were summoned before the golden throne and asked what I wished for most, I wouldn't have to think twice: Give me a heart of stone! What other people achieve with their emotions, I would say, I'd like to accomplish with my reason. In future I won't care who dies on me; never again will I put up with a year like this past one.

My move to the Lepschitzes' can only have been Martha's doing. After she took me home from Father's funeral with its handful of sad little Jews, and saw me sitting there in the empty room, her heart must have burst with pity. In those days we were terribly in love. I've no doubt she meant well, even though today everything is over between us. Now when she comes into the room, I immediately wonder whether there isn't something for me to do outside. Since I've been living here, our ardor has evaporated, and you need sharp eyes indeed to discern even a vestige of it.

I haven't the courage to look around for a new girlfriend. I picture what would happen if one day I were to turn up here with a Jutta or a Gertrud—how Rahel Lepschitz would bury her face in her hands, how Hugo Lepschitz would shake his head over such ingratitude, and how Martha would try with unblinking eyes to behave as though it was the most ordinary thing in the world.

So what it boils down to is that I have the choice of forgetting about a certain kind of pastime or of moving out. Or things with Martha will right themselves. But I don't see that happening. In those days it didn't matter to me that she was a year and a half older than I was, and that some people were surprised that such a mature, adult person should waste her time with a childish creature like me. Today she seems to me like an old woman.

A year ago I would have bet anything that we would have three kids and that a lifetime of happiness lay in store for us.

A year ago I trembled at the mere sight of her coming around the corner.

I am grateful for every chore I am allowed to perform. At first I wasn't even permitted to carry coal up from the cellar, as if idleness were the best therapy for a patient like me. Whenever I wanted to take a bath, Hugo Lepschitz had to go down into the cellar and, with his puny little arms, lug coal up the stairs for the boiler. Out of sheer pity I almost stopped taking baths. In the meantime, things have improved to the point where I am even allowed to prepare supper and set the table.

I set the table. They watch TV as they do every evening. They know of no more agreeable occupation than looking for likenesses between faces on the screen and those of people they know. I can only be amazed at the vastness of their circle of acquaintances, for every evening they score hits. Once someone was supposed to look like my father, but I didn't want to interrupt my reading.

They sit at the supper table so that the TV set remains in their line of vision. Lepschitz asks his wife where Martha is; she doesn't know. He bites so vigorously into a piece of matzo that a rain of crumbs is scattered over the table. Somewhere in town there is a store that sells Hungarian matzos. Father went there only once or twice a year, but Lepschitz insists on having these brittle matzos on the table every evening. I had always found that store rather odd: no oranges, no beef, no tomatoes, but matzos for Hugo Lepschitz.

"I've been meaning to ask you something," he says as he chews.

I have never felt so uncomfortable in this apartment; yet nothing has happened. Time has passed—that's all—much too much time. There is a crackling in my head. Not that I hate the couple, God forbid; it's just that I don't love them all that much and I'd like to get away and don't know how.

"You're not eating," says Rahel Lepschitz.

The TV program is about back trouble: a red-haired man explains how the pain can be reduced by strengthening the dorsal muscles. And a young woman in a leotard demonstrates the appropriate exercises. In Rahel Lepschitz's eyes, this is nothing but a scam. Her husband asks: "Where's the scam?"

"Exercises like that," she says, "can only be done by someone who has no back pain. You might just as well advise a person with one leg to run ten kilometers a day."

How would someone living as I do, like a housefly, find a new girlfriend? I attempt nothing, so nothing can go wrong and nothing can take a surprising turn for the good—I'm not yet twenty, for God's sake! My father, who wasn't all that active himself, would never have stood for this. He would have insisted that I keep moving, that I leave the apartment at least once a day. He was a prodder. How old can a person be and still be called an orphan? When you're sixty and your parents are no longer alive, nobody's going to be very surprised, but where do they draw the line?

"I've been meaning to ask you something," says Lepschitz. "For several weeks now, it's been obvious that there's something wrong between you and Martha. Is there some way we can help?"

"Please, Hugo," says his wife.

"No, there isn't," I say.

The question makes it clear that Martha hasn't confided in them, and I'm not surprised. At the time, they must have believed they were taking into their home their daughter's great love, Martha's one and only. Suddenly, instead, they are saddled with a boarder, a sad sack of a boarder who doesn't have enough tact to make himself scarce after love has grown cold. The TV gymnast resembles a woman in the

4

building across the courtyard; I'm surprised they don't notice this.

"You must understand," says Rahel Lepschitz, "that we're concerned."

"Of course."

Every day I expect a letter from the university. I haven't much doubt I'll be accepted; my grades are good, and both my parents were victims of the Nazi regime. So what can go wrong? I intend to major in philosophy.

If Father had had his way, I would have to study medicine; he always wanted an internist for a son. But he's not having his way, so I'm going to study philosophy, with no idea what it's all about.

"You can trust us. Who else can you talk to?"

"That's true," I say.

"Well then?"

"We're no longer attracted to each other," I say.

After living here for ten days, I sat down and figured out how much a month it would cost them to keep me. This was my supreme effort of the past year. Since then I have been transferring a certain sum to their bank on the first of every month. In the beginning they refused to accept a penny, but I couldn't allow that, and not just because I have five times as much money in the bank as they do. I argued that no relationship can last in which all the sacrifices are made by only one side. Martha, who happened to be listening to us, murmured something about "precocious." After Lepschitz had haggled thirty marks off, they agreed.

"Why won't you answer?"

Like a rescuing angel Martha floats into the room. She floats past my back, tapping me lightly on the shoulder, kisses her mother, kisses her father, and lands securely on a chair. Myriad drops shine in her hair, which is brown and smooth

5

and inordinately long. I realize that at the mention of her appearance, I still sound like a lover. She apologizes for being late and tells us who held her up.

"We were just talking about you," I say.

This is not nice, of course it isn't, I say it more out of spite than for the sake of clarification.

"It wasn't that important," whispers her mother.

"I told them we're no longer attracted to each other," I say casually.

Her father sends out waves of displeasure, but I refuse to be intimidated. I read once in a Russian book that people who have trouble coping with themselves tend to be spiteful.

"They'll have noticed that even without your explanation," says Martha.

"Well, they didn't."

"But how could that happen?" asks her mother, seizing the opportunity.

Martha and I look at each other for a long time after this question, and, believe it or not, we smile. "Just look at those two," I hear Lepschitz burst out. Where does this remnant of affection suddenly come from, this residue in a pot I had thought was empty? The smile shows me that we can never be enemies, and Martha must be thinking exactly the same thing, to judge by her eyes.

"Just look at them," says Lepschitz.

My room is as crowded as a Number 9 bus. Every object is in its place, yet in the way; I brought too much. I had to leave behind so much stuff that I was incapable of judging my real needs. With record cabinet, dresser, armchair, chest, desk, library stepladder, rocking chair, all I have ended up with is too little space. For months I have been laughing about the stepladder, yet at the time it was nothing but a dark brown object that my father bought for a song in a junk

6

shop, when I happened to be with him. There are similar explanations for almost everything else. The only thing I might one day find useful is the desk.

I lie down on the bed, as I do ten times a day. I turn on the record player to drown out the sounds of the family. Sometimes I feel that my helplessness in those days can't be explained by grief alone. The situation was more than I could handle, and, although my father's death cost me about half my reason, the fact remains that even the two halves together wouldn't have been enough. But I don't find it so odd that someone whose father has been dead for a few days and whose mother has been dead for years and whose sister is in a mental home and who has only just finished school doesn't always do the right thing. Yet a few mistakes less would still have been plenty, I must admit, and one mistake in particular was too many: I should never have sold the cottage. Giving up the apartment was okay—they talked me into that—but to get rid of the cottage was unforgivable.

For days on end I had to listen to: *Why should you saddle yourself with that shack way out of town? It's much too isolated to live there. Don't forget you're only eighteen. Sell it, my boy; not only will it bring you in some money but you'll have disposed of a problem.* That sounded sensible enough.

If I still owned it, that cottage, the world would be a different place today for Martha and me. I won't say we would never have had our differences, but the end of all our efforts would not have come so soon. I'm sure of that. No place on earth was more important to us. It was in that cottage in the forest that we touched for the first time, I mean touched each other, and it was only there that shyness and embarrassment were dispelled. A decision to go out to the cottage always meant we were going there to make love. No one can imagine the elation I felt on my way to the cottage.

These days a writer spends his weekends there. A few

weeks after my move, Martha gave up her study of Germanistics and entered drama school. That was the next disaster. With incredible speed, she lost one attractive quality after another. She started using strange words, rolling her eyes, reading different books, using eye shadow from "the West." And from one day to the next she stopped wearing a skirt and switched entirely to slacks. If the cottage had still been there for us, I might have been able to do something about it.

I have the only vaguest idea of what happened to my father and, after his death, to me too. I suppose one must begin by creating the clearest possible picture of the events that should be erased from one's memory; and this probably applies even more to the memories one wishes to preserve. But I simply let everything wash over me, the memories came and went at random, while I just sat there.

Martha comes into my room and asks whether I wouldn't like to have a glass of wine with them.

"A person isn't just a riverbed, is he?" I say.

"A what?"

"A person isn't a riverbed."

"When did you find that out?"

"This very moment."

She nods and goes out again, as if she has received the information she wanted.

I used to go out to the cottage without Father's knowledge. I asked him for the key, but he wouldn't give it to me, saying that right now it surely wasn't too much to ask for me to stop fooling around and get down to some studying. Yet with only two tests left, my final exams were almost over. I was sure he didn't like Martha, although there seemed no reason.

The first time I was refused, I took the key and went to the locksmith to have a duplicate made. After that, I could decide for myself when to go to the cottage, even though I always asked permission.

Martha and I became expert in removing traces; my father never had the slightest suspicion. Not that we took any special care while we were in the cottage, but before we left everything was put back in its place, every hair picked up, and the radio turned back to the old station. Our efforts were excessive, because Father seldom went out there; besides, he was trusting by nature. But Martha insisted. Now and then he allowed friends to stay in the cottage for a few days. Once, we were lying in bed when we heard someone at the door trying to get in. Never have I seen Martha so relieved as when it turned out to be a burglar. I climbed out the window and, grasping a heavy stick, crept up to him from behind. He fled in terror and was three times as scared as I was.

Behind me in the interurban train, someone was listening to the news: Secretary-General Walter Ulbricht's condition was still serious, and those goddamn French had set off another of their hydrogen bombs in the South Pacific. Someone muttered that the Russians were no better. It was a Sunday.

For once we didn't go together. Martha had promised to drop off a book at the home of a friend in the suburbs, so we agreed to meet at the cottage. I was early, either from impatience or in the hope that she might get there sooner than expected. Because love made us hungry, I had brought some sandwiches. We had to take the train to Erkner, then a bus to Neu-Zittau, and after that there was still a twenty-minute walk through the forest.

Father had bought the cottage when I was a baby and Mother was still alive. He must have been rolling in money at the time. The cottage itself may not have been all that expensive, but the renovations must have cost a fortune: pure copper gutters were fitted to the roof, because galvanized iron was unobtainable in the fifties; three of the four rooms were paneled in beech; each room was equipped with electric floor heating. The first time Martha saw the cottage, she was so impressed she forgot I was there.

Father never told me how he acquired his wealth, long since used up, but from remarks dropped carelessly through the years I got some idea. Right after the war he must have been involved in some shady business. Not that he was one of those fellows with a turned-up coat collar who sold their stuff on the black market and in dark doorways—far from it. He was probably involved in deals between the military occupation zones—buying goods that Western dealers were not allowed to supply to the East and spiriting them across the border. Steel, for instance. Occasionally I heard him say: "Things weren't always as cut and dried as they are today, my friend." And once when I asked him to come to my

10

school and, as a living witness, tell the history class about the postwar period, he looked at the kitchen dresser, sighed, and said: "Now he's really taken leave of his senses."

A special feature of this forest was that it often smelled of mushrooms—great quantities of morels and chanterelles—although scarcely one was to be found. People were always showing up with empty baskets, kitchen knives, and disappointed expressions, especially on weekends.

From some way off I could see that the day was ruined. A car, a revolting yellow car, was parked outside the cottage; it belonged to Gordon Kwart, a friend of my father's. I couldn't understand why Father had kept quiet about his visitor, lecturing me instead about my exams. I had to keep out of sight, for of course Kwart would report me to Father. And the obvious next step would be the question: What was I doing hanging around the cottage without the key? So I thought I might as well walk to meet Martha, curse my father, and consider what to do with the rest of Sunday. I threw away the sandwiches.

After about ten steps, I decided to turn back. I approached the wall of the cottage and listened. Martha might already have arrived and, suspecting nothing, be waiting for me inside. Or Kwart might be making a brief visit and soon be off again.

Below my favorite window, through which the trunks of the pine trees look like a solid fence, I pressed my ear to the wall and tried to screen out the sounds of the forest. Seconds later I heard a little scream, not especially alarming. I must have smiled, thinking: That fellow Kwart! For the scream sounded to me like the love-making kind, and Kwart was almost as old as my father, in his late fifties, probably.

Then came a second scream, a little louder, and this time it had nothing to do with passion, but, rather, with pain. I was scared at the sudden unknown goings-on in our cottage.

11

An agitated voice, which I didn't recognize, called out something. I took the key from my pocket, opened the door, and stood in the dark hallway. The movement was coming from the main room, but the door was closed. There were plenty of reasons not to fling it open and call out: What's going on here? I stepped into the corner behind the wardrobe, the only piece of furniture in the hallway, and got a second shock. There was a smell of urine.

By then I was determined to speak to Father about this outrage, even if it meant revealing my betrayal of his trust. And if I was really prepared to do that, I thought, moments later, then I could also confront Kwart here and now, for dirtying our nice cottage, the pig. We would have to air it for weeks in order to breathe in it without wanting to throw up!

Then I heard Father say: "Can we go on now?"

That was the worst: my father beyond the door.

The answer was a low, drawn-out whimpering that sounded as if someone were searching for a difficult musical note.

A man whose voice I didn't know said: "Give him a little time."

My father said, in a loud, reproachful voice: "He's had enough time."

There must be at least four of them in the room, I thought: my father, Kwart (silent, so far), the stranger who had spoken, and this person they were talking to. After all, it couldn't have been Kwart who had whimpered like that.

I heard my father say: "For the last time, are you going to talk?"

"What do you want to hear?" someone asked in a scared voice.

The first unfamiliar voice: "How many of them were there?"

12

"Eight or nine. I already said that."

"You'll say it as often as you're asked."

"Eight, then?" asked my father. "Or nine?"

"Eight," came the answer after a pause.

"Who picked out the men?"

"I don't know."

I heard a sound that was unmistakably a blow, a dull thud on back or chest; it was also obvious from the groans that followed. My God, who was hitting whom? Never in my life had my father laid a hand on me. And who was the victim? A few old men had apparently lost their senses and were behaving like the heroes of a nightmare. They were holding someone by force, grilling him, and were not satisfied with the answers. That much was clear.

Out of the bathroom—no, the kitchen—came Gordon Kwart. The wardrobe no longer hid me. He saw me instantly and raised indignant eyebrows.

"What are you doing here?" he asked.

"What am I doing here?" I said, as brazenly as possible. "This is my house too, you know."

But he wasn't going to accept any sophistry and shouted: "Arno!"

The hope that the room might contain a man with a voice amazingly like my father's was shattered. There was no point in trying to knock Kwart down and escape; I would have had to kill him.

My father opened the door to the room. He looked toward Kwart; I was still in my hiding place, not visible to him. He looked exhausted and surly. The part of the room I could see was empty, but the smell came from there.

Kwart indicated me with his chin, saying: "We have a visitor."

Father strode across. I cursed my curiosity when I saw how the sight of me shocked him. His shirt was soaked with sweat;

13

wet patches reached from his armpits down to his hips. Kwart stood there irresolutely as if wondering whether it wouldn't be better to leave father and son alone.

My father grabbed me by the collar so violently that a button came off and a seam tore audibly. We stood for a long time face to face, myself a head taller. His teeth were clenched as if in a vise. Finally he thrust me against the wall; then he let go and buried his hands in his pockets, as if to restrain himself from an unconsidered action. At last Kwart disappeared, perhaps merely to close the door so I couldn't see inside.

I was sure that the first question Father would ask me would be how I had got into the house, and I decided to stick to the truth. I was much too confused to invent a good story. I put my hand in my pocket, meaning to reply by pulling out the key. Instead, he asked: "How long have you been standing here?"

"Long enough," I said, letting go of the key.

"What does that mean?"

"Who was that screaming?" I asked.

Then something completely crazy happened. He hugged me. What had I done to endear myself? I could feel his heart pounding. I heard him whisper sadly: "Oh, Hans, Hans . . ." which meant: What devil had to bring you here? When he let go of me, his face had resumed its look of fury.

"Why aren't you at home studying?" he asked.

"Because I know everything," I said.

Father made a strange grimace, sucking his lips deep into his mouth and squeezing his eyes shut. He stood there nodding his head, looking more at a loss than I had ever seen him. His decision to take me by the arm and usher me into the room must have been a hard one.

"This is my son," he said.

The explanation was directed at two strangers, who were

14

staring at me. One of them stood beside Kwart at the window. He was at least seventy years old, stout, tall, and bald-headed except for a narrow fringe of snow-white hair. Spectacles were pushed up on his forehead. The other man seemed to be a few years younger. He was the one who stank; his shirt, once white, was stiff with spilled food. He was sitting in an uncomfortable position on an iron bed, his feet bound together with a leather belt looped around one of the bedposts. Although he could move his hands freely, this was obviously temporary, for hanging from the bedstead were handcuffs, with the key in place. The bed didn't belong in the room; I had never seen it before.

The stranger by the window asked Father: "Why did you have to bring him here?"

"I didn't," said my father.

"So how come he's here?"

"Ask him!"

There was a chamber pot under the bed, and on the prisoner's pants, between his legs, a wet patch—I couldn't help looking. On the mattress were some dark spots, probably blood. It went through my mind that I had last seen Father a few hours before, at home, and that I hadn't noticed anything unusual about him.

"We are waiting for your explanation," Father said. The man on the bed couldn't decide whether I was friend or foe; yet the fact that my turning up was making the three men uneasy seemed to give him a ray of hope. We couldn't stop staring at each other. Suddenly I knew that I must not betray the presence of the key in my pocket.

"He wouldn't tell me either," Kwart said to Father.

They must have so intimidated the man that he didn't dare remove the strap around his feet, although his hands were free. To me he said: "These men have kidnapped me, and now they're torturing me."

15

"Who's torturing?" Kwart asked from the window.

After a moment's silence, my father walked over to the bed, struck the prisoner's chest a few times with the back of his hand, and asked grimly, as if for the last time: "Are we torturing you?"

"No."

Father glanced at me, saw my horrified expression, and turned back to the man. "Now tell him why you're here."

The man answered reluctantly: "Because I . . ."

At that moment I knew what it was all about.

With every syllable, Father jabbed his finger at the man's breastbone as he prompted him: "Because I . . ."

". . . was a concentration-camp guard," the man finished.

"And where was that?"

"In Neuengamme."

"And now tell him what Neuengamme means."

"I know what it means," I said.

"Just a moment," said the stranger at the window to Father. "Does that mean there are now four of us?"

"Well, he's here now," said my father angrily.

All the monstrousness was perfectly camouflaged in the camp guard's face, behind a deeply lined forehead, gray dark-circled eyes with no brows, a stubble of beard just beginning to curl, a small pale mouth that barely opened even when he spoke.

"I can see that for myself," said the man at the window. "But where do we go from here?"

"Have you any suggestion?" Father asked him.

I had seen such people only in photos and grim movies, but now he was sitting as large as life on the bed, looking disappointingly feeble.

"These gentlemen refuse to accept that in those days there was a different law," he said.

16

My father pointed his finger threateningly at him.

"Don't ever utter the word 'law' again in my presence!"

I wasn't sure whether he was playing the role of spokesman or whether his behavior was merely due to my presence.

"How did he get in?" the stranger asked my father. "I thought you had the only key."

"You're getting on my nerves," said Father. "You want to find out something from him, yet you keep asking me."

"I happened to be walking past, and the door was ajar," I said.

"The door was ajar?"

Both men cast withering looks at Kwart, who promptly shook his head. "Impossible," he said. "I closed it. Don't I know how to close a door?"

"So how did he get in? Through the chimney?"

"How should I know?"

In all this confusion, the thought of Martha was the only bright spot, my only consolation. Perhaps she was already somewhere near the cottage, waiting impatiently for a signal from me. I had to go to her; the only question was, would they try to stop me? This stranger and Kwart and Father were involved in something that required the utmost caution, but it was unthinkable that they would use force against me, Arno's son.

"Tell the truth, boy," said Kwart. "How did you get into the house?"

"I already told you."

"But the door wasn't ajar."

Kwart looked at me in disappointment. Suddenly he turned to Father. "I'd like to see what's in his pockets."

"What could there be in his pockets?"

"That's what I want to see."

The prisoner was sitting bolt upright with tension.

Father didn't seem convinced by Kwart's proposal. He asked me: "Do you have anything in your pockets that might interest us?"

"No."

"A key perhaps?"

"No."

"I believe him," Father said to Kwart. "If you're not satisfied with his answer, you'll have to deal with him yourself."

I considered which of two possibilities was the better: to say that I wanted to leave now and leave, or simply to leave. The first seemed to me a shade more conciliatory, so I said: "I have to leave now."

Without waiting for their consent, I walked to the door, not looking at anyone of course. The stranger rushed over from the window and blocked my way, saying to Father: "He can't just leave like that before we've decided anything!"

I walked around him, out of the room, and out of the cottage. Behind me, voices continued, but I was so concerned with leaving that I didn't catch the meaning of the words.

What was best was the air outside. I peered behind a few bushes and softly called Martha's name, knowing I was probably being watched through the window. When it became obvious that Martha hadn't turned up, I started off toward the bus stop; that way I couldn't miss her.

I had believed that after thirty years they could live like normal people, and then suddenly that room: as if for thirty years they had merely been waiting for a chance like this; as if, behaving normally, they had only been wearing masks.

I made up my mind to persuade Martha to do in the forest what was impossible to do in the cottage now; I could think of no better distraction. I was sure she wouldn't resist if I could bring myself to suggest it. I tested the forest floor; it was dry as tinder. The idea excited me. We had never made love outdoors. Whenever we were in a forest, it was this one,

18

and the empty cottage was always close by. I remembered a good spot, over toward Wernsdorf, where we would be as hidden from view as if behind seven walls. At the most inappropriate moments, Martha liked to tease me about my shyness. The sky looked as though the sun would go on shining for years.

One thing needed to be decided at once, however: whether or not I should tell her about what I had seen. At first I thought: Absolutely. Then: Absolutely not. My decision changed from step to step, but not as the result of deep thought, for I wasn't thinking at all. When I realized that we couldn't possibly make love after such a disclosure, I decided to keep the secret to myself, at least for that day. Otherwise she would keep hold of my hands and refuse to believe that I could be thinking of such a thing at such a moment. And if I waited till after to tell her, she would take me for an even worse brute. She must comfort me without knowing why I needed comforting.

At the bus stop I sat down in the grass and kept my eyes on a dog that was standing beside the shelter looking at me. Father had always seemed to me a level-headed person, fanatically logical; all through my childhood I had to listen to his insisting that cool reason was more useful than hot blood. Whenever I threw a tantrum, which mostly happened when I was frustrated about something, he would lock me in the dark bathroom and tell me to call out when I had come to my senses again.

Martha turned up on the next bus. She was glad to find me waiting, but not surprised. She put her arm around my waist, stuck her thumb in my belt loop, and we started off. Every other step, her breast would rub against me, so for a while I said nothing. She explained why she hadn't been able to come sooner. I said nothing until we reached the fork where we had to leave the path to go to the cottage.

I paused there and said: "There are some people in the cottage."

"People?"

"Father and someone else."

"You've been there already?"

"Yes, I have."

She looked at me expectantly, as if there was more to come. And I knew that the expression in my eyes wasn't as natural as I would have liked. I took her hand, and we walked on in the other direction.

"Why didn't he tell you before?" she asked.

"Because he didn't know I'd be coming," I said.

"That's the risk that goes with being furtive."

Her apparent lack of concern annoyed me; she couldn't have any idea of where I was taking her, yet she wasn't disappointed. I would have given a lot if the suggestion of finding a good spot in the forest had come from her. Although it amounts to the same in the end, there is a tremendous difference depending on who makes such a suggestion. Just a hint, I implored her in my mind, and I would jump at it and say all the rest myself.

"Did your father see you?" asked Martha.

"God forbid!"

We passed a few cottages similar to ours. A little girl had tied an elastic cord to a garden fence and was standing with the end on the other side of the path; the result was an almost invisible obstacle. She was solemnly waiting for us to step over the cord, and we did her the favor. From the window of another cottage came the smell of cooking.

"Anything wrong?" asked Martha.

"Everything's fine," I answered. "What makes you ask?"

"Your shirt's torn."

"Must've happened on the way here."

"I believe you're keeping something from me."

"Then you know more than I do."

"Where we're going, for instance," said Martha, but in a different tone, as if changing the subject.

"For a walk, of course," I said. "Or do you suppose I have another cottage in this forest?"

She stopped and gripped both my arms. I had to meet her eyes before I was allowed a kiss. After that she asked what I thought about going back into town to see a movie; we hadn't been to one in weeks. I agreed. That was probably the smartest thing to do.

The next-to-last in a loathsome series of tests—the swim test—was scheduled for the morning. I couldn't sleep that night. To get a B in physical education, I needed an A in swimming, and for that I had to do a hundred meters in less than 1:40. I tried to persuade myself that it was possible to lead a contented life even with a C in P.E.; the longer I lay awake, the more convinced I became.

When I switched on the light at two and looked at my watch, Father wasn't back yet. The last few nights he had come home very late, but I had assumed he was playing billiards. Father was a keen billiard player.

What were they planning to do with that man? Did they want information about some particular thing I knew nothing about? Did they intend to question him until he made a confession that could be handed to the public prosecutor? Did they mean to scare him, torture him, or keep him prisoner for God knows how long? Or—the thought kept haunting me—did one of them intend to kill him? Certainly not Gordon Kwart. He was a dull, good-natured person, tenth- or twentieth-desk violinist in the radio symphony orchestra, a man who was afraid of the unexpected and for whom peace and quiet were the equivalent of happiness. About the third man, the stranger, I knew nothing except that he was very suspicious. And I did not believe my father capable of violence. Yet a few hours go I had looked on while he treated the prisoner with hatred and brutality.

Although I had said that afternoon I knew what Neuengamme meant, now, in the night, I realized that for me it was little more than an evil word. I got up, went to the encyclopedia, and read the brief entry. I learned the few figures it contained by heart, as if I must have them constantly at my fingertips over the next few days—above all, the figure 82,000. Sleep was still out of the question, so I read the articles on a few other concentration camps. That kept me busy until I heard Father come in. I turned out the light; he tiptoed down the passage and disappeared into the bathroom. Obviously they must loathe the camp guards; obviously it must make them ill when such a man claims that in those days there was a different law, that he had always acted only within the law.

But today there actually were different laws, different courts, and different police. The police could be blamed for whatever one liked, but not for one thing: that they were too easy on former concentration-camp guards. Why didn't Father and his friends simply report the man to the authorities and rely on what was, after all, reliable? Why did they bother to speak to him at all?

It was true that I was totally ignorant of what had happened. Maybe the guard had made them angry; maybe he had behaved in a manner that, even after thirty years, they found intolerable. Maybe they had been carried away because the opportunity had been so uniquely favorable. Maybe one of them had recognized him.

But they had laid claim to a right to which no one is entitled, not even they. And even if he were my father a hundred times over, how could I approve of former victims

23

seizing their former torturers? They had only themselves to blame for the fact that in that foul-smelling room I could feel pity for the guard but not for them.

It was quite likely, of course, that they didn't care about the opinions of others; that in their eyes it was a matter solely between the guard and themselves. And if they were found out, well, then they would have to take their punishment. Possibly they speculated that, if the worst came to the worst, the punishment would not be all that severe.

Yet wasn't it also true that so much time had elapsed between action and counteraction that emotion could no longer be regarded as an extenuating circumstance? Is it legitimate for someone who was beaten up when he was thirty to hit back when he is sixty?

No one can choose the moment when he loses his reason. Because I had never seen Father beside himself with rage, I had drawn the conclusion that he could never be beside himself. Now it had happened. Perhaps the three men had been amazed themselves at the extent of their rage. Perhaps they had thought their lust for revenge was long since extinguished, until they came upon this man, one unlucky day.

I heard Father come out of the bathroom and shuffle along the passage as far as my door. Cautiously he opened it and came in. I pretended to be asleep. He didn't turn on the ceiling light, so I kept my eyes open a slit and saw him against the dim light from the passage, but I closed them as he approached. He stopped beside my bed; he used to do that every night. He stood there for quite a while, as if wanting to test the limit of my self-control. I had no trouble keeping my face completely motionless. I breathed deeply, as if asleep, and as I breathed I could tell that he had brought that foul smell home with him.

After he had gone to his room, I felt that he would have

24

liked to sit with me. As long as they were occupied with the camp guard, perhaps everything had seemed logical, but later, when they found themselves alone, they were forced to think again.

I didn't give up my hope of doing a hundred meters in under 1:40: it is better to be successful. I wasn't very far from swallowing the first sleeping pill of my life. The only reason I didn't was that I was afraid I might still be drowsy when the time came for me to be at the pool, in a few hours.

Where did they get those handcuffs? I'm sure there isn't a single store in the whole country that sells handcuffs. The prisoner is probably kept permanently with his feet bound to one end of the bed and his hands handcuffed to the other. When they're present, they release one half of him: hands or feet, whichever they feel like. They feed him and push the chamber pot under him, though not often enough. Is one of them in the cottage at all times? Do they take turns guarding him, or only go there together and rely on the restraints the rest of the time? Have they thought about what will happen if one day they arrive at the cottage and the prisoner is gone?

Father was coughing in his room, which meant he was smoking, although he had promised both the doctor and me to stop. Tomorrow we would sit down and discuss everything calmly, after the swim test. We had to talk; we couldn't pretend that something had happened that wasn't worth mentioning.

Would he defend himself? He didn't like talking about himself and his affairs; he always behaved as if I were the only one whose affairs were of interest. His response might well be that I shouldn't stick my nose into things I didn't understand.

I still didn't know, of course, what I was going to say to him. Everything that had been churning through my head

25

amounted to: Stop the whole thing. That would hardly be enough. If I merely appealed to his sense of justice, he would give me a friendly pat on the shoulder, as if, despite my endearing efforts, I were too dumb to realize what was involved. I had to attempt something I had never yet achieved: to convince him.

Lepschitz is at work, Martha is at drama school, her mother is out shopping, and I am carrying the garbage downstairs. For the past week I have been doing this whenever I see the mailman leave the building. I am still expecting word from the university. Although I don't expect to be turned down, news of my acceptance would reassure me. I take three letters out of the box: one for each of us except me. I put them back and, carrying the pail, run through the rain to the garbage bin, which is so full that I have to heap up a little mound on top.

On my way back, I pick up the letters. As I drop them on the kitchen table, the handwriting on the top envelope seems familiar. I pick it up again, and I am right: my sister, Elle. What can Elle be writing about to Martha? Why doesn't she write to me? She knows how I love getting her letters. Or didn't I ever tell her? I haven't been to see her for at least two weeks. Is Martha seeing Elle behind my back?

I take the letter to my room. On a few of my visits to the mental home, I took Martha along, usually when the weather was fine. I can well remember Martha's amazement after our first visit; it had taken a lot of persuading for her to go. But Elle was highly intelligent! she claimed, as if I had said anything to the contrary. It was incredible and outrageous, she went on, that such a bright person (that was her expression) should have to rot away in that home! Her words sounded as if she were reproaching Father and me for not having done enough to obtain Elle's release. Yet I know that Father sweated blood trying to get her out. Sometimes I even believe that his efforts on Elle's behalf have consumed all his paternal love, and that's the only reason there is nothing left for me. Presumably he began his shady postwar deals because of Elle, since he needed contacts and money to drag her around to all the specialists who had been recommended to him. But for Elle's case there were no specialists: for no apparent reason she would attack complete strangers, pummeling them, clawing their faces, and trying to poke their eyes out with her fingers.

The external characteristics of the people she attacked were analyzed, as a way of keeping them and Elle apart, but no common factors were found. She attacked men as well as women, people with blond hair as well as brown and black hair, short people and tall. Sometimes weeks would go by between attacks, sometimes only hours. It was found that children were never among her victims, but our parents couldn't very well move with her to an area inhabited only by children. Elle herself refused to give any information. Everyone assumes that wartime experiences account for her behavior, but to this day no one has uncovered the exact connection. I was twelve years old when I was allowed to visit her for the first time, and she was already thirty-one. The day before that visit, my father revealed to me that I had a sister. We took to each from the very beginning.

To read the letter would mean stealing it from Martha: I can't hand her an opened letter. I vow that I will open it and read it and then get rid of it, but there is one problem: Martha will go to see Elle, Elle will ask about the letter. Martha: What letter? Elle will tell her about the letter, it sounds a bit confused, she often jumps from one thing to another. Martha will soon believe that there never has been any letter, she will think: Oh, well, she's a bit odd anyway. And intuitive Elle will suspect the role played by her brother.

I take the letter back to the kitchen, go to Rahel Lepschitz, and ask when Martha is expected home.

In the afternoon I knock on Martha's door, and she lets me in. She is sitting at the desk, barefoot and in her slip, reading a blue book by Engels or Marx. On the floor lies Elle's letter, the tiniest handwriting one can imagine.

"Oh, it's you," Martha says.

I wish she were more fully dressed. I point to the letter and say: "I brought it up with the mail."

"So?"

"You went to see her?"

"Have you any objection?"

"None whatever."

She stands up and pulls on her yellow sweater; it is quite chilly in the room. Sometimes I sense that it annoys her to recall that she once liked me. As she raises one arm to pull on the sweater, I notice that she has shaved under it. Maybe this is mandatory at drama school.

"So now what do you want?" she asks as her head emerges.

"I have a request."

"Yes?"

"That letter . . ."

"Yes?"

"May I read it?"

"Why?"

The question takes me by surprise. I look at her bare feet which I once loved toe by toe and say: "I don't know anyone who writes such beautiful letters as she does."

"Maybe so," says Martha, her tone indicating that she is still waiting for my explanation. I hate myself for being too cowardly to take the letter and walk out with it.

29

"I can read it aloud to you," she says.

She picks up the letter, not doubting that I will agree to her suggestion. I cannot believe there is any secret between her and Elle. Although in our previous life there were a few occasions when I read Elle's letters aloud to Martha, I would never have minded if she had preferred to read them herself. Besides, Elle isn't her sister.

I can think only of rude things to say, so I leave the room before the performance begins.

The swim test. I woke up before the alarm went off and felt as rested as though I had been hibernating. Other mornings I had to cope with vestiges of dreams, but not this time. I picked up the encyclopedia, which was still lying there, and put it back on the shelf.

I had timed myself for the hundred meters a few weeks ago. Martha had sat at the edge of the pool, looking at her second hand, and claimed that I had managed only 1:43, but at one point I had had to swim around a whole bunch of kids.

In the kitchen I fixed my breakfast, as I did every morning, but I left it untouched, because one can probably swim faster on an empty stomach. Father's jacket was hanging from the window latch, swallowing up half the light.

On arriving at the pool, I had half an hour to spare. The fat cashier pointed to me and asked: "Grad test?" I nodded; she took pity on me and waved me through the turnstile. All the lockers were unoccupied, the doors open at the same angle. I decided on Number 71 because I had first met Martha in 1971. Before exams I always think up magic numbers that can influence the result.

I entered the pool area and climbed up onto the diving platform. Since no one was in the pool, the water lay motionless and mirror-smooth. As I dived I could see each in-

31

dividual green tile on the bottom and thought with horror: No water! I flew and flew—unimaginable how long it took to drop those five meters. The thought of my damned impetuosity would have been the last one of my life if the water hadn't finally met me. I was so happy about my escape that I began to believe this was my lucky day.

This time, too, my trick with magic numbers worked: I swam 1:38, although I had no strong competition. With each stroke I thought: If you make it, the business in the cottage will work out okay. Mr. Sowade, our P.E. coach, winked at me and called out: "How about that!"

Exhausted, I went into the shower room. First I let the hot water splash on my head and shoulders in needle-sharp jets that seemed to penetrate the skin; then, to maintain the exquisite agony, I slowly increased the temperature to the limit of the endurable. I tried to figure out a program for the day: Talk to Father? Go out to the cottage and see what happened next? Prepare for my last exam? Spend the day with Martha? None of these appealed, not even Martha. I needed someone to advise me, someone who didn't need long explanations, who knew more than I did, who could think more clearly and didn't immediately panic when the situation became confused. But although the day had started so well, I couldn't think of anyone.

A swarm of graduating students crowded into the room to stand under the showers and pull off their swim trunks. As late as yesterday I would have splashed and guffawed just as they were doing. Today they seemed like kids who grated unbearably on my nerves; they were from another school.

One, a short, husky fellow, touched me on the shoulder and pointed to a sign on the wall that said trunks were to be removed before showering. His face was full of pimples, which matched his officious manner. I carefully washed the place where he had touched me and turned away. But he wasn't satisfied and went on: "Can't you read?" To this day I can't understand why I got so upset over that busybody. Suddenly I felt that he was one of those bullies who love to torment and only stop when they find themselves confronted by someone stronger. I remember wondering whether I should hit him low down or high up.

"Hey, you," he said in a challenging tone, "I'm talking to you."

I swung around and punched him in the face. I must have closed my hand and made a fist, because my knuckles hurt for days. He gave such a yell that everyone turned to look. Even as he staggered back and fell, my rage dissolved.

The others threw themselves on me; a regular fight ensued for the privilege of grabbing me. Finally, four students held my arms; the others surrounded us, with their bare behinds and peckers, ready to jump like a pack of vicious dogs on leashes. I didn't resist; apart from the fact that it would have been futile, I didn't consider it necessary. Someone asked what had happened, but no one could tell him.

The pimply fellow slowly got to his feet, holding his nose with his hand. Dark red drops lay on the tiles, but his chest looked positively alarming: blood on it blended with water to form a delta. He stared at me with respect as well as anger. I liked him better without that camp-guard look. "This fellow is crazy," he said. Then he examined the palm of his hand, stepped under one of the still-running showers, and washed off the blood.

One of the boys roughly twisted my arm. I told him to stop, and the pressure actually subsided. Pimple Face came closer; he was now cleaned up, but a mustache of blood remained, which he prevented from growing by constantly sniffing.

"What's been going on?" someone asked.

"I'm afraid that if you hold onto me much longer, he'll get his courage up," I said.

"They don't have to hold you for that," said Pimple Face.

Mr. Sowade and a man I didn't know came hurrying into the shower room, and the students let go of me. Somebody turned off the showers, and Pimple Face started telling the teachers his version of what had happened. I caught only the first few words before I left the steamy room and went back to the pool area. Why I didn't go back to the locker room and get dressed I still don't know. The last thing I heard was Sowade sternly calling my name.

In the pool area everything was remarkably quiet. Swimmers waiting for their test stood or sat around solemnly; each seemed to want to save his strength by not moving unnecessarily, so the pool was empty. I jumped into the water and thought about why I had hit that boy. How had I reached a state in which a stupid loudmouth managed to make me lose my self-control? I had the uneasy thought that it might be a symptom of the same disease that in my sister's case was already far advanced. Granted, I had never before punched anyone in the face, not even when I was attacked, but it could also mean that the disease had a long incubation period.

I had not jumped into the big pool but into the one for nonswimmers. Sowade had no trouble finding me; he stood at the edge of the pool and beckoned. I pretended not to notice him, although that was impossible. I swam in a gentle curve and then under water toward the opposite end. But there he was again, squatting above me. The two stopwatches hanging around his neck dangled between his legs, close to my eyes. "What's the matter with you?" he asked.

There would have been no point in answering, especially since I hardly knew myself. A few years before, I had fallen from the crossbar during P.E. Sowade had caught me and broken his little finger in the process. I was not hurt. I understood why he had to pursue this business, the other instructor would do the same. I shrugged and looked solemn, so he wouldn't think I was taking the matter lightly.

"Do you mean to tell me that you smashed his nose for no reason at all?" he asked.

"Is it broken?" I asked.

"Probably not. But no thanks to you."

"There was a reason."

"He says he drew your attention to a sign, that was all."

"Not true. He did it three times."

"You don't say!"

"You should have seen his eyes when he did it."

"His eyes?"

Sowade put his hands on his knees, as if about to get up, then blew air through his nostrils and assumed an indignant expression.

"You must have a screw loose," he said. "Who gives you the right to punch someone just because you don't like the look in his eyes?"

I had already reached this point in my own thoughts, and I could see no sense in contradicting him. So I said, "Nobody."

"We don't have to make a big deal out of it," said Sowade, straightening up. "His name is Norbert Waltke, remember that. Now go back to the shower room and apologize to him. He'll accept that, and the incident will be forgotten."

"Must I take off my trunks to apologize?"

"I see nothing funny about all this," Sowade said as he walked off.

I got out of the water and headed for the shower room. Sowade was speaking to the students at the starting blocks but looking across at me. Probably, I thought, this is the last time in our lives that we'll ever see each other. My mouth filled with ashes.

If I'd been on the receiving end of the punch, I wouldn't have given a damn about an apology. Sowade pursued me with a policeman's stare, convinced that my misdeed could be atoned for with a few lying words. Ought I to have hugged the disgusting fellow?

By this time there were some kids from my own class in the shower room. Somebody asked me a question that indicated that news of the incident had not yet spread. As I walked through the steamy air toward Norbert Waltke, he turned his back, as if he didn't want to be found that easily. He had finished his shower long ago and was probably only standing there in order to forgive me.

I went and stood under the next shower, played around with the taps, and allowed some seconds to pass before asking: "Do you have a moment?"

"What for?" he asked, with a poor pretense of innocence. The left half of his face was red, his nose swollen. I felt no satisfaction at this sight; on the contrary, it embarrassed me.

"That business just now," I said, "I mean, the way I behaved. That wasn't right."

"I agree," he said.

"I'm sorry," I said. "And I hope you'll excuse me."

From the opposite row of showers, one of his pals, an especially hefty youth, called out: "Everything okay, Norbert?"

"Sure," he called back with a wave of his hand. Then he looked me over, as if to find out whether I deserved his leniency. I passed this test too. He said: "Forget it. But next time be a bit more careful."

Because his loudmouth manner annoyed me again, I said: "We'll see, next time."

I turned off the shower, shook myself like a dog and, with everyone watching, went toward the locker room. Pimple Face followed me, not with any evil intent, apparently—he was simply going in the same direction. On the way I loosened the string of my trunks, while Waltke carried his and wrung them out as he walked.

I stopped in front of locker Number 71 and felt for the key I had hidden in a crack between the lockers. Waltke walked past me, and I thought I was finally rid of him. But no. After a few steps he stopped, turned toward me, and said: "If I had known about it, I wouldn't have bothered you, of course."

"What do you mean?" I asked.

"I wouldn't have pointed at the sign."

"What do you mean by 'If I had known'?"

He smiled like someone who wouldn't be taken in. "Just forget it," he said, and walked on. I looked at his back, which was even more pimply than his face, until he disappeared into a side corridor.

As I was drying, I tumbled to the meaning of his words. I could almost hear what Sowade must have said to placate him: *That sign—you're quite right—does apply to everyone, no question, and that means him too. But there's another side to the matter that you couldn't know about: and that is: Hans is a Jew. There may well be sensitive areas there of which people like us have no idea. I hope you understand.* It must have been something of the kind, for no other explanation would fit. For twelve years I had got through school unscathed; in other words, I had always been treated in a normal way, and now, in the final swim class, this. In the onset of my anger I wanted to rush back to the pool, but what could I have said to Sowade?

A theory of my father's, which I had heard on various occasions, ran as follows: There were no Jews at all. Jews were an invention; whether a good or a bad one was debatable, but it was certainly a successful one. The inventors had spread their rumor with so much conviction and persistence that even those who were directly affected and suffered from it, the alleged Jews, fell for it and claimed to be Jews. This in turn endowed the invention with greater credibility and a certain reality. It was becoming more and more difficult to trace the lie back to its origin; it was covered by layers of history that had become impervious to arguments. But what was most confusing was that so many people not only had adjusted to their role as Jews but were positively obsessed by that role and would resist to their last breath any attempt to take it away from them.

While I was dressing, my anger subsided; it belonged to a dimension that I was now leaving behind. As I combed my hair, I looked into each of the four aisles of the locker room, but Waltke had left. If I hurried, I might catch up with him on the street, and then? I thought of what I might have said to Sowade in parting: *I would not like to disappear from the school without correcting an error that I have only been made aware of today: Contrary to your assumption, I am not circumcised. I had no superior motive for hitting that fellow, only an inferior one. I hope the misunderstanding did not persuade you to press your stopwatch a few seconds too early.*

Even as I was walking down the stairs, the cottage loomed into significance again, with Gordon Kwart, with the suspicious stranger at the window, with the man shackled to the bed, with my poor father. I stepped out onto the street, undecided which way to go. I had forgotten why I had wanted to keep the whole disaster from Martha, the only person I trusted; I only remembered that I had to. I would make it up to her with the story about Norbert Waltke and Sowade.

Today I miss the mailman: today the pale green letter from the university arrives. Rahel Lepschitz offers it to me like a holy relic, whispering: "I hope it brings you what you want!" Then she leaves me, so as not to distract me at such a moment.

My desire to go to university is not as immense as she seems to think. I can imagine many occupations that would be quite bearable: carpenter, male nurse, farmer, gardener, watchmaker. Anyway, I don't know what kind of work one is expected to do as a certified philosopher.

The letter contains the expected: they are happy to be able to inform me that I have been accepted by the university; enclosed is a half sheet of *Practical Suggestions*. It remains to be seen whether philosophy will benefit; I am not yet prepared to exclude the possibility. At the moment it is I who am benefiting, but now I have to find someone to provide me with a room. Whatever happens, I don't want to embark on my university career from this apartment. Given the magnitude of the problem, four months doesn't give me much time. One has heard of people who spend longer than that searching for a room, of waiting lists a mile long. I sit down and write to Werner Klee about my good luck; we are almost friends. He is a soldier, pining away in barracks near Prenzlau, and needs some good news.

During supper the TV news is turned on, with the sound off, for which there can be two reasons: one, they are waiting to hear what was in the green letter; the other, the familiar speech on the anniversary of the Liberation is being given in some big hall. Hugo and Rahel Lepschitz always look toward the screen when it shows the audience, which looks incredibly attentive.

I hear Lepschitz say: "That blond fellow in the third row . . ."

"Where?" asks Rahel.

"How many third rows are there?"

"What about him?"

But Lepschitz sulkily falls silent and turns back to his food; the picture has changed, so there's no longer any point in saying who the blond fellow looks like. At home we had no TV, either in the apartment or in the cottage. I was all for buying one, but Father controlled the funds. When I complained to him that there were discussions every day in class about things I had no knowledge of, he said: "So what kind of knowledge is that anyway?"

While keeping his eyes on the soundless speaker, Lepschitz says: "I could tell you why he isn't saying anything."

"Why?" asks Rahel.

A glance is shot at me to see whether I have understood that they are talking about me.

"He's saying nothing because they've turned him down."

For several seconds I am given the chance to refute this supposition—I let it pass unused. The longer I keep them guessing, the greater will be the relief.

"I could also tell you why they have turned him down," Lepschitz goes on.

"Why?"

"Because he was too proud to enter on his application that he is the son of a victim of Fascism."

That was precisely what I *had* entered in the space provided

40

on the application, even though I hadn't felt comfortable about it.

"What's that got to do with pride?" I ask.

"If you prefer the word 'stupidity,' by all means," says Lepschitz.

"But you're mistaken. I am not the son of a victim of Fascism."

Simultaneously they ask: "What else are you?" and "Are you out of your mind?"

"By the time I was born, he had long ceased to be a victim."

"One remains a victim for the rest of one's life, my boy," says Lepschitz. "One never gets rid of that."

And Rahel Lepschitz says: "A person can't choose whose son he is."

"But he can choose what kind of a son he is."

"I have my doubts about that too," she says, and Lepschitz shakes his head over so much foolishness.

I refuse to be dragged into an argument that would never have arisen without my lying. I say nothing for a while. Perhaps I really have been accepted for that reason alone, but I don't care. I *would* care if going to university were important to me and if I had to think that my good luck was due only to extenuating circumstances.

Father loathed being regarded as a victim. Although we never discussed the subject, certain remarks of his permitted no other interpretation. For instance, I remember a quarrel between him and Kwart in which he accused Kwart of being a sponger. Kwart had brought him the news that recognized victims of Fascism didn't have to pay radio license fees, whereupon my father fell into a rage that surprised us both. I was eleven or twelve at the time and very impressionable; I remember how as the quarrel proceeded my sympathies shifted from Kwart to my father. He accused Kwart of having no sense of embarrassment. Not having to pay the fee, he shouted, was nothing more than a humiliation, and Kwart, the idiot, allows it to be palmed off on him as an act of kindness! "They're making a sponger of you, and you even thank them for it!" When Kwart persisted in finding nothing wrong in claiming the benefit, they refused to speak to each other for weeks.

"I can't imagine why you're making such a fuss," I say. "Of course they accepted me."

"They *did*?"

"Were you in any doubt?"

For several seconds I am the only person at the table who goes on chewing. Tears are sparkling in Rahel's eyes, but she's overdoing it; happiness has a different face. But for Hugo Lepschitz the matter is not yet finished.

"Kindly explain why you've kept us on tenterhooks for so long," he says. It sounds as if he's repeating the sentence for the tenth time.

Rahel lays a placating hand on his arm and says: "Try to understand—he just wanted to enjoy our suspense. Don't be hard on him now, just when everything's turned out so well."

"I see it differently," says Lepschitz.

"How do you see what?"

"He's implying that his affairs are none of our damn business."

"Hugo, please!"

"And that's not all," Lepschitz continues. "He wants to show us that he finds our interest a nuisance! We're not supposed to imagine that we have any claim on his confidence."

"For heaven's sake, Hugo, what are you saying?"

Lepschitz is now a person who, after having been silent far too long, has finally exploded. Even Rahel seems to sense that there is something in what he says; she would be glad if I could refute the accusation. She nods at me as if urging me to do away with the misunderstanding as quickly as possible. I decide to do her the favor, although Lepschitz is right. You don't have to be that smart to draw such conclusions. He merely has to believe what he sees every day. But I must hasten to assure them of the contrary. I owe that to both of them since, after all, they'd had nothing but the best intentions in taking me in.

So I boldly say to Lepschitz: "You're wrong in what you're saying."

"Where am I wrong?"

"The only reason I didn't mention the letter is because I don't think it's that important."

"You don't think it's important?"

"There you are!" Rahel cries in relief, as if I had smashed the suspicion into atoms. But Lepschitz isn't that easily convinced; he shakes his head, with tiny, swift movements that look more like trembling. A piece of matzo crumbles as he spreads it with butter.

"Maybe you're surprised that someone isn't glad to be accepted by the university?" I say.

"Yes, we are surprised," says Lepschitz. "Why did you bother to apply?"

"It wouldn't have been the end of the world if they'd rejected me."

"Brilliant explanation."

"Why don't you stop picking on him?" Rahel says. And to me: "Do me a favor: I'd like to read the letter."

I go to my room for the letter. The sole crime of Hugo and Rahel Lepschitz is that they are what they are. How long must I go on reproaching them for having believed a year ago that I, with my nice inheritance, was the right man for their daughter? We all believed that. I go back and hand Rahel the letter.

While she is reading, Lepschitz says: "Answer me one question: If you didn't care about the result of your application, why did you go every day to meet the mailman?"

I have to get away from here, beyond any doubt; I need a room as quickly as possible. I must be blushing under his gaze. I've never known him this determined, this searching. To my surprise I find myself saying: "Not every day. I sometimes do go to the box when I'm expecting a really important letter."

"From whom?"

Rahel has finished reading; she has not been listening. She innocently places the letter in front of Lepschitz and waits for him to express a little pleasure too. But he has no intention of doing that. He pushes the sheet of paper aside and turns his gaze on the soundless TV speaker; with each passing moment he seems to intensify his gaze, as if he could read the words on the man's lips. Rahel makes soothing gestures in the belief that the resentful mood will subside. Then she folds up the letter and lays it beside my plate.

I steadily go on eating. I have recently developed the art of thinking of nothing; the only thing in my head is a faint buzzing that, I imagine, spreads like a protective layer over my brain to keep all activity from it. At such times I don't react to words spoken at normal volume; it is easier to reach me by nudging me. I eat, and practice my art.

A little cry from Rahel penetrates the armor: she is holding her hand to her mouth. What has happened? Lepschitz has switched to a West German station. Willy Brandt has just resigned, she cries out.

I remove my protective layer and hear Rahel and Hugo arguing. She is bemoaning the fact that our politicians in East Berlin couldn't keep their hands off such a level-headed man, and Lepschitz is convinced that there are spies everywhere, and only certain ladies with their housewives' horizon would swoon with pity. She protests, of course; I don't hear her words. I pick up my green letter and leave as unobtrusively as possible.

After leaving the pool I hesitated outside the building. Suddenly I was afraid to go home, where Father would be sitting in the kitchen sipping hot tea from a saucer and reading *Neues Deutschland*. But equally I dreaded hiding from him, let alone playing the innocent and chatting with him as usual. It was up to me to take the offensive, but how? If I couldn't come up with anything better than to say that what they were doing at the cottage was wrong, I might as well give up.

I went to visit my sister Elle at the mental home, that was the solution. She was the only person I could talk openly to about yesterday's events; strange that I'd taken so long to think of her. On good days she spoke so sensibly that one wondered why everyone else wasn't in the institution, why Elle of all people. It was pointless to lie to her or to keep something from her: either she saw through you with incredible accuracy, or you felt like a cad. If there was anything to be kept from her or lied about, it was no use even going to see her. Yet on other days she was unapproachable; she would nod a lot and smile, like a mother who seems to be listening to her prattling child while her head is full of worries.

The gatekeeper with the huge goiter gave me a military

salute; we had known each other for years. Father once loudly
took him to task because Elle had come to meet us a long
way from the home. Why had they bothered to install him
in the gatehouse if everyone was free to pass through the
gate? he said. Ever since then the gatekeeper had taken every
opportunity to show that he had nothing against me, as distinct from my father. I must add that, in dealing with people
over fifty, Father tended to be unjust and rude.

Elle's is a gray, one-story building with an unfinished look
to it. As long as I can remember, it has been surrounded by
piles of bricks and stacks of cement, as if the builders were
waiting for it to be vacated for them to complete it. Inside,
however, it is completely furnished, if somewhat austerely.
Yet the park surrounding the place is wild and luxuriant.

I went to the room labeled "Head Nurse." We greeted each
other by name. I didn't have to explain why I was there. As
usual, I went to the visitors' room and waited for Elle to be
brought to me. We were permitted to walk in the park.

But this time the head nurse came, not with Elle but with
a doctor I had never seen. "You are her brother?" he asked.
I nodded, and we shook hands. Something was wrong; that
was clear. At the other end of the room, two patients were
playing Halma, one of them laughing immoderately, perhaps
over a stupid move on the part of his opponent. Screeching
and shrill laughter were not uncommon sounds in this place;
by now I had learned not to show alarm. The doctor told
me I couldn't talk to Elle today. I begged him to let me. I
was in urgent need of her advice, I said, something quite out
of the ordinary had happened. "All the more reason not to,"
he replied.

I felt flattered that he treated me like an adult and took
time for me. I had the feeling that the final word hadn't been
spoken. On previous visits I had noticed that the doctors'

decisions often concealed the fact that they were at a loss; it happened to be their job to give orders here, whether they were sure of what they were doing or not.

He told me they had had to give Elle a tranquilizer, and that as a result she was tired and hardly capable of carrying on a conversation.

"What does that mean—'had to give'?" I asked.

By way of reply he opened his shirt, baring his neck to the shoulder. I could see a crimson scratch that began at his throat and ended in the area of the collarbone. There was no need to ask questions, nor did he explain; he gave me a few seconds to take in the sight. I was shocked, but curious, too, for this was my first encounter with someone Elle had attacked. His, then, was the kind of face she couldn't bear. For me, personally, there was nothing alarming about his face; it was quite an ordinary face, pale and inoffensive. I asked him how often Elle had met him before.

For a moment he looked at me, puzzled; then he smiled and said: "No, no, you're jumping to the wrong conclusion."

Yesterday, while walking in the park, Elle had attacked an elderly woman who was visiting another patient. She had torn out a handful of her hair and, when the woman fell, began kicking her. The doctor had come running, and it was during his attempts to restrain the enraged Elle that he had been injured.

Because I couldn't think of any way to persuade him to change his mind, I apologized for my sister. "How can you be blamed?" he said. "How can anybody be blamed?" I liked him better than any doctor I had met so far, and I said: "Please—do let me see her!"

"By all means," he replied, as if we had been talking at cross-purposes. "But she should be spared any sensational news. She really is tired. She has had to take so much of the stuff that anyone would feel tired too."

On the way to her room, he told me he had been working for only two weeks in this section, and that he had already grown very fond of Elle. It sounded as if he was trying to explain his leniency, but that wasn't necessary. How could anyone not like Elle?

She looked as if she had been doing some work that had gone beyond her strength. As I walked in, her eyes were fixed on the door. She placed her hands on the arms of her chair as if to rise, but then broke off the movement. I held her in my arms for a long time and stroked her hair. I can't imagine that anyone had ever felt such pity for anyone as I felt for her. Father had told me that sometimes he went out to the home just to hold her in his arms for a little while.

I pulled up the other chair and sat down; the window was open in front of us. There was a smell of tar and new-mown grass. Whenever I dreamed of our mother, she always had Elle's face. I hated the medication. Although today she had been given an exceptionally strong dose, the fact remained that she had to take those damn pills every day, under supervision, because she wasn't reliable. The medication controlled her permanent agitation but left almost nothing of herself behind.

She took my hand and said: "Yesterday it happened again."

I didn't quite know how to react, since she never talked willingly about her attacks and shriveled up whenever I mentioned them. Would it be better to pretend ignorance now, or was I supposed to know what she was talking about?

"What happened?" I asked.

"You mean you don't know?" she asked, losing a little of her fatigue.

I quickly said: "Oh, of course I do."

She nodded, as if she couldn't have imagined anything else.

Then her eyelids began to droop again, and I could see that the doctor's advice had been sensible.

"How did it end?" I asked.

"As always," she replied, infinitely weary. "People came and overpowered me."

"It's the most normal thing in the world to hate certain faces," I said. "I feel the same way, it's just that I can control myself better."

"But that's a big difference. And you know what?" she said. "While they're still hanging onto me, I'm thinking: They're right, of course; I know that."

I told her that the doctor had been injured too; I didn't want to keep anything from her. The fear of treating her the wrong way dogged me; I described the scratch he had shown me, but she was hardly listening. She didn't even answer my question as to whether he'd made the same good impression on her. So I suggested she take a nap; I would wait and find something to do.

Elle nodded. She walked to the bed, lay down, and was probably already asleep by the time I went over and drew up the covers. I was hungry, so I opened her cupboard and found some cookies. In principle I find hospitals and similar institutions repulsive and would never want to eat there, but this room was Elle's home.

In her bookcase were books other than those brought her by Father or me. As soon as she finished a book she would give it away; there was no stopping her. But she may also have swapped books. I picked up one, sat down in her chair by the open window, and read. Whether because of the swim test or because of last night, I quickly fell asleep too.

We were wakened by a nurse. I was sitting with my back to the door and pretended I had been looking out the window, but as I turned around the book fell to the floor. The nurse looked from Elle to me and asked softly whether Elle didn't

50

want any lunch today. I asked whether the meal couldn't be brought to the room, by me, for instance, and just then Elle said: "I feel sick to my stomach, and you two are talking about food."

The nurse left us alone. Elle got up and drank from the tap. She claimed that the water there was excellent, and I wondered what other water she could compare it with. She ate the rest of the cookies. In response to my look of surprise she said: "It was the only way to get rid of her."

We sat down again by the window. I waited patiently. Her nails were cut right down to the quick. Her tiredness hadn't yet left her; she should have slept ten times as long. Smiling encouragingly, she asked: "Tell me quickly—what's the name of those things you keep drinks warm in?"

"Thermos flasks?"

"That's right," she said. "How about bringing me a Thermos of coffee next time you come? Suddenly you can't buy coffee here anymore."

I got up, but she said I needn't try, there really was no coffee anywhere, not even in the little grocery store. We sat in silence for a while. I found it quite understandable that she couldn't instantly recall the names of things she never had anything to do with.

I gathered up my courage and said: "Something happened to us in town too, yesterday."

"Forgive me," said Elle. This was her way of expressing her regret that so far we had discussed only her affairs and not mine. She tilted her head to the left until her ear touched her shoulder, a sign of special attentiveness. I knew from Father that she used to do this even as a little girl.

I told her what had happened. I began by telling her about Father's refusal to let me have the key to the cottage, and confessing to the existence of the second key. Her reaction was a wave of the hand, which could only mean: Never mind

51

the details. My date with Martha, the yellow car outside the cottage, the strange noises I heard on creeping up to my favorite window; how I believed the first little scream to be harmless, and how the second one had sent shivers down my spine.

Even at this stage of my story, while everything might still prove to have been harmless, Elle's eyes showed that she was expecting the worst. Her head rested on her shoulder, all trace of sleepiness gone. Even when I made a long pause, her attention didn't waver.

My story contained only one lie: I suppressed the fact that I was discovered by Father, Kwart, and the third man. Instead, I entered the cottage, stood there as if invisible, and disappeared unnoticed after I had seen and heard all I needed. Keeping to the truth, I left the cottage to intercept Martha; I didn't want her, too, to become a witness. I quoted everything that had been said by the prisoner and his kidnappers, as far as I could remember it, leaving out only the words addressed to me. I described the iron bed, the handcuffs, the horrible smell; I didn't want Elle to be deprived of a single detail. My story ended with the information that, when I met Martha, I didn't tell her a word about the episode.

On my way to visit Elle, I had thought of two reasons why I should not tell her I had been discovered. One was that I wanted her to believe it would depend on her advice whether or not I confronted Father. From my version, she could also conclude that the affair didn't concern either of us, that Father was old and wise enough to make his own decisions. The second reason was that I pictured Father's next visit to Elle. Quite obviously he wouldn't tell her about what was happening in the cottage; but if Elle believed that Father knew nothing of my having been a witness, she wouldn't feel nearly as excluded.

When I came to the end of my account, she remained for

a few moments with her head resting on her shoulder. I could see in her face the transition from listening to pondering. Soon she got up, rummaged in her bedside table until she found a cigarette, and lit it. Years ago, long before my first visit, she told Father she wanted to smoke and had been forbidden to do so. Father had managed to negotiate a compromise with a senior doctor that she be allowed to smoke in her room, and only there, and to this she had agreed.

She seemed to be thinking hard but not coming to any conclusion. But although I allowed her plenty of time, she said nothing. Perhaps she was hoping to be let off, to have nothing to do with the whole business. But I continued to wait, I wanted nothing to do with that business either, and after all she was my older sister.

Finally she said: "Would you mind going out and getting me a hot dog or something from the kiosk?"

Clever. When I came back, she ate the hot dog devoutly, as if any distraction might spoil the taste. I felt isolated. Suddenly she turned toward me and moved one hand up and down: I was not to become impatient.

As I moved to the window, she said: "Please move away from the window."

I asked whether I should go outside and come back a little later.

"I'm almost finished," she replied.

That sounded as if in her mind she had to check off a certain number of points, and that the last of these points was already in sight. There had indeed been no coffee at the kiosk. The saleswoman knew nothing about any new regulation; she had simply not been supplied with coffee for the past month and was annoyed about it herself.

Something was stirring in Elle. I sat down in front of her and watched her. Our knees were touching. She was wearing the dark red running pants I had outgrown in grade 10. She liked to touch me, liked to hold my hand, she would hold onto my arm, brush against me frequently; it was often meant to look accidental, but I was aware of the intention and always felt a little honored.

More time passed before she said: "There is nothing pleasant about your story. I'm surprised I never heard of it happening before. It's against all probability, isn't it? But then, people can show incredible patience when things start to improve for them. And now Father."

I deliberately did not interrupt her; I understood enough to know that the advice I was waiting for hadn't yet been given. She said I shouldn't sit there like a supplicant, and I changed my position, I forget how.

Elle tapped me on the knee for attention and said: "All right: you simply have to tell him what you saw."

"Tell who?"

"Father, of course."

"And then?"

"Just do that first. It's more important than you think."

I had to be careful not to show my annoyance. She wasn't to blame for the expectations I had brought with me. When she asked whether I was disappointed, I stopped pretending and said: "A bit."

She raised her hands as if to say: What can you do? Her advice had nothing to do with me. It had been given for Father's sake, not for mine: Father ought to know that there was a witness. What good did that do me? Instead of becoming my ally, she had mistakenly come to Father's defense.

"How is Martha?" asked Elle.

"Do you really want to know?"

She looked at me in surprise, so I quickly told her how Martha was. As I spoke, Elle went over to the bed and lay down on her back. Closing her eyes, she said: "Please go on talking, I'm listening."

I knew she would soon fall asleep; even on normal days, long conversations tired her. When she lay there with her eyes closed, there was a resemblance between us; otherwise I couldn't see any.

Her face looked relaxed; all signs of the effort I had imposed on her had disappeared. It would have been easy to animate her again. I had only to mention that Martha and I had been to the movies. She loved to hear movie plots, since no films were shown in this institution. She had become familiar with at least fifty movies this way, and often I had to repeat many times the story of one she particularly liked. She probably knew the movie *The Cranes Are Flying* better than I did.

I went on talking until I was sure she was asleep. Once, in the park, I had overheard her telling a couple of other patients, two young men, the story of *The Stone Flower*; she had blushed when I made my presence known. Her lips now parted ever so slightly. Believe it or not, I liked watching her as she slept. Ah, that habit of mine of looking for the guilty: things just happened the way they did.

What could she know of the outside world? She lived beyond time, in an environment that was linked to the outside only by books, by me and Father, and by the radio—only by words. Had I gone crazy, to ask her, of all people? Law courts, restitution, guilt, Neuengamme, retribution. In her quiet world there were only meals, visits, trifling events. Maybe her habit of occasionally clawing a person's face made me regard her as an expert.

But it would have been nice to hear the all-clarifying suggestion from her, to receive the help that would end my indecision. She looked indescribably peaceful.

On entering our apartment I heard the bathroom door click shut. Either he hadn't heard me or he was avoiding me. I called out: "Is that you?" He called back: "Who do you think?"

I went into my room, leaving the door wide open in case he had any idea of sneaking out. He's sitting on the edge of the tub, I thought, trying to figure out how he can give me the slip.

The best of all possibilities was that they had set the man free; that, after my appearance, the risk had been borne in on them and judged unacceptable. The prisoner went straight to the police—and then? When the police went to check out his story, all trace had been removed: the cottage aired, the iron bedstead on a garbage dump. Three statements versus one. The accusation was so lacking in credibility that no one would plunge three honorable men into disaster on the strength of it. Who knows what that fellow has been up to the last few days? That was one way to get rid of him, the only way. And if they hadn't thought of this yet themselves, it was up to me to see that they did.

Father came out of the bathroom, by no means quietly, and called out to me to come into the kitchen. Is he trying to turn the tables on me, I wondered.

He was standing in front of the open cupboard and said:

"You didn't do any shopping—there's no food in the house."

I opened the refrigerator; that was empty too. I was about to dash downstairs, feeling very guilty, but he said: "In the first place the stores are all closed, and in the second there's been nothing here all day."

In a corner of the cupboard I found two cans of herring in tomato sauce. I told Father that I had been to see Elle.

"Your offer to go shopping now does you credit. But what with? I'd like to see how much housekeeping money you still have," he said.

"It's almost the end of the month."

"According to my calculation, there's still a week to go," he said. "Are we supposed to starve that long?"

"I've already told you that I'm willing to go out and buy something."

"Then show me the housekeeping money. Put it down here on the table."

"I'm not a child anymore."

"That's not the problem," he said. "The problem is that you're already out of money. That you're using it for something other than buying food."

He wanted to stop my mouth before I started to yap. The trouble was that his assumption was correct: it was true that being short of funds forced me to resort to minor embezzlements, which by the end of the month often led to a food shortage. I said: "If you'd rather, you can do the shopping yourself in future."

"I wouldn't rather," he said, artificially suppressing his artificial exasperation. "What I would like best is to be able to rely on you."

I wondered whether the opportunity for the talk I had in mind hadn't now passed; that much, at least, he had achieved. He put on the kettle for tea and looked far from unhappy. A confession from me would probably have improved the atmosphere in my favor, but I couldn't force myself. I opened one of the cans of fish: he waved it away. No matter what I began to talk about now, it would look as if I were trying to distract attention from my own misdeed.

"And another thing," said Father as he shook some tea leaves from a caddy into the teapot—too much, as always. "If you don't like what I'm doing, go to the police and report me."

He looked at me with interest to see the effect of his words. I hadn't even mentioned the cottage, but he was lashing out as if I were his mortal enemy.

"That's no way to talk," I said, getting up and leaving the kitchen.

"Isn't it?" I heard him call out after me.

I needed some comfort, quickly. Martha? If the subject was so repugnant to him, he didn't have to talk to me: how could I stop him if he left without a word? But no, he had to pitch into me. Obviously his remark about the police hadn't been serious. His idea had been to challenge or abuse me.

I dialed the Lepschitz number. It was busy. Our phone was in the passage, and the cord was so short that it couldn't be carried into any room. Martha sometimes accused me of sounding absurdly stiff on the phone.

During my next attempt, Father opened the kitchen door and said: "Just a moment."

The tea was ready, and he was sipping the hot, bitter brew as he waited for me to join him at the table. He had a habit of not looking at me when taking me to task, but when he listened he never took his eyes off you.

"Since we're on the subject," he said, "would you mind explaining how you got into the cottage?"

"I told you that yesterday."

"Then be good enough to explain it again. I was upset

yesterday, as you can imagine, and I didn't take everything in."

I knew what was about to happen, I knew it as well as if it had happened already. And still I had to repeat: "The door was open."

"The door was open?"

"I happened to be passing by. I saw the car parked outside and I wanted to . . ."

"You happened to be passing by?"

"For God's sake, I just said so!"

"Don't shout. I have more reason than you, yet I'm not shouting."

He was forcing me to keep repeating my lie until it sounded childish in my own ears. If I didn't soon think of a counter-thrust, I was lost; it was now just a matter of standing my ground. I felt like someone whose hands are being tied before the actual fight begins.

"So how did you get into the cottage?" he asked.

"I suppose you've become so accustomed to talking like an interrogator that you can't stop doing it at home!"

He dunked a cube of sugar in his tea and put it in his mouth. At that moment we had become total strangers; we sat there like adversaries, each watching for the enemy to make a false move.

When he was tired of waiting, he said: "The door was not only not ajar, it was locked. Kwart wasn't sure because, just before you came, he had gone to get something out of his car, which made him the last person to come in. After that I locked the door myself, without telling the others. You may wonder why I said nothing? Because I didn't want Rot-stein to insist on searching you. He's a suspicious type, as you saw. Just imagine if he had found the duplicate key."

Pretending to run out of patience, I said: "For the last time, you're mistaken. The door was open. After all, I did go in."

Now he'd had enough of my lying. The look of superiority vanished from his face and was replaced by outright fury. For a moment it seemed as if he was going to yell at me, and I was ready to walk out deeply offended. But he didn't do me the favor. He said coolly: "You traveled thirty kilometers because you were counting on the door being open. Is that right?"

He put the piece of sugar still in his hand back in the jar and stood up, saying: "So you think *this* is the way we should talk?"

He wasn't interested in my reply; he went out of the kitchen and left the apartment. I took the damn key out of my pocket and threw it in the garbage pail. Minutes passed before I pulled myself together enough to do something: eat up the fish. If I could have thought of some safe haven, nothing would have kept me in the apartment, I swear it. I had the childish desire to run away, to give him a chance to miss me. Now we had to pay the price for always having talked only about superficial, inconsequential matters.

I moved a chair to the phone and tried my luck again. Rahel Lepschitz answered and wanted to know how my exams were going. It was hard work till Martha came. "Where'll we meet today?" I asked her.

"Nowhere."

"And when?"

"I mean it. We can't."

"What's happened?"

"Nothing's happened; just that we've had an invitation."

"We?"

As luck would have it, she had to go with her parents that evening to visit some friends. The invitation had only come today, so she hadn't been able to mention it to me yesterday; I could see that. She didn't care for my suggestion that she let her parents go alone; she asked for a valid reason. I offered my undying love, but that didn't convince her. I think she would have agreed immediately to meet me if she had realized my anguish. In the end, she said I could join them if my love was causing me that much pain, she would explain to her parents. Needless to say, I refused.

The tea was now lukewarm; I poured it down the sink. I wished I could fall asleep and wake up years later. Father's room, which I seldom entered, was a mess. The side of the big bed that hadn't been used for eighteen years was covered with newspapers, underwear, books. I opened the closet to find out whether the stink I dreaded was already present, but everything smelled as usual. I rummaged among his things without knowing what I was looking for. On the table were a lot of photographs of my mother. I had seen them before, but he usually kept them in a drawer. My mother as a tiny schoolgirl, as a shy bride; with Elle in her arms; wearing a Jewish star; my mother after the war, standing in her fur coat on a street full of rubble; on vacation by the Baltic Sea; my pregnant mother, with me in her huge stomach. He had spread the photos out as if from now on they were to be part of the furnishings of the room. I wondered what this meant.

I went to my room and opened my biology book, because suddenly I was scared of not being properly prepared. Meaningless words were scattered over the pages, and, when I did happen to understand a sentence, the little I knew immediately began to melt away. I soon gave up the struggle and exchanged the biology book for a thriller, but the two books were oddly similar. I regretted having refused Martha's charitable offer. I forced myself to read the chapter on the ontogeny of multicellular organisms—my weakest spot. Maybe some of it would stick.

The ringing of the phone sounded like rescue. I rushed to tell Martha that I would accept her offer after all. It was a man wanting to speak to Father. I told him Father wasn't there, and the man asked where he had gone. I said I didn't know. It was the truth, although not the whole truth. The man asked: "Am I talking to his son?" When I said yes, he went on: "We've met. Tell him Rotstein phoned."

Rotstein's call made one thing clear: Father hadn't gone to the cottage, so he must be at the Eckstein, a kind of bar plus billiard club—where else? If this evening had been like any other, I would have assumed that he was there. For years he had been strangely attracted to billiard tables; he played carom billiards and on good days he would score an average of over four. I remember his highest run was forty-three points and that he was almost bursting with pride the first time he told me about it.

I left a note saying Mr. Rotstein had phoned. Underneath, I wrote that one accusation, the one about the housekeeping money, was justified; the other, the one about the key, was not. I put the note on the floor in the passage. I was hoping that at some point doubts would rise in his mind if I went on denying long enough.

I went downstairs. It was barely eight o'clock. Out on the street, on an impulse, I decided to look in at the Eckstein. After a few steps I turned around and went back to the apartment, where I tore up the note because it seemed too ingratiating. Then I set out once again. My behavior was not based on reason; it was arbitrary and random, corresponding to the emotion of the moment, regardless of where that came from. So as not to admit to myself that I was looking for Father, I took a big detour and on the way made up my mind several times definitely not to go to the Eckstein.

When I entered, he was reaching diagonally across the billiard table, which stood in the middle of the room, and he made a stroke that failed to come off. As he straightened up he saw me standing at the door. For a fraction of a second he hesitated before walking to his table and sitting down with his back to me. I sat down, too, at a table not far away. The place wasn't crowded—Monday night. I knew the Eckstein well. There was another big room at the back with three more billiard tables. When I was twelve or thirteen, Father used to bring me here: I hadn't wanted to stay home alone, and he didn't see why we should sit around being bored every afternoon. When the place was empty, I was allowed to take a billiard cue and try various strokes according to his instructions. My last attempt ended in my tearing a hole in the green felt as I tried to give the ball a back spin. The owner had seen it coming.

A man with a few drinks under his belt called across the room: "Arno, isn't that your son?"

I heard my father mutter: "Yes, unfortunately."

It wasn't too pleasant sitting there with the eyes of the players and customers on me. I coped with that by going over to the counter, ordering some coffee, and remaining there until the little pot was pushed toward me. Everyone knew now that there was tension between Father and me, and everyone could see that he was the stubborn one. I decided to wait until he had finished his game; if he began the next without favoring me with a glance, I would leave.

The fellow who'd been drinking came over, put a hand on my shoulder, said Arno's son was his friend, and asked what I'd have. When I replied that I didn't drink schnapps, he laughed and loudly called for two vodkas. Father, who happened to be standing at the blackboard marking down his score, said: "Leave him alone." It sounded threatening, especially because his back was turned to us; it sounded as if he didn't want to have to say it again. There was a short silence. The man shrugged and shuffled back to his seat, and everything went on as before.

After finishing his game, Father came over to me. Without

a word he took me by the arm and led me, like a prisoner, into the back room. There he let go of me, asked why I had followed him, and sat down to wait for my reply. A solitary player was practicing at one of the three billiard tables, always bringing the balls back to the same position and paying no attention to us.

"How can you treat me like this?" I said.

"Right now I am taking insults and deceit very seriously," Father said.

"What are you talking about?"

His face twisted with impatience: he was showing how much he had to control himself. "Why did you come here?" he asked again.

"To tell you that Mr. Rotstein phoned."

Someone stuck his head through the door and asked whether Father wanted to go on playing or not. "Some other time," he answered.

I followed him back to the bar, and he went to the counter to pay. I heard him tell the woman not to forget the coffee, and her say: "He's quite the young man now, isn't he?"

Meanwhile, it had grown dark outside. We walked in silence from one street corner to the next. He chose our direction. When we had to stop at a red light, he put his arm through mine. It must have been many years since we had walked together like that.

"First of all, let's get this straight," he said after a while. "I don't want any advice from you."

"I wouldn't know any," I said.

We reached Friedrichshain Park and sat down on a bench facing the street, with the dark park behind us. My right arm and his left were still linked, as if forgotten.

"What did Rotstein want?" Father asked.

"He didn't say. I was just to tell you he phoned."

"You know who Rotstein is?"

"Yes."

He lowered his voice as if talking to himself. "I know I'm not a very considerate father."

I made no comment, surprised, yet smart enough to keep my mouth shut.

"You have no idea how much trouble you've caused me," he said.

"With Rotstein?"

"Never mind," he answered. "Start asking. What do you want to know?"

I was unprepared, so I asked him to tell me how the kidnapping had come about, from the very beginning if possible.

"From the very beginning!" he repeated, amused. "From my boyhood, perhaps?"

He looked at me as if I were a child incapable of understanding such a momentous story. Then he stood up and walked away, not very fast, as if he wanted to stop himself from making a big mistake. But in that case why walk into the park instead of away from it? That's how he was: complicated enough to drive you crazy; at any given moment everything could be different from the moment before.

I followed him, slowly enough for the distance between us to remain the same. In my mind I turned over questions to ask him. In the middle of the park, beside a black pond where swans floated in the daytime, I found him waiting for me. "Why don't you and the others simply report the man?" I asked.

"Because we don't want to."

"Are you afraid that he'll get off too lightly?"

He pretended that this problem had occurred to him for the first time, then shook his head and said: "Not in *this* country."

"What other reasons are there?"

A final hesitation; he still had to overcome some lingering

misgivings. Then followed a hair-raising explanation: he, Kwart, and Rotstein agreed that they were living in an inferior country, surrounded by second-rate people who didn't deserve any better. He could imagine, he said, how such a view would surprise me, yet why should he have discussed it with me before? Unfortunately, I had to learn to deal with these creatures; there would have been no point in representing my surroundings to me as unbearable. It was true that the concentration-camp guard would be severely punished if they handed him over to a court of law. But on what basis? Solely because one occupation power rather than the other happened to have conquered the country. If the border had been drawn slightly differently, the same people on either side would have opposite convictions. Anyone strong enough could impose his convictions on this German rabble, whether his name was Hitler or something else. That was why they had decided to take matters into their own hands. If there were a court of law they could recognize, such an idea would never have occurred to them.

By that time we had strolled around the pond. Although my eyes were now used to the darkness, I couldn't make out a single swan. I was careful not to interrupt Father; he was speaking of things I had never thought about and that made me uneasy. I was hurt that he had kept such important views from me. According to him, this had been for my sake, but couldn't the reason also have been a low opinion of me?

"Does that answer your question?" he asked.

I was aware that I was no match for him, like a layman daring to instruct an expert in his own field. Nevertheless, I said: "Have you thought about what will happen if what you're doing gets out?"

"Yes."

"I don't mean what will happen to the man, but to you and your friends?"

66

"We have thought about it."

I could clearly hear his reluctance to continue the conversation. Should I stop? My fears increased. I couldn't behave as if they had been dispelled. So I went on searching for arguments, although today my efforts look pathetic to me, like trying to blow out a fire with your mouth.

"And even if you believe a hundred times over that the people and the courts and the country aren't worth a damn, what gives you the right to place yourselves like princes above them all?" I asked.

He scratched his head. I knew that gesture; the way other people count to ten, he scratched his head. Then he said: "Let's drop the subject."

"Doesn't it always lead to trouble when people lay claim to rights they're not entitled to?" I asked.

"Maybe."

"If you assume the role of judges of this man," I said, "then you're not only breaking the law . . ."

I stopped, not knowing how to continue the sentence. The door was wide open to me, and I couldn't go through. Father allowed me plenty of time; probably he sensed that I was in no position to make use of it. The pause was humiliating.

Finally he said: "Why don't you forget about giving me advice, even though you find that difficult?"

He put both hands in his jacket pockets and walked off. The last thing I saw was his white head as it seemed to float through the darkness. I hadn't made much progress.

On the pond, circles formed, caused by fish mouths breaking the surface of the water. Never again would I stumble so blindly into a discussion with Father, with no valid argument, no prospect of success. For the first time I began to suspect that there was only one way for me to exert any influence: by going to the police, as he had suggested.

Rahel and Hugo Lepschitz are scowling; the TV set has broken down. I remain in the living room, not merely out of curiosity but also out of sympathy: in misfortune one must draw closer together. I sit with my nose in a book and wait for some diversion—that's how low I've sunk. This afternoon when I helped Lepschitz carry the TV to the repair shop, he drew my attention to every obstacle, every curb. When the woman in the shop told us the repair would take four days, he groaned. He managed to get her down to three.

"I suppose the news today will be about the resignation of your Willy Brandt," says Lepschitz.

"What do you mean, my Willy Brandt?" asks Rahel. She is making use of the opportunity to mend some underwear, including mine.

At times during the past year I've puzzled over whether the people around me really are as terrible as Father said they were that night at the swan pond. Not that his judgment made me lose any sleep; it was just that I wondered from time to time how much he might have been exaggerating. To this day I don't know the answer.

Since I have never been beyond the borders of our country, I have no basis of comparison. During this last year I had the time and money for a trip abroad, but I wasn't really all that interested. The problem is made worse by my knowing hardly a soul even within the country. The Lepschitz family, Kwart, Werner Klee, Martha of course, and a few schoolmates, a few teachers—how can I possibly form any judgment based on them? Perhaps it's just as well. Suppose I did come to the conclusion that Father was right, that they *are* inferior— then what?

"Oh, Hans, we forgot to take our vitamins!" Rahel said.

I go into the kitchen and bring back the brown pillbox. They're forever taking vitamins, during the winter months three a day, in summer two. The fact that they are still alive is, in their eyes, incontrovertible proof of the efficacy of the pills.

Rahel holds up the box, smiles seductively, and asks me: "Wouldn't you like to try?"

I shake my head, as always when she asks me this question.

Over the top of the newspaper Lepschitz says: "He'll only take them when it's too late."

"Do you know the advantage of vitamin C?" asks Rahel.

I nod, whereupon she explains: "Every other vitamin is harmful if you take too much of it. It accumulates in your organs and gradually causes damage. Only vitamin C has the wonderful quality of leaving nothing behind. You can take as much as you like. What your body doesn't need is eliminated."

"But that's hardly a good enough reason for taking it," I say.

"Nobody says it is."

"Can't you see he's trying to annoy you?" says Lepschitz.

"It's good for anything to do with colds," Rahel continues, unfazed. "Look at me: I haven't coughed once in two years."

"Nor have I," I say.

"And Linus Pauling—I suppose you know who Linus Pauling is?"

"Yes."

69

"Linus Pauling takes a thousand milligrams of pure vitamin C every day," Lepschitz says irritably. "Why do you think he does that?"

The thought that I might have saved Father if I had confronted him more decisively continues to haunt me. Yet I still don't know what I could have done, even if I had realized what was at stake.

No one had taught me how to resist, no one had shown me how to do what one feels is the right thing. At school I had always been merely a quiet listener; as early as the first grade I discovered how wonderfully easy it is to get ahead if you follow the teacher's opinions. An added advantage of such behavior was that it suited my lazy nature. I needed to find out the opinions of only a single teacher to know those of all the others. Between the worlds of speaking and thinking there was a wall, and I would have considered myself the greatest idiot if I tried to break down that wall. To this day I panic when I find myself alone with an opinion. Luckily I rarely get into this situation; that's the good thing about being withdrawn.

Even Father hadn't exactly made a fighter out of me. Although he didn't teach me to keep my mouth shut, he never encourged me to open it. I don't believe he really taught me anything at all; he wasn't interested in me.

A few months after I was born, my mother died of blood poisoning, incredible as that may sound, and Father was left with the baby. Her death made him apathetic. At the time of their marriage they were both nineteen. I must have been a constant trial for him, what with my screaming and my constant hunger. He hired a nurse, who was not very reliable. On discovering that she drank and some afternoons took the baby buggy with her to a bar instead of wheeling me around in the park, he fired her. Instead of looking for a replacement, he grimly took on all the work himself. I didn't hear this from him; Elle told me about it. At that time she was the only person to whom he could unburden himself or, as Elle once said, "air his soul." In emergencies he could deposit me with an old woman living in the next building. I remember her well; her name was Mrs. Halblang. She had only one eye and died five years ago. She didn't take any money for looking after me but would accept gifts such as coffee or candy. A few times I even spent the night at her place, sleeping on a sloping couch with two heavy armchairs pushed against it so I wouldn't fall off. I remember the shock I got when I saw her one morning without her teeth.

How relieved Father must have been when, as the years went by, the necessity of caring for me and watching over me gradually diminished. Well, by the time I was at last able to occupy myself, he no longer had the strength to concern himself with how I spent my time. It suited me not to have to account to anyone. That was how my few opinions were formed without his being involved. I have never succeeded in going deeply into anything; whatever I take up, I merely poke around in it briefly and soon move on, as if there is harm in concentrating too long on one subject. From physics to astronomy, from medieval history to music, and so on. Yet I believe that the only people who can lead an exciting life are those who are committed to one thing.

Lepschitz is reading a newspaper article aloud. He didn't ask for our permission: we wouldn't dream of listening to him. I look at Rahel; she glances up from a shirt and meets my eye. She smiles, as if to encourage me. I consider how I might kill time if I went out. The reverse method, of first going out and then thinking about what to do, has never worked.

Rahel leans toward me and whispers: "How long does that kind of study take?"

"Four or five years," I whisper back. "I'll find out."

"And then what does one become? A philosopher?"

"Either you listen," Lepschitz says, "or I can save myself the trouble of reading to you."

"I only asked how long he'll have to study."

"Please go on reading," I say.

But he folds up the newspaper; he's not angry, but seems to be more interested in our conversation than in his article. It concerned some incident: a helicopter lost its bearings on the Chinese-Soviet border and landed on the wrong side. I'll read the details later. With exaggerated slowness, Lepschitz puts the newspaper down on the table.

"You know I never interfere in your affairs," he says. "But since we're on the subject, what in the world made you choose philosophy?"

This is the very thing Rahel has been wondering. She sighs, resumes her sewing, and says resignedly: "It's all been decided anyway."

"What have you got against philosophy?"

"*I* have something against philosophy?" says Lepschitz, pointing all his fingers at his chest. "All I want to know is, what use is it?"

"Wouldn't it have been more sensible," Rahel asks, "to study medicine, for instance?"

"That's what Father thought too."

"That doesn't make it wrong, does it?" says Lepschitz.

I explain that I have no idea where my studies will lead me, but that I'm curious to find out; that this curiosity, while not limitless, is still greater than the interest I have in any of the other disciplines.

"Mysterious," says Rahel.

"Indeed," says Lepschitz, "very mysterious."

"Besides," I say, "I'm not a very cultured person. With any luck, that will change by the time I've finished those studies."

"We wish you that with all our hearts," says Rahel.

They leave it at that, but Lepschitz looks dissatisfied as he picks up the paper again. It's the same old story: they worry about me, they want the best for me, and I curse them both for it. I can recall only one instant when I found their sympathy welcome: at my father's funeral, suddenly there they were. Hugo Lepschitz had taken a day off work and sacrificed a day of his vacation. And Rahel had prepared a feast, unannounced, just in case I had no place to go after the funeral. Then, as we sat at table, with the candles burning, when Rahel put a slice of carp on my plate, I had a sense of being cared for as never before.

Martha comes in; she's still home. Her appearance is unfamiliar, for instead of slacks she is wearing a close-fitting green dress with a pattern of white flowers, in which she looks the way she used to. She stands in front of Rahel, in need of help: her zipper is stuck. She seems not to be aware of me, but I have barely started to rise when she says: "Don't get up, I'm leaving right away."

A few weeks ago, when for the first time she openly went out without me, she was embarrassed. By now we've all become used to it. I have no trouble adjusting, much less than her father does. I'm tempted to ask who she's meeting. We'd all like to know who our Martha has taken up with, but each of us can imagine how such a question, coming from me, would be interpreted.

Hugo Lepschitz's eyes challenge me to do battle. How can anyone put up with such a disgrace, his eyes shout: you're losing her and you're not lifting a finger! Rahel, too, is far from pleased, but the zipper leaves her no time for significant looks. If a vote were held in this family on whether Martha and I should turn ourselves back into a couple, the result would be two to two.

When the zipper is fixed, Martha tells us not to wait up

for her; she blows a kiss in the air and leaves. We who are left behind resume our occupations, which none of us finds easy. The floor trembles slightly when the apartment door is slammed shut. Only then do I realize that apart from Martha no one spoke a word as long as she was in the room. That can't be pleasant for her either.

Her parents are furious that I show no jealousy. I'll outwit them: I'll begin to suffer until they realize that I have no choice but to move out. The idea seems so smart that I promptly heave a big sigh, which immediately draws a pitying glance from Rahel.

The phone rings; I am the only one who can reach it without getting up. Lepschitz whispers. "I'm not here." He's often "not at home" for no reason at all. I pick up the receiver; a man asks to speak to Martha. "She's on her way," I tell him.

When I came into the kitchen on Tuesday morning, I found the breakfast table already set. Father stood smiling at the stove, where he was putting eggs into boiling water. He asked if I wanted one or two, I was confused; there were fresh rolls in the basket, and there was a smell of coffee. When I sat down, savoring my good fortune, he asked: "Am I mistaken, or is this your last day of exams?"

That's how it went. We chatted quite casually, not a word being said about the previous evening. He asked me in detail about my visit to Elle, and I saw no reason not to tell him about the incident in which the doctor was scratched. Father said it was encouraging to note how rare such incidents had become. He was in an exceptionally good mood. Where had it come from so suddenly? He said he felt quite certain that I would pass the exam with ease, and I called that a bold prognosis. He asked me to let him know sometime what kind of a graduation gift I would like from him. I suddenly suspected that he was merely employing new tactics. He never so much as mentioned the missing housekeeping money.

During breakfast I learned that he intended to go off that afternoon and be back in the evening. For the hundredth time he tried to convince me of his method of eating boiled eggs:

peel two lukewarm soft-boiled eggs, place them in a glass, shake about a pound of salt on them, and then poke around with a teaspoon to produce a homogenous, pale yellow mush. He invariably expressed surprise at my refusal.

When he left the kitchen I went to work on the garbage pail; in the smell of fish, under coffee grounds, eggshells, and tea leaves I searched for the key to the cottage that I had thrown away the day before—too hastily, it now seemed. Father's voice from the passage asked what I was looking for in the garbage, and I replied casually that I had thrown away some notes for my exam by mistake. For a moment the suspicion flashed through my mind that he had long since found the key and was asking with feigned innocence.

What a relief it was to feel the key between my fingers. After a glance at the door, I pulled it out of the garbage. I put it in the sink and washed first my smelly hand and then the key.

Father had gone to his room. Through the slightly open door I could hear radio music, accompanied by his strangely cheerful humming. As I was about to leave, he stuck his head out and asked whether I had found my notes.

"No, unfortunately," I replied.

"You'll manage all right without them," he said confidently.

Now that I knew he would stay in the apartment until afternoon, I decided to go out to the cottage as soon as the exam was over. Of course there was the risk of running into Kwart or Rotstein. I'd have to check that out when I got there and, if necessary, disappear unseen. But if neither of them was there, I wanted to speak to the prisoner. The idea of freeing him was distasteful to me.

I was determined not to spend too much time on the biology paper, not more than two hours. The risk was limited because

I'd had straight A's, so even a really bad exam paper wouldn't be disastrous. But an angel was watching over me. The subject chosen was one I was thoroughly familiar with, "The Cell as Transmitter of Hereditary Factors." While most of the others were still exchanging forlorn glances, I was already writing. I believe it was the first time in my entire school career that I hurried at the beginning of a paper and not just at the end. While I was busy writing, a cry for help came to me from Werner Klee, who was sitting behind me. I had no choice but to pass him a crib, but even so I needed only a little more than an hour. When I handed in my work, the teacher nodded as if at a model student. Not for a second did the solemn thought occur to me that my schooldays were now behind me.

Later I discovered that my departure had been interpreted as arrogance. Werner told me about it, and because I couldn't let on why I had left so quickly he shared this view. All the others had gathered in a café, in accord with tradition. Werner said the get-together had been quite emotional, and I had only myself to blame for the memory the others would retain of me.

At the interurban station I phoned Martha. She congratulated me before I had even said a word; then she said she had a surprise too. "Why is it a surprise that I passed my exams?" I asked.

She ignored that and asked whether access to our cottage was still blocked by visitors. When I confirmed this, she groaned; she knew I liked that. She wouldn't talk about her surprise on the phone. "Not till you're here," she said.

Then she said she could tell from the noises in the background that I must be at a railroad station. Where was I going? My explanation that I had an errand to do for Father satisfied her. By this time I was so good at lying that I might have done nothing else all my life. "Too bad," was all she said,

77

without knowing that those words almost caused me to give up my plan. Another sigh from her and I would have postponed the trip. My hands grew hot with desire. At that moment it was clear that I had to release the prisoner as quickly as possible so the cottage would once again be available to us. A man banged on the window of the phone booth.

"I can hear what's happening," said Martha. "Are you coming here this afternoon?"

"Absolutely."

As I left the booth, the impatient man was already extending his finger to dial. There would have been enough room for us at Martha's, but the eyes and ears of her parents were waiting around every corner. Everyone knew that residents of East Berlin were not permitted to rent hotel rooms in the city. If there had been enough housekeeping money left over, I would have tried anyway. The sky, on which we depended so much, refused to turn blue; it looked like rain, and it was cold.

On the way I wondered who the prisoner was placing his hopes in, assuming he hadn't given up all hope: in me, probably; in every unexpected visitor; in the police, to whom his disappearance would certainly have been reported, by his wife, by anyone he was living with; in his kidnappers' coming to their senses. Perhaps he screamed himself hoarse as soon as they left him alone.

Then I realized that he had every reason to fear the police like the plague. Elsewhere, former camp guards might be treated leniently, but in this country they were regarded as monsters. Here he could not count on leniency, here they would tear him to pieces. He couldn't shout for help. Indeed, he couldn't report Father, Kwart, and Rotstein even if he succeeded in escaping. He could only pray that nothing would happen to attract the attention of the police.

Given the camp guard's desperate situation, it followed

that the danger my father was in was less than I had assumed. Had a kidnapped person ever feared discovery more than his kidnappers did? It shocked me to think how firmly he was in their grasp. He could only hope for their mercy—in other words, for a miracle. If I went to the cottage, he would be in my grasp too.

When I left the train at Erkner, another train, going in the opposite direction, was standing enticingly a few feet away. I had to force myself not to return to town. One way or another, the man was in my grasp, whether I went on to the cottage or back to town.

This time the forest didn't smell so strongly of mushrooms; the wetness had its own smell. It was raining, but, because there was no wind, only a few drops penetrated the treetops. It was like walking under an umbrella full of holes. The closer I got to the cottage, the stronger my aversion became—to the stench there, to the man, to what I was doing. It would have been a relief to find one of the captors there. But there was no car outside.

I crept up and listened under each window but heard nothing suspicious. After a while it seemed safe to assume that the prisoner was alone.

Cautiously I unlocked the door. At my first visit it had not been locked, as Father had claimed; I know that for sure. His mistake had reinforced my denial.

I entered the dark little hallway. As I stood there, I kept telling myself that there was no need for me to be so agitated. What did I have to be afraid of?

I stood listening for a long time, hearing nothing but the rapid beat of my heart. Then came the moment when my fear was transformed into determination, and I opened the door to the prisoner's room. He was lying there asleep. As I had expected, he was wearing handcuffs, with the chain wound around a bedpost. His feet were tied with a leather

79

belt to the foot end of the bed, as before. He was lying on his back, the only possible position; his body seemed to be stretched. In the room the stench was stronger than in the hallway, of course. The chamber pot was still under the bed. What good was it to him, if he couldn't move?

A sheet was draped over the window. Since the window faced the rear rather than the path, I removed the sheet. To do that, I had to push a chair up to the window, and that made a noise. But even in spite of the light he continued to lie motionless. I took a good look at his face. With a shock, I realized that he might have fainted or even be dead. I gave the bed a sharp kick.

Except for his eyelids, which opened wide, no part of him moved. His gaze immediately focused. I could find no fear, no pleasure, no surprise in it, nothing. But there was no mistaking the moment at which he recognized me. "You're the son, aren't you?" he asked. And when I didn't react, he went on: "Are you going to help me?"

I wasn't born to be master over life and death. It seemed to me that, of the two of us, I was the one most in need of help. During the two days since our first encounter I had told myself over and over again that I must not let myself be influenced by pity, but now I felt not the slightest pity. This much was clear: if I ever did help him escape, it would be for Father's sake. I felt tempted to tell him this, that I hadn't come out of pity. In addition to the stench, I was bothered by his immobility.

"Do other people come here, too, to speak to you?" I asked.

"Other people?"

"Apart from my father and those two men?"

"No."

"Do they come at set times?"

"Twice a day."

"When?"

"Once in the morning, then again in the afternoon or evening."

"Have they been here today?"

"He was here. The bald one, calls himself Erik."

"Alone?"

"In the mornings, only one of them comes. Gives me something to eat, shoves the pot under me. Doesn't say a word. Later, in the afternoons, two of them come, or all three. They call it interrogation, sometimes it goes on till late at night."

"How often do they feed you?"

"That part's not so bad. But d'you think they ever let me get up? I've been lying here for five days! Don't even give me any paper to—in plain language—wipe my ass! I can smell the stink in this room the same as you do, but what can I do about it?"

His voice had risen, and his eyes swam with tears. I don't believe he intended to rouse my compassion; he was just utterly appalled by what was being done to him.

"It began five days ago?" I asked, and he nodded. If he had asked me to untie his feet, I would have done so.

I went back to the window, this time to open it. Fresh air was one reason, but I also wanted to be sure that he wouldn't take it into his head to scream.

As I grasped the latch, he said: "Why are you opening the window?"

"Why do you think?" I replied.

On the white paint of the windowsill a cigarette had left a burn mark that had not been there a week earlier. I pushed a chair close to the bed and sat down. Some distance away I could hear a dog barking. He raised his head as high as he could and in a low voice said: "The open window is not a good idea."

"Would it upset you if someone found out you're here?" I asked.

He blew air through his lips, as if after a joke that doesn't deserve a good laugh. Then he dropped his head again, briefly closed his eyes, and said: "Things are more complicated than you think."

"In what way?"

"Have you ever thought what will happen to those three if I'm found?"

"You want to remain undiscovered out of consideration for them?"

"Not so loud, please," he said.

When I closed the window again he asked nervously whether I was leaving already. I didn't answer.

"Of course I'm thinking of myself too," he said.

"What would you have to be afraid of if you were found?" I asked.

"As if you didn't know!"

It was an effort to ask him not to mention my visit, but I had to. He promised with a grin. But then his face grew serious again, and he asked whether I hadn't come to help him.

"What's your name?" I asked.

"Arnold Heppner."

I didn't know how to free him, even if I'd wanted to. The handcuffs looked so sturdy that it would have been a waste of time to fool around with them. Maybe one could take a hammer or rock and smash the bedpost to which they were fastened, but that would have left him with manacled hands. I had no intention of helping him outside the cottage, through the forest, through town, all the way to his home.

"Aren't you going to release me?"

Suddenly I was furious at how brutally they had chained him up: like some wild beast that can't be allowed so much as an inch of movement. I could see, of course, that it wasn't enough to lock up the cottage; it simply wasn't escapeproof. But why hadn't they tied him up in such a way that he could sit like a human being and turn and perform essential functions? It seemed to me that they had made themselves guilty of unnecessary cruelty.

I untied his feet. I recognized the leather belt; I had worn it myself. The prisoner lifted both feet together to make the job easier. The bonds had cut two grooves into his thin ankles. I made a mental note of the bedpost and the method of tying him. His shoes were new; only the middle of the soles showed wear.

He waited until I was in the chair again before seeking a more comfortable position. He pulled himself up until his head touched the iron rods and bent his elbows. Then he flexed his legs. Groaning with relief, for a little while he was occupied with himself. I decided to tie the belt more loosely next time.

"What about my hands?" he asked.

"I can't free them."

"Where there's a will there's a way," he said.

"Perhaps I don't want to."

He looked at me for an uncomfortably long moment before saying: "You don't want to double-cross your father. I can understand that."

I went to the kitchen and drank some water from the tap; I could never have brought myself to use one of our glasses.

The prisoner, not knowing what I was doing, called out: "You aren't leaving, are you?"

The kitchen was a pigsty: soiled, moldy dishes everywhere, on the table some dried-up bread and curling slices of sausage, plates and saucers full of cigarette butts, and a sour smell coming from half-empty beer bottles. This filthy state seemed to me to be the inevitable result of such an undertaking, and

I still believe that. There had been times when I had had to listen to Father lecturing me for not leaving the cottage tidy enough after my visits. When I closed my eyes, I saw Martha and me as we lay in each other's arms.

He was obviously relieved when I went back into the room; he was sitting upright, propped on his arms behind his back. I reminded him that two days ago he had claimed that he was being tortured, and I wanted to know what all that was about.

He looked at me meaningfully, as if to indicate that I must prepare myself for something extremely unpleasant. Then he said: "They like beating up people."

"Who does?"

"Sorry to have to tell you this: Your father is the worst."

"He's the only one who hits you?"

"Well, no, but he hits me the most and the hardest. The bald fellow hits me too. Only Kwart hasn't touched me yet. That's because we know each other. We go to the same café."

"You saw the others for the first time here?"

"Yes. Kwart tricked me into coming here, making me believe I'd been asked to play skat. I like playing skat."

"Why do they beat you?"

"They ask questions, and if they don't get the answers they want they beat me. Trouble is, I'm not psychic."

"Where do they hit you?"

"Usually in the stomach and the chest. In the face, too, but only with the flat of their hands. Open up my shirt and you'll know what black and blue means."

He was probably telling the truth. It may sound unbelievable, but I was relieved that he didn't have worse things to report. "But with you people, things must have been much worse," I said.

"What do you mean?"

"In Neuengamme."

He looked at me, surprised, almost offended, as if he hadn't expected such an allusion from me. But he didn't protest; he said nothing, because I was the last person he wanted to annoy.

I saw a pair of eyeglasses under the table and picked them up; one of the metal side pieces was damaged. I asked whether the glasses were his, and he nodded. I put them back under the table. I still had some questions that had less to do with him than with my father.

"I'd like to know why they are interrogating you. Is there something to be cleared up, or what? They could have reported you, couldn't they? What do you think? Why have they brought you here?"

He shrugged and said: "For days I've thought about nothing else. I could understand it if we knew each other personally—I mean, if one of them had been an inmate of Neuengamme. But we've never seen each other, and after thirty years, all of a sudden this! Do you know what I suspect?"

He stared fixedly at me, and I turned away until he went on speaking.

"That the whole thing is due to a kind of persecution mania. I don't want to offend anyone, but isn't that the most reasonable explanation? They still feel trapped; they think that our kind are waiting for a chance to shove them back into a concentration camp. I told them till I was blue in the face what a nobody I was in those days. But they refuse to believe me."

"Has there ever been an official investigation of your case?" I asked.

"There is no case."

"Then why are you afraid to call for help?"

Several times he seemed about to answer but always stopped. I got up, took the belt, and indicated that he was to slide down again. He did so without protest and held out his legs.

While I was wrapping the belt around his ankles and the bedpost, he asked me to believe that he regretted the deplorable events of those years, even though he bore no responsibility for them. When he began to tell me how he often lay awake for nights on end because of the memory of the camp, I pulled the belt tight with all my strength. He understood, and fell silent immediately.

I hung the sheet over the window again and put the chair back in its place: otherwise I had changed nothing. His face was filled with dismay. All the questions I might still have asked seemed meaningless. I had learned nothing, I had achieved nothing that would be of any importance to anybody. Meanwhile, I have realized that it was only for my own sake that I had gone to the cottage: to prove to myself that I wasn't closing my eyes to this nightmarish situation.

I noticed that I had tied him to the wrong bedpost. When I undid the belt, he said fervently: "Thank God!" But he was silent when I tied his legs again, this time to the correct bedpost; he held just as still as the first time.

"I hope you know that I can't make any trouble for your father?" he said when I had finished. "I mean, assuming that I get out of here."

"I realize that," I said.

"Why did you come here?"

I went to the kitchen to have a look around, although I hadn't touched anything there but the tap. It would be a long time before I could use the cottage again with Martha, even if he were to disappear today. To clean it and air it suddenly didn't seem enough, but what else? A huge fly emerged from an open jam jar. I heard the man call, asking me to come back again. It wasn't nearly afternoon yet.

When I stood beside the bed, he said: "I'd like to make a suggestion."

"I have to go now," I said.

"If you'll help me, I'm prepared to make it worth your while. You would have to come back with a file or, better still, with a heavy wire cutter. You know what a wire cutter is?"

It was not the moment to demonstrate my sensitivity: since I wanted to prevent his betraying me to Father I must not deprive him of all hope of my help. So I asked: "How much did you have in mind?"

"I've managed to save a bit over the years, and I'm prepared to give it all to you. Between you and me, I'd be glad if in this way I could draw a line under the damn past. I wouldn't regard it as a loss, believe me."

"How much?" I repeated.

"Five thousand marks."

I had the impression that he had intended to mention a larger figure, so I pretended to think over his offer. It must have been a tense moment for him.

"If I tried very hard, I might be able to scrape up another thousand," he said.

A notion came to me, so absurd and despicable that I wished I could blot it out immediately: whether it wouldn't be a good solution to accept the money and let him escape. Since I had been considering releasing him anyway, no further effort would have been involved. And wasn't there some justice in the money passing from him to me, I found myself thinking?

"One more thing," he said. "I can imagine that eventually I'll be killed. Not that they are intending to do this at the moment, but how else can it go on? Soon they'll reach the point of not knowing what to do with me. In a few days they'll be tired of the whole thing, then they'll find it a nuisance to keep coming here. Do you believe they'll untie me then? How can they? They'll never bring themselves to do that."

I had to admit that his fear was not unfounded. During many days of pondering, he had come to the conclusion that the worst of all possible outcomes was at the same time the most likely. Later I was surprised at how unmoved I was while he was fighting for his life.

"I'm merely telling you this," he said, "so you won't think we have unlimited time."

"If those three are told that I've been here, they'll change the lock. Then the rest would take care of itself."

"Do you think I'm crazy?" he said.

The door to the room had to be firmly closed, the kitchen door left ajar, the front door double-locked. As I emerged from the cottage, a little dog dashed away, as if it had been listening under the window, a terrier, its owner nowhere in sight; not far off there were dozens of other cottages to which the dog might belong. For a while I stood in the porch, scanning the area. I'd have given a lot to know how Kwart had come by his knowledge. The prisoner could hardly have been reckless enough to choose him, of all people, for a confessor. I was beginning to feel annoyed, because I wouldn't be able to bring myself to accept the six thousand marks. As I approached the edge of the forest, the rain grew heavier.

That was it, more or less.

A coincidence: Martha was opening the window to air the room, saw me hurrying through the rain, and was standing with outstretched arms as I entered the hallway downstairs. At that instant, my visit to the forest prison became a thing of the past. We stopped on every second step to kiss until we reached her landing. I had arrived an hour ahead of time, but not a second too early.

Her mother called through a door to ask who was there, and Martha pushed me into the kitchen, took my right hand, and held it out for her mother to shake, saying: "Be nice to him, he's so shy."

Rahel made a remark about her daughter's sense of humor. Then we went to Martha's room, and I showed her who was shy. We embraced, and everything I had hoped for from Martha in that godforsaken cottage proved to be true. Martha pointed to my shoes and asked whether I had walked across a field.

I never felt really comfortable in that room; we were only there when we had no other choice. On one such occasion I bolted the door, but Martha had looked so unhappy that I resolved never to do it again. I took off my shoes as well as my wet socks. We sat down on the rug, carefully avoiding the bed. Martha took my foot and rubbed it between her hands as if I had come from the depths of winter.

"Now for your surprise," I said.

Martha was in no hurry. She proceeded to rub the other foot until she considered it warm enough. Then, after crawling on all fours to her desk, she stood up, and her eyes began to shine as if our life were about to change the very next moment.

"It's a pretty big surprise."

"I can't stand the suspense," I said.

From the desk she picked up a fat pink binder and handed it to me. I read the words in large letters on the cover: *The Years before the Beginning*. Although it's easy enough with hindsight to maintain that from the first moment I felt an aversion to it, it's the truth. Martha sat down again beside me; my hesitation had lasted too long for her. Impatiently she flipped back the cover: it was a film script.

"What is it?"

She let me leaf through it for a bit as if not wanting to deprive me of the pleasure of finding out for myself. No matter what the page, there was dialogue everywhere: a name, a colon, followed by sentences, vast quantities of sentences. I glanced at Martha to see whether she was expecting me to read line for line, but her finger firmly directed my eyes back to the script. As I turned the pages, something red kept cropping up: all the lines to be spoken by a certain Rahel had been marked in the margin with a red pencil.

"Doesn't anything strike you?"

In the text I saw the words "SS man," in various places, from which I concluded that *The Years before the Beginning* referred to the Nazi period. Martha's smile would have faded had she known I had come straight from an SS man, and a genuine one at that. He had been a nobody, he claimed. I could believe him or not; it made strangely little difference. I could not muster any hatred, no matter how hard I tried.

He was a tiresome problem in my father's life, hence also in mine—no more, no less.

"I said, Doesn't anything strike you?"

"Do you mean the red markings?"

"What else?"

She took the binder from me, pushed me down flat on the rug, lay down beside me, and began to explain. We lay stretched out side by side as if in a double coffin. Did I remember, she asked, that she'd been invited out with her parents the previous evening? I did. The man they had gone to see was Roland Minge—no doubt the name would mean something to me. "You went to see a man?" I asked. But she was in no mood for jokes. It turned out that Roland Minge was a movie director, apparently a well-known one, who was about to shoot a new movie, *The Years before the Beginning*. Martha asked if I was now able to continue the story in my own words. Because I went on lying there like a corpse, she solved the riddle herself: he had offered her the part of Rahel.

Of course I had seen this coming. "Because you're such an excellent and experienced actress?" I asked.

"Perhaps because he likes me a lot," said Martha.

She sat up and smiled down at me, as if it was all too easy to understand that I was jealous. Hence bad-tempered. "Have you never had something offered to you that was beyond your wildest dreams?"

She had already accepted. They were in a hurry because some actress or other had fallen ill, so Minge had asked Martha to make up her mind quickly. If it hadn't been improper, she told me, she would have accepted then and there, but for the sake of appearances she had asked for a script, had read it that night and phoned Minge a few hours ago.

"That means the child has already fallen into the well?"

"What child? What well?"

"Why didn't you speak to me about it first?"

"If you'd objected, I'd have been in a nice fix," she said.

We heard Hugo Lepschitz come into the apartment. Martha laid her head on my chest; we listened until all was quiet in the passage. She took my hand in a gesture of reconciliation and played with my fingers; we were simply not used to any tension between us. "It's like a journey into the unknown," she said. "What's so hard to understand about it?"

I sat down at the desk and began to read the script; I don't know why. Perhaps I wanted to show Martha that I was concerned about her affairs even when I wasn't asked. I had to turn many pages before coming to the first red marking. Rahel was described as a pretty woman of thirty, with short hair and a straightforward expression. I broke out in a sweat. Although it was no concern of mine how old Mr. Minge thought Martha was, were they really going to cut her hair short?

"What's going to happen to your hair?"

"To my hair?"

"It says here quite clearly that she has short hair."

Martha bent over the script; I pointed to the place. "Well, imagine that!" she whispered.

"I thought you'd read the script?"

"During the night," she said. It seemed to me that she was taking the whole thing much too lightly.

"Are you going to let them cut off all your hair?"

"Why not?"

Uneasily I went on reading. The story was about a Resistance group, of which one member was a Jewish girl—Rahel. All the members lived with false documents and were in the same danger. Consequently it made no difference to Rahel that she was Jewish—at least that's how I took it. There was one scene in which the group kidnapped the child of an in-

92

dustrialist, to obtain money for their underground activities by blackmail. In the next scene Rahel and Anton, a young Communist, were guarding the child in a remote barn. Anton was in love with her. The script said: *For the first time she notices the fire in his eyes and surrenders to it.* While they roll in the hay, the little girl is able to escape.

I mustn't think, said Martha, that acting was done for nothing; she'd be paid plenty for it. She forced herself between me and the script and acted the part of a rich woman, with weary eyes, curled lips, and fat stomach. I imagined having accepted the six thousand marks and being able to say: Forget it, Martha, let's go on a nice trip instead, I've got money to burn. We had never traveled anywhere together, for God's sake, to Cracow or the Caucasus. How could she resist?

"I'll be paid three hundred marks a day," she said, sitting down on my lap, almost as if trying to distract me from the script. "Minge thinks," she said, "that I'll be needed for ten days, but it might be as many as fourteen. That would mean a minimum of three thousand of the best. What do you say now?"

"I never knew you were so keen on money," I replied.

She passed her hand over my face as if it were a blackboard she wanted to wipe clean of unnecessary words. When I held on to her hand, she said: "Then it's about time you got to know me."

And she closed the script behind her back so I wouldn't go on reading. Nor did I want to as long as she was sitting on my lap; never had anyone been more willingly distracted. I put my arms around her and left it entirely up to her how sensible we would be. For a few moments things looked favorable, then she gave me a final kiss, with a significant look at the door. I asked whether I should say hello to her father, and Martha thought that was a brilliant idea.

When I came back, she was standing by the window, the script open in her hands. She proceeded to read aloud a scene: Rahel's arrest by the Gestapo. Then she asked me my opinion, and I told her I didn't know enough about it. She nodded, as though I had given precisely the right answer. Simultaneously we saw my shoes and socks lying on the floor, and we both wondered how I could have gone barefoot to see her parents. The scene wasn't original, I thought: of course they will be arrested, what else can be expected?

Martha said she would probably never have been offered the part if Minge and her father hadn't known each other for years. But Minge was lucky, she said, for she happened to be talented. Although she was trying to give the impression that she was talking about something not very important, I could tell how serious she was about it.

Suddenly I felt tired, my head demanded a respite. It was being forced to give an opinion about everything; at school, at home, in the forest, now here, it was constantly being required to make decisions. My head ordered me to drop on the bed, and I obeyed.

"Aren't you feeling well?"

"Could be," I had to say.

Martha showed no alarm. She stood silhouetted against the window until I closed my eyes; then she crossed the room. Her fingers touched my temples and drew little circles, feather light, to bring me back to life or make me fall asleep. It was almost unbelievable that she had allowed herself to be so dazzled. She gave one reason after another for why she had been hired for this movie, except the obvious one: that she looked the way Mr. Minge imagined a pretty Jewish girl looked. I could understand his dilemma: young Jewish girls are few and far between, and here Martha suddenly turns up on his doorstep.

I held my tongue. By this time I was past master at keeping

quiet, added to which there was my fatigue. She sat down on the bed without interrupting the gentle circling of her fingers; probably she was holding her face close to mine. I could smell her mouth. But I didn't move, I didn't even open my eyes, I wanted everything to stay exactly the way it was.

We go up into the attic, Rahel Lepschitz and I, to hang up the laundry; she can't handle the big pieces alone. We begin by wiping the clotheslines, which are black with the dust that sifts through the roof. Father and I never did any washing; we always took our stuff to the laundry, an unheard-of luxury. I have already had one disappointment today, one not altogether unexpected.

In the morning I had gone to the student counseling office, where I had told a man about my housing problem. He said wearily that he'd be glad to put me on the waiting list for the students' residence. It didn't sound too promising; nevertheless, I accepted the offer and thought: Just in case. When the man had a look at my identity card, he gave a laugh and said: "But you're from Berlin, the residence was built for everyone except Berliners." I said: "But I don't have a place to stay!" The man: "Where are you living?" I: "With strangers." The man: "Renting a room?" I: "That's right." The man: "And why don't you stay there?" Then he said that, strictly speaking, it made no difference; for cases like mine the university wasn't responsible anyway, and maybe I should try the housing authorities. When I didn't immediately get up from the visitor's chair he said: "Always these exceptions, everyone claims to be an exception."

First we hang up the small items, one working from each end, each piece as close as possible to the next, to leave enough room for sheets and other bed linen. I notice that Rahel has paused and is staring at me. Why? I try not to grin when I catch on: I happen to have picked up Martha's panties. Rahel sees this and is thinking: How must the poor boy be feeling now!

I can't think of anyone I might turn to for help in finding a place to live. The one good thing is that it was only yesterday that I decided to look for a place, and today I'm already looking. By my standards that can be called breakneck speed.

She heaves a huge sigh and keeps looking at me while she smooths her husband's shirts. I simply cannot understand why Rahel and Hugo Lepschitz want me, of all people, for a son-in-law. Because they like me? Because I've inherited a little money? Because they suspect that Martha will bring home a non-Jewish boy? Because I happen to be around? I see Rahel rummaging in the basket of wet laundry, I'm sure she's putting aside all the items that might shock me.

The plastic clotheslines are so limp that our sheets hang only a few inches from the floor. I suggest that we wring out the large pieces to relieve them of some of their weight, but in Rahel's opinion the distance from the floor is irrelevant; the main thing is that they don't touch it. There'll be nothing to prevent my coming to see them from time to time if I'm living in a different part of the city. The one I'll miss most will be Rahel. We hang up the last sheet and stand face to face, our eyes expressing the thought that there is still time to avert the calamity.

I go to my room and do what I usually do: waste time. I read the newspaper and turn on the radio in search of music that doesn't require listening to. I read an interview with a racing cyclist:

Neues Deutschland: Did you have any problems en route? K. D. Diers: Well, yes, at first I wasn't quite sure which gear to choose. So after about six kilometers I switched to a relatively high gear. And then I was scared that with the wind getting colder all the time my muscles might seize up! ND: How was the mood of the team at the start of this year's peace rally? K. D. Diers: Optimistic. Earlier on, Hans-Joachim had some stomach trouble, but that settled down, so we were all in the best of spirits. ND: Karl Dietrich, I understand you were trained as a watchmaker? K. D. Diers: That's right, but at present I'm privileged to be doing my service with the National People's Army, I'm a corporal. ND: How did you happen to take up cycling? K. D. Diers: It was in 1965, when I took part in the Little Peace Rally, I enjoyed it and then for a long time raced for the Locomotive Güsten team, where Max Händler taught me a lot. One of my greatest successes at that time was a silver medal at the Spartacus Games. ND: At age twenty you're the second-youngest on your team? K. D. Diers: Wrong—on Thursday I'll be twenty-one!

My lack of friends is neither pleasant nor disastrous; it just happened that way. It's true that Father once accused me of being like the princess and the pea as far as friendships were concerned, but should I have accepted just anybody, regardless, merely because it's a good thing to have a friend? Needless to say, I could use a friend now, especially one who knew of a place to live.

Hugo Lepschitz thinks differently from my father about this. A few months ago he said he could well understand why my outside contacts were so limited: because our kind have to be so very particular about who we take up with.

To my question as to who he meant by "our kind," he replied: "Oh, come now, my boy, *I* know, *you* know—why waste time explaining?"

A rare visitor comes into my room, her hair pinned up, and wearing long, dangling earrings that I have never seen before: Martha. She asks whether I am very busy. I put down the newspaper. My gesture to the empty chair makes her smile. But she sits down, and gone is her cheerfulness; she looks around the room as if in sitting down she has mislaid her courage.

While waiting for her to begin, I invent a story for myself: Yesterday evening, while Martha was with her young man, she had to think about us two. Comparing me with him, she became aware of the mistake of her life. But it's not too late: there's still time. Shouldn't we try again where we left off?

"It's nothing important," Martha says. "I shouldn't even ask."

"Yes?"

"You've got some money in the bank, haven't you?"

"Any amount."

"Can you lend me some?"

"Yes."

"I would understand if you had any objection."

"Why should I?"

"I mean, it would be quite natural."

For the first time, someone wants to borrow money from me. I've never borrowed either; it is a moment of great embarrassment. I consider how best to end it quickly and ask: "How much do you need?"

But my remark appears to intimidate her. She interprets it as a warning not to be greedy.

"I'm going to the bank tomorrow anyway," I say. "Just tell me how much."

I don't want to sound boastful or excessively helpful, as if

99

I were prepared to make any sacrifice to regain Martha's favor. I don't want to sound like anything. I just want her to say how much she needs so we can bring this to an end.

"I don't really know. The thing is, Papa's birthday is coming up. I have no money for a gift, and I don't know what to give him."

"On his last birthday I wasn't living here yet."

"Maybe a shirt," says Martha. "Most of the shirts he wears are pathetic."

"How old will he be?" I ask.

"Let's see. Born 1914—what've we got now? For heaven's sake, he's going to be sixty!"

My bed hasn't been made. I get up and, in passing, pull up the cover, since the sheet doesn't look quite clean. I open a drawer that has never contained any money, look in, and say: "No, I really have nothing here—sorry."

"There's no hurry," says Martha. "Could you spare a hundred marks?"

"You can have more if you like."

"A hundred will do. I'll need it for three weeks. Is that all right?"

"Pay me back whenever it suits you."

Martha rises and says: "Maybe it had better be a hundred and fifty."

She smiles at so much helpfulness and goes to the door. My eyes assail her from behind: the blue jeans, the dark blue shirt, the brown hair. Martha is walking away, but already her pace is slowing. Who is to hold her back if not I? In a moment she'll stop. She will ask softly: That's how you seize the opportunity? But she is leaving, leaving, I must be out of my mind. I cling to what I know for sure. Fifteen minutes ago it was still true, so why not now?

"Wait," I say, as she reaches the door. "If he's having such an important birthday, shouldn't I give him a present too?"

"That's up to you," Martha says, but she stops.

What else? I can see surprise in her eyes, a small, cool gleam. She knows me well; if anyone can decipher my expression, it's Martha. I must be careful: long pauses can tell tales too.

I nod, it is over. The emotional seizure is over, now she can go or stay, the only thing still to be settled is Hugo Lepschitz's present. Where does an attack like that come from, and what makes it disappear? She'd love to know why I'm suddenly so relieved, I can tell from her expression. But she'll never know.

"I have a suggestion," I say.

"What is it?"

She lets go of the door handle, a sign that she is not in a hurry. I know how curious Martha is; in our good times she never made a secret of it. Last summer she used to look through my diary, merely out of curiosity, not mistrust.

"You'd like to suggest," she says, "that we buy a joint gift for him?"

Again I nod. "In that case," I say, "we still wouldn't know, of course, what to get him, but we'd need only one inspiration between us."

That convinces her. On Father's last birthday I gave him a photo album. He thanked me effusively but never used it. We think about what would appeal to Hugo Lepschitz.

I received a letter from Elle. It was undated, but I believed it was written before my last visit. She didn't say a word about the episode in the cottage.

> *Dear Hans*
> *please read this letter at night*
> *it was written at night too*
> *there are strangethings going on here*
> *that force me to stay awake at night*
> *only unfortunately I don't always manage to do that . . .*
> *Just imagine you wake up onemorning*
> *and find you have been robbed that's exactly what happened*
> *   to me*
> *there is nothing more silent than thieves they float*
> *around the room like elves . . .*
> *I wake up and the beautiful picture*
> *that yougave me has vanished*
> *then it occurred to me how often something has been missing*
> *a cigarette a match a page from a book*
> *that particular thief goes about his work so carefully*
> *that at first glance there is Never anything to see*
> *which this time . . .*
> *But since I have been staying awake nightafternight*
> *he has Never come again*

I read or write to stay awake
and would like to surprise him
but he is so clever
or he sees the light under my door
but as soon as I turn it out I'm asleep
so how can he ever be caught . . .
I hope you remember Albert who is still
my friend
when I told him about the thefts he
understood immediately for overtheyears
many of his things have disappeared too
Albert is a most understanding person
but his advice is useless
you will laugh when you hear
what he advised me to do
he said I should tie down all endangered articles
because apparently no thief has enoughtime to undo a
    thousand knots . . .
But that is Not so much funny as sad poor Albert
he has a mind like a razor but
always turned in one direction inwardly
outwardly he Never succeeds . . .
In the dining room I hear that Others
have been robbed too
that pleases me inasmuch
as I am Not the only victim
I thought I might discuss with the other victims
how to set a trap for the thief
but then it occurred to me
that this person was probably also sitting in the dining room
only when the staff notice something missing
will anything be done
I hope it will be too late then . . .
Enough of that tell me about your big exam

Father has told me
how hard you have to work
and how convinced he is that you will make it
of course I let him go on believing the first part
only I am Not as proud of you as he is
actually you are Not working all that hard
learning comes easily to you
you have a brain
that seems made for study
you have a remarkably good memory
but you have another characteristic which
offsets that and hampers you
you know what I am referring to
your superficiality
you constantly believe that there is more to be found some
     place
Other than where you are
you lack the desire to linger
in this respect you might follow the example of
Yoursister for I am still here
in this nuthouse after so much time . . .
But it is beautiful at night
Should I be grateful to the thief for this
it is a time that everyone should try
including you
through the open window this bird is singing
I have read how much its song is praised I wonder why
I assume that in this praise
allowance is made for the night
As for me I prefer to hear only the rustling of the trees
Now I do Not even know
are there trees outside your window or Not . . .
Now in conclusion I must ask you
to treat the theft affair confidentially

in other words to keep it to yourself
because I do Not know what it may lead to
I would Not like to be the one who makes
a mountain out of a molehill
perhaps there will be some harmless explanation
even though I do Not believe that . . .
Between ourselves
I have long since ceased to care about the loss
but apart from ourselves no one needs to know that
Yoursister

I have never given Elle a picture.

Without knocking, Father opened my door. I was still in bed. I had read the letter four or five times and saw no reason to get up. He had come to lecture me about my slovenliness: there wasn't a single clean dish left, the furniture was thick with dust, and so on. He said I would do better to pay attention to my household chores than stick my nose into the business of strangers. He actually said "strangers."

I locked myself in the bathroom and stayed there for an hour. It wasn't clear to me whether he was really that annoyed about the state of the apartment, or whether he only wanted to shut me up for the rest of the day. Then it dawned on me that I had also been given a concealed message: If he was aware of my visit to the cottage, he would have mentioned it right away.

After I returned to my room, he came in, carrying a cup of tea, and sat down.

"I see you did find a clean cup after all," I said.

"I had to wash it," he said.

I started to dress and ran into a problem: on the one hand, I didn't want to stand there naked after being lectured; on the other, I didn't want to hurry. I couldn't send him out of the room; it would have been unthinkable.

"Would you be kind enough to tell me how your exams went?" he asked.

"They're over," I replied.

"May one hear the results?"

"I don't know them myself," I said, "but I imagine they went all right."

For a few moments I concentrated on dressing. When I looked at him again, he had put down his cup and was reading Elle's letter. He appeared to be reading every line twice. The interest I noted in his eyes made me jealous. I went into the kitchen.

There I got busy washing the dishes. No one meant more to him than Elle, even though he went to see her less often than I did; he felt it keenly that she didn't show more warmth toward him. When he realized that I came first with her, he stopped going to the home with me and went alone.

While the water was running into the sink, I tiptoed back: he was still sitting there with the letter. I could see only his back, but his posture seemed to denote an inner turmoil.

In protracted negotiations we had split up the housework between us. It was strictly laid down who was to do the shopping, the dusting, the vacuuming, and the dishes. This month, shopping and washing the dishes were my jobs, and I didn't want to give Father a chance to put me in the wrong whenever he felt like it.

After finishing the glasses I noticed that he had sat down at the kitchen table. I went on washing. He had come in order to talk to me, not to check up on my housework—I sensed that. He never came to me without a reason, never, for instance, because he might have enjoyed my company.

"Does she write to you often?" he asked.

"Sometimes not for months," I replied without turning around, "then sometimes every other day."

"Why didn't you ever let me see any of these letters?"

"Why should I show you my mail?"

A few seconds passed before he said: "That's not your mail, nitwit."

"What else is it?"

"She's never written to *me*," he said.

That surprised me, I had taken it for granted that Elle was writing to him too. How sad for him, I thought. He must be convinced that, out of some strange habit, she addressed all the letters intended for both of us only to me, so that he had the same claim upon them as I did, and that I was constantly withholding the letters from him.

I heard him sigh, and I wanted to say something comforting, but when I turned around he was gone. That's how it always was: One of us forever being hurt, and the other forever having to toil at undoing the misery.

When I entered his room, he was sitting with folded arms in his armchair, and the look he gave me implied that I had been taking my time. I didn't know whether I should give him all Elle's letters to read now. One result might be that all those letters would depress rather than please him.

But he wasn't waiting for words of comfort. He indicated a chair with his chin.

"What do you want?" I asked.

He affected surprise, spread his fingers on his chest, and said: "Did I call you?"

"Do you want me to leave?"

I only hope I have not inherited his compulsion to complicate every discussion and burden it with an extreme touchiness. It has often turned the simplest conversation into sheer torture.

"I had no idea she doesn't write to you," I said. "Otherwise I would have . . ."

He interrupted me: "Save your sympathy for a better occasion. I imagine that you wish to speak to me about something else."

"Then your imagination is at fault."

"All the better."

Here was another of his habits that interfered with normal conversation: When you told him something, he would constantly interrupt with conjectures as to how the story would go on. Sometimes I had to fight my way through his interruptions and prognoses before being able to come to the point. This trick of his was time-consuming, but quite often I also found it entertaining, since sometimes his assumptions were an improvement on my original story.

I was prepared to remain silent for hours, but finally he said: "A little more anger on your part toward villains and murderers wouldn't come amiss."

"What are you talking about?"

"Why are you so unconcerned?" he asked. "Why don't you get angry when you think of their victims? I don't mean only the dead; I also mean people like me and Elle. A little more indignation, if you please."

He patted his pockets as if looking for cigarettes; then he remembered he had stopped smoking and gave up the search. "Don't you know what led to Elle's illness?"

"Nobody knows that."

"How can you say such a thing?"

There followed a description of Elle's childhood that I was hearing not for the first time. Cool and skeptical, I sat facing him while he became submerged in memories. The predictable emotion overcame him at the point where his little daughter was sent away to be hidden by money-grubbing strangers. And when, after the Liberation, his little Elle, always so merry and bright, had turned into a hard, suspicious, irritable girl, he had to fight back the tears. Although Elle had never brought up the subject, for Father there was no doubt that she regarded the people she attacked as the kind from whom she had once had to be hidden.

When he was done, I asked whether they had come to any decision about the fate of the prisoner. Father stared at me as if my question was preposterous.

"You and your friends have taken on a load with that man that you can't carry," I said. "You're doing yourselves in and don't even realize it."

"It is rare to meet an eighteen-year-old who knows as much about life as you do," said Father.

"You have maintained that the courts are not competent to handle a case like this," I said, "that they would only condemn the man because they have no alternative. And that's simply wrong."

"So let it be wrong."

"You can't seriously maintain that the courts secretly sympathize with concentration-camp guards! They would condemn the man simply and solely because of their belief that such a man *must* be condemned."

Father looked at me mockingly and nodded, as if to encourage me to spout more such nonsense. Then he said: "I'll explain it to you once again. The reason they can't condemn him out of their belief is that they have none. All they know is orders. Many of them imagine that the orders they are given correspond to their own opinions. But who can rely on that? Order them to eat dog turds, and, if you're strong enough, they'll soon come to regard dog turds as a delicacy."

"That's just talk."

"Look around you," said Father, pointing to the window. "Where in this country can you find anything original? Show me something these people might have made solely because they thought of it themselves."

110

"The point is that, no matter how they behave, you just can't stand Germans."

"That's hardly surprising."

I could see from his face that he regarded the conversation as closed; I was becoming a nuisance. I felt tired and powerless, unable to stop him. I asked him what the interrogations had produced. I could hear how listless my question sounded, like an attempt to keep a flagging conversation going. He replied that the results were disappointingly meager—he had to admit that—whereupon I said that anyway the prisoner told them only what they wanted to hear from him.

He smiled and said: "Too bad we don't have you with us there, with all your expertise."

"And what'll happen when you've finished the interrogations?"

He looked at his watch, got up, and showed surprise at how late it was. "Some other time, my boy, some other time."

In passing he patted my shoulder. At the door he turned and said: "And in future kindly give me the letters to read right away."

That day I tried three times to phone Kwart, and three times he wasn't at home. The phone was always answered by Wanda, a harpist with whom he lived, who invariably asked what I wanted from Gordon. Each time she sounded more impatient, as if offended that someone wanted to talk with him rather than with her. Not even Father knew whether the two were married. Wanda had the biggest gap between her front teeth that I have ever seen and was at least twenty years younger than Kwart. On the few occasions I saw them together he seemed afraid of her, but, when I mentioned this once to Father, he tapped my forehead with his finger. I wouldn't have felt free to tell her what I wanted to discuss with Kwart, even if I'd been sure of what I wanted to say. I didn't doubt that he was keeping the kidnapping a secret from her. So at my third attempt I lied, saying that it had to do with some trivial information that only he could give me, a question about music history in connection with my exams. In my haste I forgot that Wanda was a musician herself, although unemployed, and that in this way I had added insult to injury.

Finally, at my fourth attempt, Kwart lifted the receiver; by that time it was evening. I told him I'd like to talk to him, and he didn't ask: What about? As if the reason for my call were perfectly clear to him, he reeled off a schedule of his concert dates and rehearsals that left only Saturday and Sunday. I asked him whether he couldn't find a little time this evening, half an hour at most; the matter was quite urgent. He told me to wait. When he returned to the phone he asked if I would like to have supper with them. I told him I would rather come after supper, if he didn't mind, and he said: "All right, then, come at nine."

Kwart opened the door himself, gave me a conspiratorial handshake, and gestured toward his room. I could see Wanda standing at the far end of the passage. She responded ungraciously to my greeting and disappeared. Kwart closed his door behind us and said: "I take it you wish to speak to me alone?"

In the middle of the room was a music stand; in front of it, a chair with his violin lying on it. He put it away in its case to clear a space. There was no other chair, only a couch. I had once heard Kwart tell my father that it was his bad luck that Heifetz and Oistrakh happened to be Jews: everyone expected big things from him too, but unfortunately he was only a run-of-the-mill violinist.

He asked whether I had told Father about this visit.

"He knows nothing," I said.

At that he pulled a face, and I reassured him by saying that my visit was not a secret, and he was welcome to tell Father about it if he thought he should. "Thanks a million," he said.

He placed the violin case on a shelf, sat down on the chair, crossed his arms, and leaned back, like a spectator before the start of a performance from which he doesn't expect much. I had to move into a corner of the couch because the music on the stand hid Kwart's face from me. His pose didn't suit him; I knew him for a softy: shy and awkward, embarrassed, a mouse of a man.

"It's about the camp guard," I said.

From my conversations with Father during the last few days, I scraped together those sentences and phrases that seemed to me best suited for putting the kidnapping in a bad light. Not a single new point occurred to me. Still, it didn't seem altogether hopeless to try to drive a wedge between the kidnappers; it was conceivable that one or other of my words that had bounced off Father would score with the weak Kwart. And if I managed to instill just enough fear in him to make him recoil at himself, mightn't that create a new situation for the other two as well?

I must have hammered away at him for a good ten minutes. With Father, I had felt upset, at a disadvantage, whereas now I was in charge, at least so it seemed. I never took my eyes off Kwart, in order to see from his reactions where I could get at him and which of my arguments were falling flat. Today I know that I underestimated him.

He didn't interrupt, but endeavored to maintain an intimidating pose: narrowed lips, cool stare, rigid expression. His arms lay across his belly as if on a balustrade; he didn't even allow himself to blink.

We measured each other with long looks. I still hadn't given up hope that mentally he was preparing to back down. When I was about to continue, he stood up, opened the door a crack, and looked cautiously out into the passage. Then he sat down again and gestured to me to carry on. I felt that he had calculated correctly: somehow this hiatus had caused the luster of my words to fade.

I, too, soon heard footsteps in the passage, followed immediately by the sound of the apartment door closing. Kwart bit his lip and for a few moments was busy with his own thoughts.

"Wanda's gone out," he said finally. "Pay no attention."

He was so sure that he didn't bother to check. I was silent, and a few rumblings from him sounded like sighs of profound anxiety. He looked at me again and recalled what I had been talking about. "Yes," he said, "yes indeed. You've expressed yourself very clearly. I have no comment to make."

Was this weakness or strength, or was it neither? My puzzled expression encouraged him. He told me point-blank that I had found my father a hard nut to crack and was now having a go at old Kwart, who perhaps would be easier to crack. The thought almost made him smile; his tone became flippant. Now, he said, I must hurry off to see Rotstein, as a finishing touch. Then I would have completed the job and could start worrying about my own affairs again.

Suddenly he was the stronger and I was the weaker: where had I gone wrong? I started over again by saying that the prisoner couldn't cause them any problems if they let him go; they could still report him. He was sure to be convicted, and then it would be up to the prison authorities, not them, to deal with him.

Kwart seemed to hesitate between laughing out loud and despairing. He patiently agreed with my assumption that Heppner would most likely keep his mouth shut if they let him go. But if they reported him, he said, and it should come to a trial, why should he spare them?

I had to disregard the fact that Kwart was right. I repeated the same arguments that had already failed: that even victims have no right to set themselves above the law, that I would be afraid to live in a country in which everyone appointed himself a judge, and so on. I talked until Kwart interrupted me by saying: "It's all right, my boy; you've done your best."

He sat down beside me on the couch and patted my hand. I simply couldn't understand where he found his confidence. He was behaving like someone who is accustomed to being in command. His affability made him seem even stronger than Father. "You'll have to accept the fact that we have our own ideas," he said.

"Have you considered the possibility that Father, you, and Rotstein may all end up in jail with the camp guard?" I asked.

"Yes, we've thought of that," he replied. "There are worse things."

"Father at least offers some reasons. I find them all ridiculous, but at least they're reasons. You say nothing. You listen to what I have to say, shake your head, and that's it."

"He was in camp, and I was in camp," said Kwart. "Why should we have different reasons?"

"Then you also believe that camp guards should not be judged by a German court of law?"

He shifted away, so as to get a better view of me. Solemn and arrogant, he looked me in the eye. In all the years I had known him, he had never once raised his voice, but that evening anything was possible. Father had once called him a donkey in sheep's clothing.

"Let's not talk about that," he said.

Then, with a groan, he got up, all of a sudden remembering that he was an old man. He moved the music stand aside and said he had an instinct for knowing when a conversation had come to an end.

"I want to know," I said, "whether your opinion of the Germans is the same as Father's."

Kwart picked up a single sheet of music and slowly moved his finger along the lines, as if looking for a certain place. Pretending to have found it, he hummed a fragment of melody, repeating it several times. On raising his eyes again, he seemed surprised to find me still sitting there.

"Is it true that it was you who lured the man to the cottage?"

"Is that what your father told you?"

Instantly I was aware of my blunder: idiot that I was, I

116

had betrayed the fact that I had spoken to the prisoner. What could I do but answer: "Who else?"

He forgot the music he was holding and shook his head at my father's indiscretion.

Hadn't it actually been Father who had told me about the special role Kwart had played in the kidnapping? The secrecy and the need to lie had made me lose track. I should have made notes from the very beginning, for my own safety.

With a lift of his chin, Kwart bade me follow him. We went into a room where a radio was playing. On the table were the remains of supper. He switched off the set, went to the cabinet for some schnapps and a glass, and poured himself a drink.

"Why not?" he said, as if to himself, like someone who has to overcome scruples. He sat down at the table and waited until I was sitting across from him. He downed his drink and proceeded to tell me how he had discovered that Heppner, a regular at his favorite bar, had been a concentration-camp guard. For three years they had played cards together before his first suspicions were aroused. Heppner had dropped hints when he was drunk, hints that, while not pointing to any inescapable conclusion, had made Kwart smell a rat. He discussed the matter with Father and Rotstein, and they advised him to get on a closer footing with the man, if necessary by buying him drinks. "The certainty has cost us a fortune," Kwart said. Needless to say, Father and Rotstein had each paid a one-third share, but he had been the only one who drank with the man.

After finishing his story, he quickly downed two more drinks. He pushed a bottle of tomato juice toward me and one of the used mugs on the table. From Father, I knew that ten years ago, while Kwart was on tour with the orchestra, his wife left him, taking their two daughters with her. For a long time after that, the authorities wouldn't allow him to travel with the orchestra, because of the risk that he might follow his family. From time to time he would receive a letter from them in Israel. When that happened, Father said, you couldn't talk to him for days. I have often tried to imagine the moment when he returned from a trip, opened the front door, and found the apartment empty.

So how did he visualize the end of the kidnapping? I asked. On the one hand, they wanted the camp guard to be punished, whereas on the other they could only release him at the cost of his impunity. As I had been told, there were only a limited number of options.

"You told me on the phone not more than half an hour," said Kwart.

"But nothing has been clarified!"

"What's there to clarify?" he asked mildly. "The affair will somehow come to an end, you can be sure of that. And if I may give you a piece of advice: You should think hard about whose side you're on. If you can answer that, it will take care of a lot of questions."

He put his arm around my shoulders and led me out to the passage. Until then I had met him only in Father's presence. Was this why he suddenly seemed like a different person? We had to go back because I had left my jacket behind. While I put it on, he moved the music stand into the center of the room again, making it plain that he hadn't a second to spare.

"Do you actually want to practice now?"

"What do you mean, 'want'?" he replied. "I'm a mere foot soldier on the music front. I have to work harder than you imagine."

When we said good night, he held onto my hand for a long time and looked into my eyes. He had come out on top, no question, whereas I had failed miserably. Being a mere

118

foot soldier on the life front, I had not succeeded in triumphing over irrationality.

On the stairs I met Wanda coming up. She asked me whether the gap in my knowledge of music history had now been filled. For a moment I had no idea what she meant.

Just four months until university and its coeds. I'll meet one of them the very first day—I'm sure of that; I won't waste any time. The moment I close my eyes, I see an ethereal creature with big breasts I can sink my face into. I'm almost twenty, a bundle of torments and pressures. My God, what am I supposed to do? The circumstances I have to live under are certainly not normal.

I take the streetcar to my old part of town, for no particular reason. I must gradually become used to living again with the city. This past year I've spent all my time slinking like a cat around its house.

Martha and I decided to look for a gift for Hugo Lepschitz this afternoon, but, when I asked her at breakfast what time we should start, she was suddenly too busy. I was annoyed, because there was pity in her voice, as if she regretted having to deny me the fulfillment of my dearest wish. I said that was *really* too bad, I had been so *terribly* looking forward to the afternoon, and she looked at me with arched eyebrows.

The streetcar, too, is full of women wanting to be looked at by me. Across the aisle a green-and-white-striped dress, two white knees, a hand's-breadth apart. Scarcely had I fastened my gaze on them when they moved together as if to ward off an attack. The face's turn will come later. My eyes scan the floor, a pig's snout rooting for truffles.

When I come to two high heels, I stop. One of them rests on the floor, the other hangs down from a crossed leg. Then slowly upward: blue slacks that go on and on; above them, a magazine with eight scarlet fingernails. I stare at the magazine so as not to miss the moment of bliss. But by the time a page is turned without revealing the hoped-for sight, I'm tired of waiting. The knees' face: not a day older than fifteen and containing nothing that would make me want to close my eyes. Beside her, the mother—who else could it be, the way their shoulders lean together? I should have started by looking in that direction. The hair in a roll around her head, like the housemaids in movies set in the days of the Kaiser, or like Rosa Luxemburg. Over a close-fitting T-shirt she is wearing a blouse open to the navel. She doesn't see me. We have been on the same streetcar for five stops, and I remain unnoticed, although there is nothing but a little air between us. Maybe it's because my mother died so young, but the women I tend most often to gape at are between thirty and forty. They need only snap their fingers, but the idea never occurs to them.

The closer I get to my old haunts, the more unfamiliar the street names become. There's no longer a Kniprode-Strasse, no Braunsberger, no Allensteiner, no Lippehner-Strasse. I hardly turn my back, and already they find nothing better to do than change the street names. The signs now read Artur-Becker-Strasse and Hans-Otto-Strasse and Liselotte-Herrmann-Strasse and Käthe-Niederkirchner-Strasse. I see this in riding past, but I've also read about it in the papers. From a distance the whole thing didn't concern me too much, but now I feel something like pity for the renamed streets. I imagine myself living on a Kirchberg-Gasse that one morning is suddenly called Anton-Müller-Strasse. I would feel I had been forcibly relocated, never mind who Anton Müller was. If I ever write a will, it must stipulate that no street is ever to be named after me.

Mother and daughter get off. My first impression was right; the girl dissolves into thin air, but the mother sails out like a queen. Not even through the window can I manage to attract her gaze. My mother was the same age as this woman when I was born, perhaps a little older. How Father must miss her. The daughter looks at me over her shoulder, probably wondering what such a young man can see in her mother.

In the days when we were in love, Martha and I, I never saw her as a collection of various parts of the body, yet right now I find myself staring only at parts of the body. Under newspapers, across male shoulders, in window reflections, I look for buttocks, bosoms, lips. The thought that an observant passenger might interpret my glances scares me to death. The streetcar is fuller now: I get up for a man who grins at me in surprise because he is hardly any older than I am. I want to stand, to turn my back on this streetcar full of female hips and dark underarms. I go to the end and look down onto the road as it streams out from under my feet. Five more stops to be endured.

It's not enough to turn away, for to shut out all those obscene and sinful sounds behind my back I would also have to hold my hands over my ears. What kind of streetcar have I landed in? There is a constant whispering and murmuring; I can feel steaming breath on my neck. But the moment I turn around they will be all innocence and behave like normal people.

My good fairy doesn't let me down: she diverts my thoughts by presenting me with a distraction that could hardly be greater: we are overtaking Martha. I see her walking along the street with a man, but we move away too fast for me to make out his face. She was too busy to go shopping for a birthday present for her father; now she is walking arm in arm with a strange man. I reflect on which denotes the greater intimacy: walking arm in arm or holding hands the way we always used to do.

They are in no hurry. When the streetcar stops, I almost miss getting off. Someone asks me whether I couldn't have thought of it earlier, and I answer: "But it's only just happened."

I cross the street and step into a doorway. As they approach, I discover one thing after another: that the man is wearing a three-piece suit, that they are deep in conversation, that he is much older than Martha, that he wears rimless glasses. If they looked in my direction, they could see me, so I step out of my hiding place. An actor, maybe even a director, a Somebody or other from the drama school. Perhaps she actually does find him attractive. A while ago I saw a movie in which a certain Isabella was deserted by her husband and promptly entered a convent. I won't even dream of such bliss.

It has long been decided that I will follow them. I don't ask why; I only know that I would have to be crazy to let slip such an opportunity. The man is the same age as the women who need only snap their fingers.

I cross the street and follow them at a distance of twenty yards or so. I don't dare get any closer; the distance is my only cover. I imagine that Martha is laughing. Two evenings ago a man on the phone asked for her. Would I like it to have been this man, or would I prefer someone else? They stop in front of a display window and point something out to each other. At first the place is just out of my line of vision but when they move on I can see that it is a sporting-goods store.

Instead of giving Martha credit for never having brought a boyfriend to our apartment, I am angry with her. They are walking in step; I suppose that's necessary when walking arm in arm. No, I'm not angry, but I would prefer not to have to witness that happiness. They stop, I stop. Something seems to have flown into Martha's eye. The man turns her face to the light and carefully dabs her eye with a corner of his handkerchief. He is successful. She blinks her eyes a few times to make sure, then we all move on. It isn't Martha's fault that I happened to be standing at the rear window of the streetcar. I'll never find out where they have come from.

I once asked Father what it was about Martha that he objected to; it was important to me for him to like her. He answered that he had nothing against her, nothing whatever; it was just that he didn't know her well enough to be as much in love as I was. But that can't have been the whole truth, for his behavior toward her was always cool and polite. I have never been able to discover the reason. Either he was afraid that I would neglect school on her account or he felt that such an affair was premature for a seventeen-year-old. Martha never complained about his reserve, but neither did she do anything to overcome it. That surprised me. I was sure that no one she took trouble over would be able to resist her for long. At Father's funeral she was the only one who sobbed; by then it was too late.

We walk and walk; in their place I would have taken a streetcar long ago. When they reach their destination, they will disappear into a building, and then what use will my following them have been? If they were to sit down in a café, I might be able to spy on them from behind a newspaper held in trembling hands, but there are no cafés around here, if I remember correctly. I keep going, unable to make up my mind to let Martha and her friend walk off into the unknown.

As with any activity so monotonous that it can be performed mechanically, my thoughts wander. I succeed in laying bare a self-deception: I have been pretending to have no idea why I started out to revisit my old haunts, but the truth is that I have high expectations. I would like to meet old friends—I mean people who recognize me, who smile when they see me, who say surely I'm not the boy from Number 5, who perhaps inquire where I've been staying and what I've been doing with myself. And that's not all. Everything comes to light: I am hoping to run across one of those incredibly pretty girls from our street and that one word will lead to the next. When two people haven't seen each other for so long, it's easy to start chatting.

Now I realize why I waited till afternoon: it's the time when most people come home from work. Gitta Seidel from Number 30, for instance, of whom we all knew that at the age of eleven she was already wearing a bra, and for good reason; or the girl with black hair from the apartment above the coal merchant—I've forgotten her name—who was the plainest girl for miles around and one day stepped out on the street a beauty. Is it a disgrace to yearn for young women? Must I be embarrassed for wanting to be hugged and kissed after having endured life for a year in foreign parts? And around the corner, on Eberty-Strasse, lived a fantastic girl who used to lean on the windowsill for hours and once even smiled at me.

They have crossed to the other side of the street: I don't notice until it's happened. For a moment I am afraid I have lost them. We are walking level with each other, which is sheer carelessness; it would be terrible to be caught snooping by Martha. I do something without thinking, as if what follows is so obvious that it needs only to be done: I start running, go a hundred yards, then cross the street to stroll leisurely toward them. They don't see me coming. Martha is talking, the man is listening. Most people would probably consider him handsome, his face manly, but I find something stupid about it. His tie has gray and red stripes, the scent of after-shave lotion wafts from him, there is an oddly deep dimple in his chin. I say: "Hello, Martha!"

I don't see her shocked to death. I don't see her blushing with shame. She stops in mid-sentence and turns toward me—surprised, of course; she needs a few seconds, of course. Then she says: "What are you doing here?"

They stand there with no thought of unlinking their arms. He glances at his watch: incredibly, the delay is already too long for him, the man actually glances at his watch.

"Nothing special," I say. "I've been to see a friend who lives around the corner. See you later."

I walk on; not for anything would I turn around. It annoys me that I am dressed like a teen-ager, not like a man: jeans, running shoes, sweater without a shirt. Martha knows all my friends—that's to say, she knows I have none, not even around here. He will ask her who I am, and she will answer that a friend of her parents died a while ago and they have taken in the son, meaning me.

On Friday after breakfast I went to see Werner Klee, almost a friend. I had nothing special in mind; I just hoped I might be able to cope more easily with my frustration if I could talk to someone. I had been avoiding him for a long time.

That day remains in my memory as being particularly strange, full of events that led to nothing. It was the day before the opening of the World Festival, and the streets were seething with foreigners and police. I made a detour to take in all I could. I had never seen the city in such a state of excitement.

Werner's mother said her son was still in bed, but as I was about to turn away she flung open his bedroom door as if I had at last provided her with an excuse to do so. I saw him rub his eyes and yawn. Mrs. Klee pushed me into the room and closed the door behind me. Since Werner seemed about to fall asleep again, I opened the window and sat down on the chair that served him as a bedside table. He caught hold of my hand and looked at my watch. I couldn't tell whether he found the hour early or late.

Werner said there must surely be something of extraordinary importance to discuss; otherwise, after realizing how unwelcome my intrusion was, I would surely have left at once. He always had to crack jokes, it was a kind of com-

127

pulsion. If he couldn't think of a turn of phrase that seemed sufficiently witty to him, he preferred to say nothing. I had come to like this mannerism, although it sometimes tried my patience.

"Okay, if that's what you want," he said, jumping out of bed and presenting an intimidating sight. He pulled on his pants and went out to the bathroom, saying that there was no money in the room, not a cent, so I needn't bother snooping around.

After waiting five minutes I found that I'd forgotten why I had come. Outside, a baby was screaming. I went to the window and looked down into the courtyard, where a girl was shaking a baby buggy so violently that it was only a question of time before it collapsed. I was here because of an idea that seemed by turns promising and childish: to write an anonymous letter to Father or Kwart. How would they react if the letter said that their scheme had become known, and that if the man was not released by such and such a date, the police would be notified? Ever if my hopes weren't all that great, I wanted to follow up the idea, mainly because I thought it better than nothing. Perhaps it would trigger an argument among them as to what to think of such a letter.

When Werner came back I asked him to lend me his typewriter for a few hours. He asked if mine was on the fritz, and I replied: "I have to write an anonymous letter."

He nodded and didn't seem in the least surprised, as if he received such requests every day. He sniffed his socks and threw them over for me to decide whether they could be worn one more time.

I followed him into the kitchen, where he turned up a radio so loud that the floor vibrated with the bass notes; then he found himself something to eat. In a cage on the wall a bird hopped about in a frenzy of fear. As he was slicing some bread, Werner shouted a question at me: Who did I want to send the anonymous letter to?

I turned off the radio and answered: "I need it for half a day at most."

Werner explained that the typewriter didn't belong to him but to his father, and that his father's attitude toward private property was a strained one; however, he said, I could type in his room, and he would be glad to help me polish up some of the phrases. Then he asked why I didn't simply cut words and letters out of the newspaper and stick them on a sheet of paper, that being the preferred method of composing anonymous letters.

It was no use rolling my eyes. I was the guilty party; he was merely prolonging my childishness, on and on without end. I told him to forget about the typewriter, it wasn't all that important. He nodded and smiled before saying: "I can imagine that quite a lot has to happen before a level-headed type like you resorts to anonymous letters."

While he chewed, I decided not to write the letter. It wouldn't take them five minutes to figure out that no one but me could possibly be the author. The risk was far too great compared to the minimal prospect of success. I think I knew from the very beginning that the idea was useless; otherwise I wouldn't have left myself so wide open to Werner.

I asked him whether he had been instructed when and where to report for military service. His reply: He happened to know of a place on Friedrich-Strasse, right under the overpass, where typewriters could be rented by the hour.

"The sad thing about you is that you always have to flog your jokes to death," I said.

"So far I've managed to make out all right," he said, giving me a much keener look than seemed appropriate to his words.

I took a little piece of bread and stuck it in the cage, where the bird was now sitting motionless on its perch. Werner said that bread would kill the bird; to this day I don't know whether that, too, was meant as a joke. There was undoubtedly some tension between us. I repeated my question about his military service, and he said that in that place under the overpass there were little booths where you could write unobserved. I had no choice but to get up and tell him I would rather come back some other time.

When I walked to the door, he did nothing to keep me back. With his mouth full, he said: "My jokes have never been any better than that. Why do they happen to irritate you today?"

"I wish I knew," I said, and left. It must have seemed strange that I had suddenly become so touchy.

Out on the street I had my next idea. It occurred to me that there are two groups of people whom you can ask for advice without being afraid that they will pass on your secret to the authorities: priests and lawyers.

I didn't waste much time imagining myself going into a Catholic church, kneeling in a confessional, and telling my troubles to the large ear of a stranger. So the question was: What did I want to discuss with a lawyer? I needed some good advice and no legal instruction. It was true, of course, that there was a legal aspect involving myself: I was an accessory. I didn't have the same claim to a lenient sentence as Father, Kwart, and Rotstein, there being no question in my case of specific mitigating circumstances. But could an accessory be called more severely to account than the kidnappers? Then it struck me that I was also an accessory of the camp guard.

I had no idea how much reliance could be placed on a lawyer's professional secrecy; all I knew was learned from movies. And where was I to find the money for a lawyer? And what gave me the hope that lawyers, of all people, were permitted to protect me from the interests of so-called society?

While I was searching for a better idea, I remembered that Gitta Seidel's father was a lawyer. That gave me a boost, she could help me gain access to him. If I went to see a lawyer as a friend of his daughter's and not just anybody, wouldn't that outweigh my misgivings? She lived a little way up the street, and she liked me. During recess she had always stood on the playground smiling at me. There were fellows in our school who thought I was crazy because I didn't make the most of her advances. None of them knew Martha.

I had to walk past two telephone booths before finding one that hadn't been vandalized. Among the Seidel numbers in the directory I looked for the one that matched the correct address. Her mother answered the phone, or at least an older woman, followed a few moments later by Gitta. When I said who I was, she said: "Oh."

I waded right in and asked whether we could meet; there was a problem, I told her, that she might help me solve.

"Me?" she asked, and giggled.

I asked her to meet me that very day; it was extremely urgent. I deliberately exaggerated so that she couldn't tell how serious my request really was. After some proper hesitation, she suggested we meet that afternoon, without asking what it was all about. But I had a date with Martha, so I talked Gitta into coming down to the street in an hour. No one else could have achieved that so easily with Gitta Seidel: twelve o'clock sharp. The last thing she said was: "Well, if that isn't something!"

As ridiculous as it may sound, I had no money to buy her ice cream or a cup of coffee.

Across from Number 30 I sat down to wait on the steps outside a building. Punctual to the minute, Gitta Seidel stepped out onto the street, wearing a dress that was much too elegant for this minor occasion, but she was often to be seen strolling around the neighborhood dressed to the nines. We shook hands like middle-aged people. I had made up my mind to get to the point right away; I didn't want her to get any wrong ideas.

"Well, you are in a hurry!" she said, gazing into my eyes.

As soon as we moved off, I began by saying that I had found myself involved in something I first thought I could handle on my own. She nodded. But that I had meanwhile realized I needed some help. She nodded again. That was to say, the help of a lawyer. She looked at me. Although I could turn to any lawyer, I said, my case was so complicated that I wanted the lawyer to take a special interest, a personal interest, so to speak. She stopped. So my request was for her to arrange an appointment for me with her father and also to soften him up a bit in my favor.

Before we were even halfway around the block I felt I had put my case in a precise, businesslike manner. Even close up, Gitta Seidel was a lovely girl, and it was nice to know she liked me—I mean, it was flattering. She looked at me seriously, and for the first time I had a chance to determine the color of her eyes.

"So that's the only reason for this meeting?" she asked.

I had to admit this, although it was obvious that I was harming my case. The next moment, the seriousness in her expression gave way to an indignation that I should have foreseen. She told me that all she could do for me was give me the address of the law firm on Kastanien-Allee at the corner of Schönhauser-Allee. On the outside of the building, she said icily, was a sign showing the office hours, unfortunately she did not know them by heart; moreover, I could take it for granted that her father regarded all his clients' problems as his own. She probably wasn't seventeen yet; off she walked in her Sunday best—oh, it was sad!

There were hours to kill before my date with Martha. And I had no money so I would even have had to beg Gitta Seidel for credit with her father. Some distance away, her legs disappeared around the corner.

Sometimes I think Elle's condition is getting steadily worse; at other times that she could be discharged from this wretched institution in the not-too-distant future. The institution itself is constantly changing: it is sanatorium, clinic, nursing home, booby hatch, madhouse, depending on mood and weather. I set out for a sanatorium and arrive at the waiting room of a cemetery, or the other way around.

I stand behind Elle, who is looking out the open window, and massage the nape of her neck. I've been with her for half an hour; she's hardly uttered a sentence so far, which needn't mean anything. She groans because I press my thumbs so firmly into her neck muscles. When I came into her room, an open notebook was lying on the table; curiosity made me lean over it, and I read the words "once dead always dead." I said that this was indeed one of the few irrefutable truths, but Elle thought I was being nosy. She closed the notebook, put it away in a drawer, and said: "Not yet, not for a long time yet."

Is she writing a book? I suggest we go out into the park; there's not much going on in this room today. Elle seems to agree: she immediately walks to the door, stops three feet from it, and waits like a well-trained little dog for me to open it. Not for the first time, the suspicion comes to me that she is acting out something, that from time to time she takes pleasure in playing the part of an adolescent.

In the corridor, a sad, protracted wailing reaches us from somewhere, the sound of a grief that can no longer be contained. I look in every direction, but Elle walks on as if she has heard nothing. A nurse approaching us and noticing my alarm gestures with her thumb to the floor above.

I explain to Elle why I haven't been to see her for a month; I know she's waiting for this. I say: "Things aren't going too well for me right now. Rahel and Hugo Lepschitz are the nicest people in the world, but I feel like murdering them the moment I see them. They haven't harmed me in any way, that's the worst part, they've always wanted a son. With Martha, things are different—I can't explain. I only know that it would be good for both of us if we didn't see each other for the next thirty years. You've no idea how hard it is to find a place to live. I should have started to look earlier, but it's only in the last few weeks that I've realized how terribly that family gets on my nerves. A few days ago a letter arrived to say I'd been accepted by the university. They simply won't understand when I move out."

"Why are you telling me all this?" Elle asks. "You know I'll soon forget half of it."

Now we are in the park. We try to stay away from the main paths: it is a Saturday and the weather is fine, so the place is crowded with visitors. Elle takes my sleeve and pulls me in among the bushes and we wind our way through a thicket as she drags me along, oblivious to the branches that are hitting me in the face.

"A room on my floor became vacant yesterday," she says. "Not as nice as mine, though."

There is a smell of cats. Because I am walking behind her, I can't see how seriously she means these words. Is she considering my moving in with her because I'm having such a

135

problem outside? The shrubbery comes to an end, and we step onto a little meadow still covered with long brown grass from last year. We are too far away now to hear the voices and sounds on the main path; needless to say, she knows every nook and cranny. Across from us the meadow is bordered by a high, ivy-covered wall marking the limits of the institution.

"Sit down," Elle says.

I look for a rock, the ground being too damp and messy for me. She takes her time before sitting and looks down at me, expectantly it seems. Am I supposed to express delight over her meadow? When I open my mouth, she places a finger on my lips. Nowhere an animal or person I might frighten, but I remain silent, just as she wants.

She plucks at my sweater and demands it with swift movements of her fingers. I take it off, and she rolls it up into a cushion, lays it on the ground, and sits down on it: rocks are too hard for her. From her cardigan pocket she takes a single cigarette and lights it with a match that she then replaces in the box. Throughout all this she never takes her eyes off me.

Finally she asks whether I have forgotten that we were in this meadow once before, at this very spot. Even without looking around, I know I won't remember. I ask her when that was supposed to have been. A few years ago, she says, nine or seven, in the days when I still parted my hair down the middle. I take her word for it. She asks whether nothing strikes me.

Nothing, I say. And not only that, I'm getting impatient. I've had enough of this secretive behavior.

Elle bends down to my ear and whispers: "I've discovered that this is the center of the world."

"What?"

She gives me a long, solemn look. Then she nods twice, as if to inform me: That's right; you heard correctly.

"All I see is a little meadow," I say.

"That's what it is, a little meadow."

"I have no idea what a center of the world looks like," I say, "so I can't offer any comment."

"Do you think I knew this before I came here?" she asks. "Do you think the world has more than one center?"

There are several possible ways to react. I could try to change the subject, or I could make light of her discovery, or I could be amazed and praise my sister as a great discoverer. I notice that she is wearing unmatched stockings, a white one on the left leg, a gray one on the right. The third possibility is out; I am not going to treat Elle as an idiot.

She relieves me of my decision by saying that it is impossible to explain the matter to someone who is not willing. It is just like hypnotism, she says; hypnotists are far from being frauds, yet they can only put a willing person into a trance. So the point was: Did I believe that the world has a center, regardless of whether here or elsewhere?

"Do you mean a physical center?" I ask craftily. "Do you mean the center of gravity? The point from which all gravity radiates? Or do you mean a spiritual center?"

"I don't know what gravity means," Elle replies. "I mean the center."

After thinking for a moment, I shake my head and say: "I don't believe there is such a thing."

"But it is a pretty meadow, don't you agree?"

She pats the ground, looking perhaps for a dry place to lie down. A little way off, some people break through the bushes and come across the meadow toward us: three women and a man. After a few steps they notice us, stop and whisper together, and turn off in another direction. There is no way of telling—not for me anyway—which of the four persons is the one being visited. Elle pokes a hole in the decaying grass with her finger and buries her cigarette butt in it; it makes a tiny hiss. The people sit down at the opposite edge of the meadow; they have brought along some blankets.

"Isn't it possible to buy a room?" she asks.

"Buy?"

She seems surprised that there could be any misunderstanding. If I still have the money from the sale of the cottage, then surely, she says, there must be enough to pay for a room. Or have I already spent most of it? Practically nothing, I tell her.

"Well then."

The people have brought along a basket of food that they now proceed to distribute. I can see the man struggling to open the jar of preserves and how his fingers keep slipping off the little rubber tab that has to be pulled out from between jar and lid. Why hadn't I ever thought of inviting Elle for a picnic in the park? Because I'm not a woman, who knows what to put into a picnic basket? The thought that Elle now has only me left makes me want to weep with pity for her.

"If I'm talking nonsense, you must forgive me," says Elle.

"You're not talking nonsense," I say, "but rooms aren't for sale."

I explain how acquiring a place to live is regulated in our country by the government; I try to be as brief as possible, since it is obvious that the subject doesn't interest her. She nods and nods, but her nodding is a sign of impatience rather than of comprehension.

Years ago the thought came to me that I wouldn't even exist but for Elle's periodic attacks. I mean, if Elle had been a so-called normal girl, my parents probably wouldn't have decided to bring a second child into this black world nineteen years after their first. Actually I have three parents, Father, Mother, and Elle's confusion, and two of those are no longer living. They waited patiently until they were told that not much change was to be expected in their daughter's condition;

then they wanted a second child, one like Elle but without the confusion. I would have to be many years older if that were not the case. Sometimes I was furious with Father because he never talked to me about it, but then sometimes I thought: What can he tell me?

We leave the center of the world; by this time too many visitors have arrived who sit or stand around on it noisily. It doesn't worry Elle that my sweater is wet. She gestures to me to follow her, saying that there is another place we can try. While we walk along side by side, I tell her about Rahel's and Hugo's habit of watching TV every night and trying to establish who resembles whom. She has no smile to spare for this.

She walks with me straight through the institution. We stop at the kiosk where she has me buy her some chocolate and cigarettes. Then we go on. Our progress can no longer be called a stroll, for Elle strides out like someone with a definite purpose.

A construciton site not far from the main gate is our objective. She leads me between mounds of sand, stacks of boards, and piles of bricks. Certainly no one is going to disturb us here on a Saturday, but why does she want to be undisturbed?

"This isn't exactly a beauty spot," I say.

Elle looks around to make sure no one has followed us; then, sitting down on a beam, she says: "So far we've talked only about you. But after all, there's me to consider too."

I feel uneasy, although I have no idea what she has in mind; she sounds determined and oddly severe. I sit down facing her and nod. I would like to hug her; I am thinking: If she is going to reproach me for something, I will have deserved it.

"Why don't you ever talk to me about money?"

"What money?"

"The money you inherited," she says. "That's to say, the money we inherited. It's just that I never see any of it."

I don't know how I should react—amused or thunderstruck. She is fighting for Father's estate. Is it possible that she has heard a radio program on inheritance fraud? Now I really do it: I get up and hug her. She puts up with it, no more, she doesn't take back a word. With her head against my chest, she says: "Yes, yes, I know you love me. But that doesn't mean that everything belongs to you."

I have no choice but to let go of her and discuss our inheritance. As we talk, I am constantly bothered by the thought that basically she is right. I tell her that so far I've spent scarcely a penny, and I mention the approximate amount in the account. I say that not only does half of it belong to her, but all of it if she insists.

She takes me by the arm and walks off again. There is no bank in the institution, I say, but she need only tell me how much she wants me to bring her. She links arms with me and presses my hand emotionally. I understand. She is sorry for the way she has treated her kid brother. On the way to her room we silently recover from our distress. In her room she asks if I could perhaps buy a black stole for her, and sometime or other a pretty hat too.

Martha," I said, "we can't go on like this."
She agreed, but that was no help. With that bastard occupying the cottage in the forest, we hadn't been able to find a place for our love. That love increased according to a law whereby the very thing for which there is no room tends to increase.

My initial fear, that I was the only one suffering so terribly, soon proved to be unfounded. Martha was burning and pining just as much. As bad luck would have it, there seemed to be no end to the bad weather.

Suddenly I started making suggestive remarks, more blatant than I would have thought myself capable of a few days earlier, and the funny thing was that Martha seemed to like it. When we saw an elderly couple on the street, for instance, I said: "Guess where those two are going now!" And Martha said: "They've just come from there, haven't you any eyes in your head?" Ten days ago we would have bitten off our tongues rather than talk like that.

The inner city was firmly in the hands of visitors. Suddenly there were cafés, suddenly there was uninhibited talk and raucous shouting. At one intersection some blacks crossed the street against the red light, and no police whistle summoned them back. Although the sky was dense with clouds, everyone looked happy—everyone but us. Martha was continually being winked at and accosted by young men, as if I didn't exist. When she noticed my annoyance, she said: "You'll have to put up with that, with a girlfriend like me."

She invited me to a tearoom; on the strength of her expected salary, she had borrowed some money from her parents. We sat surrounded by visitors from Saxony and Mexico who seemed to be competing as to who could laugh longest and shout loudest. What mattered most was that my hand was on Martha's knee. I looked into her face and experienced something strange: I heard every one of her words but their meaning did not register.

Someone thumped me on the shoulder. When I turned around, a blond man realized that he had mistaken me for someone else, and without a word of apology walked away. Martha laughed, and for her sake I pretended to be amused. She said that from behind it would be easy to mistake me for someone else.

Before leaving to go and meet her, I had asked Father for an advance on my allowance for August. No luck. At first, chances had looked good: he had taken out his wallet and even opened it. But then he stopped and asked why I had gone to see Kwart behind his back. I said the visit had been perfectly open and aboveboard and that I hadn't accused Kwart of anything that I hadn't accused him of. His answer was to put away his wallet again. Probably he hadn't intended to give me any money in the first place. Martha nudged me, because my hand was creeping higher and higher up her leg.

So far not a single waitress had come near us, and since we felt quite rested after having sat there for half an hour we went out onto the street again. Martha said that once, in kindergarten, she had drawn a picture of a town with every colored crayon she could lay hands on, and that was exactly what it looked like now. Then she asked whether I didn't also think that we were on the outside.

142

"On the outside?" I asked, and she explained something to me. It was as if some supernatural power were forcing me not to listen to her words. It was forcing me to think of Gitta Seidel's breasts, of the pimply youth at the swimming pool, of the chamber pot under the iron bed, of anything that would prevent me from understanding. It was strange, too, the way Martha went on talking and talking without becoming suspicious. When she paused for a moment and looked at me, I guessed that she had asked a question, and I said: "I feel fine the way I am."

So we were on the outside, she felt. Whom did she mean by "we"? Us two? Or nonpolitical people like us? Or Jews like us? Or grumblers like us who are never satisfied?

"Since you're constantly talking about inside and outside, do you know where I'd like to . . ." I said.

She indignantly put her hand over my mouth. I caught one of her fingers with my teeth. She didn't let go, but I did. She rubbed the teeth marks. Everything was so incredibly wonderful between us that, no matter what happened, things just got better and better. She showed me the finger I had bitten, and instead of kissing it I bit it again.

When our feet were tired, we tried our luck in an ice-cream parlor. We stood in line and waited for an empty table. Suddenly, at the sight of Martha's innocent face, it seemed to me outrageous to keep my one great worry a secret from her. I'll tell her about it, I thought, and to hell with the consequences. I'll start as soon as we've sat down.

But when we were seated I couldn't think of how to begin. I was scared of every word, so how could I speak? I only came to my senses when Martha nudged me because my ice cream was beginning to melt right under my nose.

"Are you depressed about something?" she asked; she didn't need second sight for that.

"You know very well what I'm depressed about."

"Something's the matter," she persisted. "You keep talking to yourself."

This was my last chance to draw her into my confidence. I let it pass, as if such chances came by the hundred. Instead, I ate my ice cream and said: "You're seeing things."

A red-haired girl came up to our table and addressed Martha by name. The acquaintance must have been a fleeting one, since Martha didn't bother to introduce me. They both stood while they talked, there being no third chair. The red-haired girl had some adhesive tape on her forehead and looked unhealthy. I hoped she would stay long enough to distract Martha from her suspicions. I was about to offer her my chair when she left without so much as noticing me.

I knew Martha would pick up where we had left off, even though I asked: "Who was that?"

"Her name's Gertrud," said Martha. "But don't change the subject."

"Do we have a subject?"

She nodded firmly, then she said that she could produce a nice little scenario: My strangeness had begun five days ago—to be exact, last Sunday, when we had arranged to meet at the cottage. She couldn't help noticing how upset I'd been, she said. She deliberately hadn't asked me any questions, assuming that I would start talking when I was ready, but now she didn't believe that anymore. And since I not only hadn't told her anything but had also maintained a stubborn silence, she was now obliged to piece together my story herself.

Alarm bells rang in my head. But what can she possibly know? I thought. Nobody can come near to divining a situation like that. Either one is a witness or one is completely in the dark.

What she assumed, said Martha, was as follows: On Sunday, all unsuspectingly, I had entered the cottage with my own key and suddenly found myself confronted by Father. There must have been quite a row; perhaps Father had even used physical force. She could remember, she said, that there was a button missing from my shirt. But whether or not there was violence, the existence of that lovely key had now come to light. What a breach of trust, what a disgrace, what an embarrassment! It wasn't hard to guess that Father had taken the key away from me. And that explained why, ever since Sunday, I had constantly been talking about visitors who were supposedly preventing us from using the cottage.

"Assuming that is what happened, can you explain why I should want to make a secret of it?" I said with relief.

"I can't understand that either," said Martha. "That's exactly where the weak spot is."

I had to make an effort not to smile. I felt like an armed robber who learns after his arrest that he's been nabbed for a petty theft he hasn't even committed.

"Your story has another weak point," I said.

"Which is?"

"That it's ridiculous from beginning to end."

"You've convinced me," she said.

I took the key out of my pocket and laid it on the table. Martha picked it up, looked at it from all sides, and said: "A key."

"What do you mean, a key? It's *our* key! The key to the cottage."

"And what does that prove?" She seemed to want to taunt me.

"First you maintain that he took the key away from me. Then, when I show you the key, you say: 'What does that prove?' "

"You don't have to tell me what I said."

She was thinking, and I put the key back in my pocket. Instead of revealing the secret and creating an eternal union with her, I was becoming more and more enmeshed in my silence and in keeping her off the right track. Even if she never found out, I would always have that knowledge, I thought.

"Where there's one extra key, there can be two," she said.

I didn't need to answer that. Her theory was so flimsy, she would retract it herself before long. But all I could hear was her obstinate insistence that I was a liar, so I said: "Just carry on like that."

"Like what?"

"With your Jewish sophistry."

I no longer knew what I was saying. I made a grab for her hand, but she withdrew it. She muttered a few angry words, which I chose not to understand, and left. Through the window of the ice-cream parlor I saw her stride past, and I thought: Now it's happened.

When she was out of sight I realized that I had no money to pay the bill. I kept my eye on the waitress until she disappeared into the back through the service door, and slipped out like a shadow.

I had walked only a few steps when I told myself that it wasn't on Martha's account that I had hurried out but because of the unpaid bill. Then I ran after her. I doubt if I would have found her if she hadn't been coming to meet me. We stopped face to face, radiant with relief. From that moment on, we watched our words, at least for the rest of that day. We now knew how easy it is to get into an argument. I didn't even tell her that she had forced me to leave without paying the bill.

146

No stone must be left unturned in trying to find a room, so I go to see Gordon Kwart. The last time we met had been at Father's funeral; he was the only person wearing an overcoat in that heat, and his expression seemed to imply that he had killed Father with his own hands. When he asked me at the cemetery gates whether there was any way he could help me, his eyes had looked beyond me into the distance. I can't remember what I said.

Although my visit was arranged over the phone, he behaves, on opening the door, as if he has been expecting anyone but me. Instantly he is overwhelmed with compassion; with the door still open, he hugs me and pats me on the back. How can I help? He leads me into the room and seats me. There are two cups on the table, two plates, tea and cakes. He pours us each a cup before the first word is spoken. In response to my glance toward the door he says: "She's out of town. Gone to see her sister in the country, as far as I know."

He wants to know: how I have spent the year, what my plans are, why I never give a sign of life. I make my story as brief as possible; he nods at every third word. When he pours the hot tea into his saucer, puts a piece of sugar in his mouth, and starts sucking it with pursed lips, I am reminded of Father more vividly than I have been for a long time. He

147

asks what I'm doing these days and goes on: "Come on, I want to hear it all."

I describe the past year as uneventful, which it truly was, that I had passed through it half asleep. But my housing problem is still unsolved, I tell him, and a little later, hinting broadly that I am looking for a room, that before I can even think of university I have to leave my present quarters.

Kwart isn't listening; he has forgotten the empty saucer in his hand—it's pretty obvious what I've reminded him of. When I pause, he repeats, almost mechanically: "I want to hear it all." I must get through to him. He has contacts with hundreds of people, he plays in an orchestra, he has friends, he goes to the synagogue: he is in an ideal position to find out about a room. But for a few moments he must be allowed to think his own thoughts.

Kwart puts down the saucer and weeps; huge tears well from his eyes, Cyclops tears, not very many. He wipes his sleeve across his face: the attack has passed. I find that I am neither moved nor sorry for him; I feel uncomfortable. I think: If, at the time, he had done what I begged him to do, we wouldn't need to be sitting here now like this. His eyes are red and for a few moments seem unable to focus. I look for the damp patch on his sleeve.

"You should have come sooner," he said at last, "much sooner. But it was decent of you to wait so long."

He gets up quickly and leaves the room. I drink my tea and wonder what's so decent about my behavior. Maybe he imagines I had wanted to spare him, that I wanted to come sooner but thought each time: It's too soon for Kwart. The truth is, we probably would never have met again if I didn't need a place to live; he'll never find that out.

He comes back and checks to see whether there is still tea in my cup. I ask why I should have come sooner. He is puzzled by my question and looks at me sadly until I repeat

148

his own words. Then he nods and says: "We must stick together."

Whining, whimpering—in front of me, of all people, I who warned him while there was still time. I don't want to grieve for Father with him; I need a room. He sighs, and his eyes say: Come, dear boy, let us weep a little.

A wave of goddamn emotion mounts in me now, after all, mounts and mounts and seeks to break out into freedom through my eyes. What's happened? As a boy I used to run out of the room when I found myself in such a state, so Father wouldn't see my twitching face. Kwart is an outsider, I don't care what he sees. He's having enough trouble with himself anyway. I ask whether he has a performance that evening.

He pulls out a handkerchief, blows his nose noisily, and answers into the handkerchief: "Don't worry about me."

By now the tea is lukewarm, but still he pours it into his saucer and gulps it down. "Not that I mean to console you, but I've had a bad year too," he says.

"Your health?"

He smiles, as if fully sympathizing with my bitterness. Then he says, in a sorrowful voice, that only over this past year has he learned the meaning of self-reproach. Although he will never know to what extent he is to blame for Arno's death, there is no doubt that he is partly to blame. I am free to believe him or not, but he would willingly lie in Father's place in the Weissensee cemetery. "You warned us," he said. "I know, I know. We didn't listen to you. You did what you could. We were completely carried away, we couldn't stop. Someone a hundred times smarter than you wouldn't have been any more successful."

It had never occurred to me that Kwart might be to blame for Father's death. The best proof is that I have not been to see him until today. Nevertheless, I'm glad he has a guilty conscience, and I'll do nothing to take it away from him. In my eyes he was a fellow traveler, although at one time I was amazed at his firmness. If Father had ordered the prisoner to be drawn and quartered, Kwart would have drawn and quartered him; and if Rotstein had said: Let's let him go, Kwart would have agreed to that too. He could not change the course of events: he could either participate or leave. For Father, what Kwart did was immaterial.

"I am here because I need your help."

"Whatever you want," says Kwart.

He transforms himself into the very image of attentiveness: he grows on his chair by a few centimeters, even his ear seems to be growing toward me. So I repeat my story, painting my situation blacker than it is and exaggerating the problems of living with the Lepschitz family. Also I describe my past efforts at finding a room rather less than accurately by letting him think that I have come to him only at the end of a long, unfruitful search. He vibrates with sympathy.

When I tell him about my unsuccessful attempt to get into the students' residence, Kwart is speechless and indignantly shakes his head twenty times. Calming down, he says: "I can understand why you didn't want to remain in your old apartment. But why did you sell the cottage?"

"Do you really not understand that?" I reply, with a shade of reproach in my voice.

Less than three seconds pass before his failure to understand collapses. He lowers his eyes, raises them again, and says: "Forgive me, forgive me. What am I talking about! Of course you had to sell the cottage—the cottage above all else! I hope they gave you a decent price for it."

I don't name the amount, although he would like to know it. I tell him he needn't worry, that Mr. Lepschitz looked after the sale for me. He asks what Mr. Lepschitz does for a living. I tell him that he is a payroll accountant in a textile

150

mill. He asks whether Lepschitz is one of our people, and I say: "Mr. Kwart, I need a room."

While he is thinking, I recall a certain scene: Kwart has come to see us. I, barely seven, open the door to him. He is carrying his violin case under his arm. Father has been expecting him and says: "You can start right away." Kwart tunes his violin in the sunlit room, then tucks it between chin and collarbone. My father says to me: "Watch carefully." Kwart plays a nursery song. Then Father asks me: "Would you like to be able to play like that too?" "No," I say. They laugh, then I am told to hold the violin the way Kwart has shown me. I draw the bow over the strings and produce a sound so terrible that I never want to hear it again. I say: "I don't want to." My arm is so short that it hardly reaches to the end of the violin. Kwart guides my hand with the bow a few times over the strings. Father asks: "Aren't there such things as children's violins?" While their attention is distracted, I seize the opportunity to throw bow and violin on the floor and run out of the room.

Kwart walks up and down in front of the window, his face dark with thought. No one else has been at such pains to find me a room. Stuck in the glass door of a display cabinet crammed with glasses and china figurines are some photographs. I peer at them, having nothing else to do, and find my guess confirmed: There is a picture of Father among them, standing in T-shirt and shorts in front of a rocking chair and laughing with embarrassment. Kwart pokes me in the chest and says he has an idea, he has *the* idea.

However, he doesn't want to decide by himself, he says. He must consult with Wanda first. She'll be back in a few days, but she won't raise any objection, he's sure. He just needs to put the whole situation to her reasonably. In short, I am to come and live with them. The apartment, he says, has three large rooms and a very nice smaller one; how they will divide them up can be discussed later. As long as I don't demand the impossible, he can see no problem. He will get Wanda to agree; I can depend on that. So?

He stands in front of me, beaming, his chin raised. It is clear from his expression that he intends to wave away my imminent outburst of enthusiasm. But I can only think: Oh my God! My aversion to the proposal is so violent and so automatic that I don't even seek reasons for it. I'll describe his offer as kind and extremely generous before explaining why I can't accept it. I need an argument to convince Kwart, not me.

"What's wrong?" he asks.

"I'm so surprised!"

"Come now," says Kwart happily, jabbing me in the chest, "don't tell me you haven't also thought of this possibility!"

The longer I postpone my decisive answer, the deeper the proposal will become entrenched in his head. To rely on Wanda's objecting would be reckless.

I snatch at the first available life belt. I say that I'm terribly sensitive to noise, a foible I've inherited from my father: if there is any noise at all, I simply can't help listening to it, and in September I am starting at the university, and after all he is a violinist and can hardly be expected to change his profession for my sake; violinist and student don't go together in the same apartment, even though the proposal is very generous, indeed magnificent.

He goes to the door, beckoning me to follow, and we walk along the passage that continues behind a curtain. I have never been in this part of the apartment. Kwart ushers me into a stuffy little room being used for storage. The first thing I see is a row of shelves stacked halfway up with coal briquettes, with books on the upper shelves. The only window is partially hidden by a wardrobe that is not high enough to keep

152

out all the light. Kwart asks me to wait a few minutes, he'll be right back.

The light switch beside the door is dead. I do Kwart the favor and wait patiently. What an extraordinary day! First Elle is afraid I might rob her of her inheritance, then this business. Does Kwart believe that I'll fall in love with this repulsive little room if I wait here long enough?

He returns after an eternity and asks: "What did you hear?"

"Nothing."

"Nothing at all?"

"No."

"I've been playing the violin!" he says with immense satisfaction.

Helplessly I follow him back into the sunny living room; I've fallen for a stupid trick. I can see myself moving into this apartment because I am too shy. Simply leave, I think, disappear without turning around—that's the only way out for a coward. I'll end up believing that my mouth was closed by tact, not cowardice. Kwart hands me a slip of paper and asks me to write down the phone number where I can be reached.

"I don't want to live here," I say.

"What's that supposed to mean?"

Go on talking, don't let go, you started off all right. I am on the track of a thought that is flying around in my head like a bird. I have to catch it. I say: "To live here—wouldn't that also mean being constantly reminded of that terrible time? Over the year I've managed to calm down, but when you opened the door for me just now the memory came right back."

His startled eyes tell me that I have scored a hit. I feel like a heel. With disproportionate violence I have clobbered a tiny little opponent.

Kwart taps his forehead with his two middle fingers; he

can hardly grasp that someone else had to present him with such an obvious thought. After all, what would it have cost me to go home and call him up in a few days with the lie that I had unexpectedly been offered a wonderful room? Then he, too, would have heaved a sigh of relief.

He says: "I should be angry with you? *I* with *you*? I can only ask you to forgive me, my dear boy. Unfortunately, my brain is slowing down a bit."

He insists on making us fresh tea—he has some genuine English tea. I accompany him to the kitchen and watch him go through the motions in sorrowful silence. From an oven no longer in use he brings out the brightly colored English tea caddy. I console him in a way that is useful to both of us. Even though I can't accept his offer, I say, he could help me by asking the members of his orchestra about a room.

"I can ask around the synagogue too!"

Those he asks could likewise inquire among their own friends, I say, and so on and so on, until one day the avalanche of questions reaches the right person.

Above the kitchen table a page from a book has been tacked to the wall. I read a few lines underscored in red on the subject of music: ". . . for it is so lofty that no intellect can grasp it, and it exudes an effect that dominates everything and for which no one can account . . ."

"Goethe wrote that," says Kwart. "But as sure as my name is Kwart, within a month you'll have your room; you can rely on me one hundred percent."

Gordon Kwart had invited us for dinner. It was six o'clock before Father told me that Kwart would pick us up in his car at seven. I complained about being informed so late; needless to say, I had a date with Martha for that evening. Father replied coolly that I needn't come if I didn't want to; he'd explain to Kwart. For some days he had been letting me feel that he couldn't stand the sight of me. And yet I kept my mouth shut and behaved as if I had forgotten all about the kidnapping. I avoided him or ingratiated myself. What more did he want?

"Do you remember asking me what I wanted for graduation?" I asked.

"Yes."

"Well, in future I'd like to be informed earlier when anyone invites us," I said.

It was sheer madness. I could have asked for a trip to the Caucasus or for some money, maybe even a motorbike; instead, I released a tiny drop of the venom that had accumulated in me.

Father said nonchalantly: "I'll see what can be done."

Martha pouted when I called her. She couldn't understand what was so important about a meal with Kwart and Father. I lied to her and said Kwart had specifically asked that I be there, God knew why. We chatted for half an hour, whispering and murmuring into each other's ears. Martha also wanted to know how long the cottage was going to be occupied, and it was the truth when I told her: "Maybe I'll find out tonight."

Kwart picked us up punctually, wearing a dark suit that made him look years older. When we shook hands he winked at me, as if some secret pact existed between us. Father asked him why he hadn't brought Wanda along, and Kwart answered cheerfully that she had a job as interpreter at this World Festival, and although it was a terrible pity there was nothing to be done about it. He was in such a good mood that Father was infected by it even before we got into his yellow car.

All over the city there were detours, and on streets left open for traffic we could hardly move because of pedestrians. Kwart kept leaning on his horn, cursing all the young scofflaws and grinning broadly. When Father asked him where he was taking us, he said: "We're almost there."

But he was exaggerating, we weren't anywhere near there. His good spirits deserted him when he kept being forced to drive in the wrong direction. Finally he parked the car in a lot and suggested we take the train for the remaining short distance. Father called him a brilliant organizer, at which Kwart rolled his eyes and asked me: "How can you stand living with this Mr. Impatience?"

On the train he kept making me feel that I was the most important person of the evening: glancing at me often, waiting for my nod before he continued whatever he was saying, showing unfailing concern for me. Father didn't like that. All this attention to me made him assume the expression of someone who no longer understands the world.

The restaurant was called the Ganymed, and Kwart knew a waiter there who was holding a table for us. We had to fight our way through a group of people standing outside the entrance; they weren't allowed in because the place was full, and Kwart had to say more than once: "No need to get angry!" As soon as we sat down, the waiter placed glasses of champagne in front of us, prearranged by Kwart. I drained mine in one gulp, although Father laid his hand on my arm. Kwart said champagne was the most innocuous of all drinks.

The waiter served us so quickly and attentively, one might have thought Kwart had once saved his life. Even so, after a short time Father became impatient and asked: "When do we begin?"

I pretended to be surprised, although I had long since realized they were using the meal as a pretext to find out how great a threat I was to them, or to ensure my silence. I innocently asked Kwart what it was we were to begin. I had decided to speak as much as possible to him and as little as possible to Father.

It was quite obvious that Kwart felt Father was behaving awkwardly, so he decided to improve matters. Refilling my glass from a bottle that was suddenly in his hand, he said: "I hear you've passed your exams."

I nodded and was about to drink, but Father took the glass from my hand, put an empty one in front of me, and asked Kwart: "Do you want to make him drunk?"

A woman at the next table was watching us. I told Father I would leave right then if he didn't stop treating me like that. I took back the full glass and gulped down the contents. I didn't like the taste of the champagne, and I was already feeling the effects of the first glass. Kwart took both our hands and said he had invited us for a meal, not a quarrel.

We had no time for him; we stared at each other challengingly.

"How am I not to treat you?" Father asked.

"Like an enemy."

"But you are my enemy."

Kwart put a finger to his lips and hissed; the waiter brought the soup. He poured it out of silvery little pots into our soup plates with a twist of the wrist, as if to demonstrate that his profession required a modicum of artistry. The soup was then consumed in silence.

Soon Father put down his spoon and turned to me. "I will tell you the truth: Gordon is of the opinion that we should speak to you, so that you will understand us better. I don't share that opinion. First of all, I don't believe that you understand anything; secondly, I don't care. But if he insists, by all means. You two talk, I'll listen."

I was thinking: One more outrageous remark like that, just one more insult! Kwart sensed the threat to his splendid evening. He said to me: "Have you heard what happened to us yesterday?"

He looked at Father for approval before going on, but Father didn't notice. He was occupied with thoughts in which I featured, for his face was grim. So Kwart went ahead at his own risk.

Yesterday, Saturday, they had found the stench in the prisoner's room so unbearable that they decided to let him have a bath. They untied him, for the first time since taking him prisoner. After a few stumbling steps he walked by himself to the bathtub. They waited outside the bathroom door, the sight and smell of that naked human, or should one say subhuman, not making them, according to Kwart, anxious to stay too close. Through the closed door they heard him taking a shower. After a while they ordered him to come out, but he did not reply. They wanted to get him out, but the door was bolted. They ran into the garden and found the bathroom window, more than six feet above the ground, open. Heppner had escaped. They told each other that he must have run toward the bus stop; why would he go deeper into the forest, or to the lake? When they were in sight of the bus stop,

158

Rotstein had a brainwave: although it was true that it would be senseless for Heppner to run into the forest, the man didn't know his way around here. So they hurried back, with Kwart, being the younger, in the lead. It was he who found Heppner, beside the path leading to the lake. He was lying behind a bush, calling in a low voice for help. What had happened? In jumping out the window he had sprained or twisted his foot and hadn't been able to go any farther. He had indeed picked the wrong direction; otherwise his escape would probably have been successful. He wept with rage because his persecutors, rather than some ordinary person out for a walk, had found him. They took him back to the cottage, supporting him and for the last few yards carrying him.

At this point Father, who had so far been listening passively and with apparent boredom, interrupted Kwart by saying: "If you have to tell the story, do get it right. We didn't carry him the last bit; we dragged him to the cottage. You by his right foot and I by his left. Does that embarrass you?"

Kwart shot my father an angry look and seemed undecided as to whether to respond. Finally he said that each person tells a story in his own way. Then he continued, for my benefit:

With Heppner between them, Father and Kwart led him along the forest path while Rotstein went ahead and looked around each curve to see if anyone was coming. Kwart said I couldn't imagine the pleasure of feeling a camp guard's arm around one's shoulder. Suddenly a child emerged from some bushes, followed almost at once by its parents. They saw the obviously injured man between the two elderly men and asked whether they could help. Kwart was so scared he couldn't utter a word, but Father calmly thanked them for their offer and said they could manage, whereupon the family went off toward the lake and the three men were free to continue on their way with their prisoner. What was really interesting about the incident, Kwart said, was Heppner's behavior: he had taken good care not to utter a single syllable. He had nodded when Father told the strangers they could manage without help, and when they moved on he seemed the most relieved of all.

"But wasn't it obvious that that's how he would behave?" I asked.

Father glanced up from the menu and looked at me in disgust. Kwart said: "Yes, of course; it was obvious, all right. But when it's a matter of a few years in prison, there's a difference between whether something seems probable to you and whether it actually happens."

The waiter brought the main course. Kwart had ordered some kind of meat that was flambéed before our eyes. Here, too, the waiter performed the motions with self-important skill. Kwart watched him in proud fascination, whereas Father drummed his fingers on the table. For me this moment was a real high point, since I hadn't had a hot meal for days. So during the next few minutes there was nothing more important for me than the food.

Again and again Kwart pressed us to tell him whether we were enjoying the meal. Father merely nodded each time, but I did him the favor of praising the food every time he asked. At some point Father exclaimed: "Once and for all, it's fine!"

Not until I had eaten my fill could I detach my thoughts from my plate. Kwart was still attentive and kind to me, yet I could sense that he wasn't taking me seriously. He took notice of me only because I happened to be the son of his accomplice. There were moments when I wished I were one of them.

"Is this man being looked for?" I asked Kwart.

"What makes you think that?"

"His family must have gone to the police long ago. So they must be looking for him."

"How do you know he has any family?"

"Why shouldn't he?"

"All right then, go on."

"The police are looking for him. They don't find him. One day you let him go. He turns up at home and, for reasons we know, is forced to protect you. But that's not the end of the story."

"No?"

"Of course not. For the police will ask him: Where have you been? And what is he to tell them?"

Kwart gave Father a long and, it seemed to me, uneasy look, until Father answered for him: "Just don't worry about that."

"He's been talking like this for days—just empty phrases," I said to Kwart.

Before Father could flare up, Kwart intervened by saying it was only natural for a son to be worried about his father. Turning to me, he said I could rely one hundred percent on caution being their main concern.

"Do you think we don't know that we are moving around in hostile territory?" he whispered.

"Why bother explaining anything to this snotty-nosed kid?" said Father.

"Your caution is indeed astonishing," I said. "One day I am suddenly in the cottage; another day your man jumps out the window."

I couldn't keep back these words. Instead of thanking heaven that nothing more was being said about my intrusion, I was drawing their attention to it and even blaming it on their carelessness.

Kwart said they had learned their lesson; each day they knew better what had to be done. It sounded as if they had finally accepted the fact that I had entered through an unlocked door. But that also did not bode well for the prisoner. I asked what they intended to do about him now.

"Why do you have to know that?" asked Kwart.

"Because he's a busybody," said Father.

"Suppose we let him go—why do you have to know?" Kwart went on. "Or suppose we hang him—why do you have to know?"

"The more politely you treat the boy," Father said, "the more insolent he becomes. Didn't you just hear his outrageous remark?"

"No," said Kwart.

"First he breaks into our cottage, then he accuses us of being careless."

"Not so loud!" said Kwart, glancing around.

"Don't you know the kind of people one has to kick out of the house ten times before they leave once?" said Father. "That's exactly the kind of person he is."

The thought occurred to me that they might have conspired: that Kwart was being nice to me only so that I'd be all the more vulnerable to Father's insults.

Kwart said to me: "It's only natural that our opinions should differ. You were never in a camp."

Father had had enough of this sweet talk. He rose, looked at Kwart as contemptuously as he had at me, and walked off toward the washrooms.

"He's annoyed because you're talking to me so calmly," I said. "He thinks I should always be shouted at."

Kwart briefly touched my arm. We looked past each other and said nothing until Father returned, by which time the table had been cleared.

"Well," Father said to Kwart, "have you asked him to be patient with me?"

Over coffee Kwart told us that yesterday he had been in

162

the café where Heppner was also a regular customer. No one had mentioned Heppner's disappearance, which could only mean that no one missed him. That in turn meant that no one had been looking for him, so that at least up to yesterday nothing had been reported to the police.

Father rolled his eyes, drank his coffee, and remained silent, lips pursed.

Kwart, who felt he was being unjustly treated, said: "Who first told him about the café, you or I? Who told him which of us took Heppner to the cottage, you or I?"

It was only when Father turned away from Kwart and looked me in the eye that I realized the disaster. On my visit to Kwart I had lied so convincingly to him that he had had no suspicion. Now this devastating blow out of the blue! I had to withstand Father's interminable gaze. I had to ignore the fact that the blood was mounting to my head, that my heart threatened to stop beating. I had to look unconcerned.

When Father had looked long enough, he turned to Kwart and said: "So what if I *did* tell him?"

My relief had to be hidden, too, for why should someone who wasn't threatened feel relieved? I have never discovered whether Father didn't want to expose me in front of Kwart, or whether he actually believed that he had given me the information and at the moment couldn't remember.

A letter from Elle:

Dear Hans
today a commission was here
to investigate whether there was
any hankypanky going on
all day long there was eye noise
all day long one could see the heads of the commission
floating along one of the paths
turning a corner . . .
The nurses did Not like that
at all they were one great big tension
and even I prefer it
when everything is the way it always is . . .
And I have Not forgotten
what you in your extremity
confided tome during your last visit
I still say you must tell Father
for there is no other way
unless you forget what you saw and heard
that might work too . . .
Probably you believe that at the time
I did Not grasp the full extent of the affair

or that I had let you down
both are wrong
your eyes were round with disappointment
and how gladly I would have givenyou more helpful advice
but just because I'm yoursister
does Not mean I know everything . . .
In any case according to my nightthoughts the affair
is Not as terrible as you made out
the other way around it would be terrible and it was terrible
but that is once and for All a thing of the past
you know what I am referring to
why should one Not turn the tables a bit
why should one Not for once put
the fearofGod into these persons
and even if one of them gets Killed
it would Not really matter
so don't be afraid . . .
You will notice how
Myadvice to you is taking shape on its own and
leaving aside Father's affairs
have you Not some plans too
or have you too Not some plans
that are wonderful to carry out
but so weak when discussed
you can be sure that Nothing will stop him
at most you can get in his way
then all that is left of his rage
will turn against you . . .
I know this Not purely from reflection
but we have discussed it ingreatdetail
Father and I
but you need Not be afraid
I did Not betray you

I was as clever as an inveterate liar
your name was Not even mentioned . . .
For a moment Father hesitated and simply did
Not know whether he could discuss such a delicate matter
with an idiot like me
but then you should have seen how
he leaped over his hesitation
and how I was allowed to know everything
the only price I had to pay was
to remain silent throughout but that was child's play . . .
Two more things
first do Not forget the coffee
there is none to be had at the kiosk
the poor saleswoman is sick of hearing the same question
second I want at some time
to learn to play an instrument
I so often hear one on the radio
only I do Not yet know which
one day I like this best and the next day . . .
Yesterday I heard a bassoon
I have only recently started to pay attention to the various
    instruments
I mean to their names
before that they were just music
perhaps it should be a flute
perhaps a violin or perhaps
a bassoon
you getaround a lot and
you might recommend something different to me
I would also have to know how difficult the various
    instruments
are to learn
for I have No wish to spend months
slaving away

if I do Not misremember you started
a long time ago
to play the violin
what came of that and please remember the coffee
Yoursister

All Monday morning I had but one desire: to crawl away into a cave, under a skirt, into the blackest of black hiding places, and not be involved in anything anymore. The letter made me ill. I loved Elle to distraction, but what kind of a letter was that!

I went to see Martha, to the film studio whose address she had given me over the phone, and I was thinking the whole time of those few fatal sentences. Where did the blame lie, with Elle or with me? *You need not be afraid. I did not betray you. I was as clever as an inveterate liar. Your name did not come up at all.* . . . Now it was clear why Father was treating me the way he was. When he heard that I had drawn his poor beloved Elle into this business, he must have hated me. At first I wondered why he hadn't dealt with me as soon as he returned from seeing her; then I realized he was doing just that, but in his own way.

Ever since Elle had been in my thoughts, I had been treating her quite differently from the way Father did: I brought her as much from the outside world as possible. I knew that inevitably she was cut off from ninety percent of all outside events and that I mustn't deprive her of at least hearing about them. Father, on the other hand, believed that news from one world should not be conveyed into the other; in his opinion, confused people must not be further confused. For instance, he hesitated a long while before buying Elle a radio, although there was one in the lounge.

The film studio was located in a former movie theater. I arrived during the lunch break. A yellow-haired doorman sitting in what had once been the ticket booth asked me gruffly who I wanted to see. I told him I had an appointment with the actress Martha Lepschitz. He ran his finger down a list of names and asked, without looking up: "Who did you say?"

The theater door stood open, so I walked through it. I was in a foul mood and almost wished the man would try to stop me.

Workmen holding lunch boxes shouted to each other across the studio. I had never been in a film studio before, yet my curiosity was strangely slight. Three men in SS uniforms were sitting around a table playing cards. I asked one of them where I could find Martha. He shook his head. Two side doors stood open, leading to a courtyard where the movie people were stretching their legs. I went out and saw Martha standing with a small group, a Star of David resplendent on her chest. I pretended not to notice her, leaned against a wall, the way others were doing, and held my face up to the sun. I wanted to be found by her.

Beside me was a young man squatting on his heels, basking in the sun with closed eyes. He also had a yellow star sewn onto his shirt; his face was heavily made up. I observed it carefully and decided that it corresponded to every prejudice about Jewish looks. I immediately felt disgusted with the whole project, and all the arguments against Martha's involvement that I had thought of before suddenly seemed far too mild. Why did Jews in movies have to be played by real Jews? When Martha was offered this part, she should have replied: Only if the SS men are real SS men.

169

The young man opened his eyes, noticed that I was staring at him, and turned his face away. So I closed my eyes, too, and enjoyed the sunshine, the first in a long time. Elle was not to blame for anything; I hadn't even asked her to keep our conversation a secret from Father. Although I had taken it for granted that she would, what was I thinking of to believe that both of us would take the same thing for granted?

When an obstacle moved between me and the sun, I didn't think for a second that it was a cloud. I could smell Martha. But I kept my eyes shut until I could no longer hold back my smile. She wasn't the least bit embarrassed to hug me in front of all these people, and she held me for so long that I began to think it a bit strange.

She asked what I meant by leaning against the wall and basking in the sun instead of looking for her. She sat down on the ground, on four trampled blades of grass, and tugged at me until I sat beside her. Normally, that would have been enough to cheer me up, but I couldn't take my mind off the letter.

"The Jewish star looks good on you," I said. "Really it does."

She let go of my hand and searched my eyes to see whether I was trying to pick a quarrel. Her star was not in the correct place; it had been sewn on so that it pointed up at an angle of about forty-five degrees, with its lowest point touching the point of Martha's right breast. Just imagine if Jewish women had gone around like that in those days, I wanted to say, but I didn't.

The big-nosed young man beside me gave Martha a look intended to encourage her not to stand for such impertinence. Martha put him in his place by showing an exaggerated affection for me. She beamed at me and asked what we should do when they finished shooting for the day. I remember how her word "shooting" grated on me; it implied familiarity with these surroundings.

I told her that one thing we couldn't do was go to the cottage; last night, with Kwart and Father, hadn't changed a thing. Since this wasn't good news, I didn't have to alter my gloomy expression. I took out the extra key and called it the most useless thing I'd ever carried around in my pocket.

Martha's spirits could not be dampened. Pointing to the now cloudless sky, she asked whether the weather didn't give me a certain idea. That did it. I was appeased and said the weather was pretty suggestive. There were moments when I forgot Elle's letter, or, rather, there were moments when it no longer seemed so devastating.

A stout, exhausted-looking man, his shirttail hanging out over his pants, stood in the doorway of the movie theater, clapped his hands, and announced the end of lunch break. The people lounging around immediately assumed work faces. Martha said I was free to leave and pick her up when the day's shooting was over. Naturally, I insisted on watching her act. "Now that I'm here anyway," I said.

In the slight crush at the door she introduced me to someone, perhaps the director; his eyes, which first glanced at me fleetingly but then turned back to me, seemed to regret that a face like mine wasn't appearing in his movie.

Martha advised me to go up to the balcony, a good place from which to watch the crew at work. The balcony still contained the old rows of seats, she said, and it was much more comfortable than down below, although one was a little farther away. And I was to take care, she said, not to let those old seats creak during the shooting; in the morning, that had caused an interruption. She led me to the stairs and seemed almost to want to explain how to walk up a staircase.

Sitting in the front row of the balcony was a girl who

turned out to be the girlfriend of one of the SS men in the cast. When I sat down beside her, she moved two seats away, as if it were only a question of time before I began making passes at her. There was no one else up there. Who knows what she had already gone through?

I found myself watching movements back and forth, people calling, pushing, which had no apparent meaning to an outsider and which, I was convinced, actually had very little meaning. For instance, a spotlight was carried off three times, and three times put back in the same place. My neighbor looked down on the confusion as attentively as if she would later have to report on everything.

Why hadn't Father told me that he knew about my conversation with Elle? Because silence and contempt were part of the punishment he intended for me? With each day this miserable affair was turning more clearly against me. My behavior was reduced to secrecy, breaches of trust, lies, and I was caught out every time, I wasn't spared a single exposure. Whether I was singularly clumsy or simply dogged by bad luck, a sequence of events had led to my suddenly standing revealed as a monster, contrary to all logic and all justice.

A demand for silence came over a loudspeaker, and instantly the noise ceased. I could hear the girl next to me breathing. On a set that was marked off by two walls and represented a military office, a scene was then rehearsed. An officer, middle-aged, with a cigar between his teeth, stared fixedly at his desk. After a few moments he performed the gesture of catching a fly, a gesture that, to my mind, was made too slowly. Nevertheless, he pretended to be holding a fly in his fist. He turned a tumbler upside down on his desk, lifted it slightly to one side, and imprisoned his imaginary catch.

Then a young SS man opened the door and ushered in a civilian, whom the officer was apparently expecting. The SS

172

man was ordered to permit no interruptions. He saluted and left the two men alone. They conversed as if they were afraid of being overheard. The girl beside me leaned over the railing and cupped one hand behind her ear.

The civilian told the officer about a meeting he had had with a Jew by the unbelievable name of Turteltaub. Turteltaub was prepared to pay a large sum for exit papers. They discussed whether it made more sense to accept the money and enable the man to leave the country, or whether, after he had paid, they should arrange for him to disappear.

But where was the actress Lepschitz?

The men agreed not only to provide Turteltaub with a visa but also to offer him a fair deal: he was to recommend them to other rich would-be émigrés and thus put them in the way of some excellent business. For what could be smarter than to relieve those kikes of their money, the civilian asked, and then foist them penniless on foreign countries?

The scene was repeated several times, for reasons that were not apparent, or not to me. After each run-through, the director walked up to the two actors and talked to them so softly that his directions did not reach the balcony. The repetitions were so similar that they gave me no clue as to the nature of the directions.

In a whisper I asked my neighbor whether she could explain to me what was going on down there. She looked at me severely and shook her head, which I took to be a gesture of disapproval rather than a no. Immediately she relapsed into her exaggerated attentiveness. But I didn't want the conversation to peter out, so I inquired why, in such fine weather and with the World Festival going on, she was sitting here in the dark. At last she was prepared to reply: "So why are you sitting here?"

I learned that her boyfriend had the role of an SS man and hadn't appeared yet, although he had had to show up early that morning. The problem for her was that she had asked specially for a day off and didn't think they would let her off again tomorrow. I tried to console her by saying that I was on vacation but wouldn't come back tomorrow whether my girlfriend was going to perform or not. She probably regarded that as a sign of insufficient love.

I regretted having turned down Martha's suggestion of leaving and returning to pick her up at the end of the day. I pictured where we would go later: to the softest and most deserted of all forests. That was a mistake, for from then on time seemed to stand still. Impatience and boredom tormented me while over and over again the two men started their conversation from the beginning.

At last the spotlights were switched on and the shooting began. In a niche of the theater that had so far been in darkness I saw people watching, with yellow stars on jackets or coats. There wasn't enough light for me to distinguish their faces, but after a while I recognized Martha among them.

I remembered the scene I had observed on my arrival: the card-playing SS men. For the first time it seemed strange to me that they kept to themselves, just as the people with the yellow stars did. The fact that they were all extras apparently united them less than their roles divided them.

As I watched, I interpreted everything to suit myself: the Jews were a frightened, bewildered little group; the two actors were a pair of double-crossers who were plotting something much worse than what they were saying; the girl beside me was too stupid to grasp the seriousness of the situation. After the scene was filmed, someone drew a chalk cross on the floor. The director called out to the actor in civilian clothes that after his entrance he was to stand exactly on the marked spot, as if it mattered.

Martha's knock on the door wakes me from a short afternoon nap that had nothing to do with tiredness, only with boredom. Wearing an apron, she stands in the doorway, a half-peeled potato in her hand: I'm wanted on the phone. Male or female, I ask; within seconds of waking up, more cannot be expected of me. It sounded more like neuter, Martha replies and leaves again.

This is the first time anyone has phoned me in this apartment. Kwart? She has put the phone on the dining table, leaving the receiver dangling like the pendulum of a clock about to stop. I don't know whether Hugo and Rahel Lepschitz have left the living room out of politeness or whether they have gone out. It's Kwart, of course.

"My dear boy," he says, "I started asking around last night—a promise is a promise."

"As if you didn't have enough worries of your own," I say.

"The trouble is," he goes on, "that no one has a room to rent. But that needn't mean anything—last night we only played chamber music."

I immediately grasp what he is trying to convey: that he hasn't asked all the musicians yet, not by a long shot, that perhaps one of the trombonists has a cubbyhole to spare.

But he deems it necessary to enlighten a layman as to the

175

difference between a full orchestra and a chamber orchestra. I carefully put down the receiver, walk five steps, and hold my hand against the TV set. It is cold, which means that I am alone with Martha in the apartment. I pick up the receiver again and wait until Kwart comes to the end of his lecture. Maybe they've gone for a walk; sometimes they do that on Sunday afternoons.

"I've just thought of who can help you," Kwart says.

"Who?" I ask, and again I know what he is driving at. While he is holding forth about the bureau where victims of Fascism can apply for assistance, my gratitude evaporates. Either he is speaking in such a way that each sentence issues inexorably from the preceding one, or I can see into the future.

He enumerates the various instances in which he personally has been helped by the bureau: health-spa treatments, car purchase, vacations—even with the acquisition of a new violin. So shouldn't it be possible for the bureau to dig up a room for me? After all that's happened?

"What do you mean, 'after all that's happened'? How can the bureau be blamed for my having given up the apartment? If I am a victim, then I'm simply a victim of my own stupidity."

"Go and talk to them," says Kwart, as if he hasn't heard me.

"I'd rather not."

He insists on dictating the bureau's address and office hours, and I pretend to write them down; I repeat his information from memory. Then he says that my father had such an infinite number of good qualities that I should not pick out his only strange one, his prickliness, as an example to follow.

"Forgive me for talking to you like this," he goes on, "but the matter is too important. You've let him persuade you that such assistance is charity, and that simply isn't so. Shall

176

I give you a list of reasons entitling us to such privileges?"

"I know what they are," I say.

"Then kindly answer me: are you going there or not?" asks Kwart, with what's left of his patience.

Suddenly Martha is in the room—God knows how long she's been here. She is standing by the open china cabinet, rattling the dishes; from a stack of bowls she needs the bottom one. Each time she has to balance something, she opens her mouth and touches her upper lip with her tongue.

"If it's any easier for you, we can go together," says Kwart.

"I'm not going to that place," I say.

"And may one know how else you intend to find somewhere to live?" Kwart asks in a voice now completely devoid of sympathy.

I mustn't keep him waiting until Martha is out of the room, and anyway what can she possibly pick up from disconnected words? I ask Kwart: "Would there be any point in advertising?"

"You'll be snowed under with offers," he says.

The apartment is Martha's and not mine; she can go on rattling her dishes as long as she likes. I have just thought of saying loudly into the phone that someone has come into the room and I'll call back later when she closes the door of the cabinet.

I say to Kwart: "If I were asked what his best quality was, I wouldn't hesitate to name that strange prickliness."

As she leaves, Martha looks at me in surprise, as if she has just noticed that I'm on the phone.

"That's very strange," says Kwart.

She is carrying the bowl in one hand and a little tower of cups in the other, and no one is there to help her, so she has to pull the door shut with one foot, a bare foot. Five scarlet toenails disappear from the room as a rear guard.

He goes on and on and once again offers to discuss my

problem with Wanda. Patiently—no, impatiently—I again explain why that is out of the question.

"You don't want to go to the bureau," says Kwart, "you don't want to move in with us. I hope you don't only like rooms that are not available."

I find Martha sitting at the kitchen table cutting beans. The way she doesn't look up tells me she's been expecting me. Where is the bowl and the tower of cups?

I pick up a knife, sit down beside her, and ask how to cut beans. Her reply consists in holding a bean up to my face and snipping off both ends. Maybe Martha believes one word from her and everything could go back to the way it used to be.

She lets me practice on a few beans before asking me what kind of an ad I was thinking of inserting. She knows nothing, my instinct tells me; she has only picked up a few words. I am busy with an invention: lining up ten green beans side by side and then, in a single motion, cutting off the ends. Probably it is my silence that implies there is something fishy going on.

"Of course no one can force you to tell me anything," Martha says.

"That's right," I say.

The varying lengths of the beans present a problem; either I cut them all to the same length, which would result in considerable waste, or I realign them before my second cut.

For a long time now I have been noticing Martha's increasing patience with my occasional testiness, as if quarreling were a sign of affection. If my status as a guest didn't prevent me, I would have already advanced to the limits of her tolerance—I wouldn't put that past me.

"I hear you've been accepted by the university?" she says.

I nod and decide to cut the beans Martha's way. A barely

perceptible odor of perspiration emanates from her, which, in our good times, used to send shivers down my spine. She notices my change of mood—she has her eyes everywhere—and smiles.

"Congratulations," she says. "Where? Here in Berlin?"

Again I nod. Her catechizing annoys me. I consider whether I shouldn't forestall her by reeling off the few details she still has in mind to ask me. Whenever I want to show Martha that it is possible to have a normal, relaxed conversation with me, it misfires.

"The long beans," she says, "can be cut in half."

"To return to your first question," I say, "I'm looking for a room. Hence the ad."

How calm she remains! She does look at me, yes, not with boredom, no, but there's not a trace of concern in her eyes, or of surprise, let alone dismay. The kind of eyes a waitress has when she is taking your order. But I'm glad to have taken the first step, the most important one. Things are beginning to move.

"I don't think you'll gain much by advertising," she says.

"Can you think of any other way of getting out of here?" I ask.

She is pondering, as I can see from the way her knife pauses in front of a bean. She puts down the knife, stands up, and gets herself some milk from the refrigerator. At least I can be sure that she won't advise me to go to the bureau for victims.

"I'll ask around among my people," she says.

"The only ones you shouldn't ask," I say, "are your parents."

She sits down again. I have no idea who her "people" are. I can see myself becoming a subtenant of that man I saw her with on Dimitroff-Strasse.

179

"Please don't give me any lessons in tact," she suddenly says. She has a milky mustache.

As if on cue, the front door to the apartment opens. It's quite possible that Martha will make a real effort to find a room for me; she has good reasons. I see Rahel Lepschitz in the kitchen doorway, contentedly observing me, Martha, and the beans. She beckons Hugo so he can see for himself that there is still hope.

An hour before shooting was due to end, when it looked as if Martha wouldn't be called today, I left the studio. Like a cop on his beat, I walked up and down the street, in a foul mood because my girlfriend was involved in a contemptible enterprise. But what mattered most was the weather. I kept looking up into the sky, the tiniest little cloud made me nervous. After all, it wasn't exactly news that the Jews had been badly treated at that time, or that the Nazis were an unpleasant bunch, but apart from that the movie contained nothing. In other words, it dealt with something that one either had known for a long time or no longer needed to know.

Martha came early, with a face reddened from rubbing off her make-up, or perhaps in anticipation. She ran toward me like a child wanting to be caught up and swung around in a circle. She apologized for not having been asked to act while I was there, though I couldn't imagine, she said, how little I had missed. Since I didn't want to spoil her mood or tell a lie, I decided not to go into the subject of movies now, not with a sky like this.

The only forest I knew my way around in was the one surrounding the cottage, and it was out of the question to go there. I could do no more than recite the names of some forests if Martha asked me to decide which way to go. But she already knew where we were going. She took me by the hand and started off. I flattered myself that she was in a tearing hurry to be alone with me, and I made a game of not asking about our destination.

The first stage of our journey ended at Köpenick station, at the taxi stand. Her response to my anxious question as to whether taking taxis wasn't overdoing things a bit for people like us was to take a few fifty-mark bills out of her purse, fan herself with them, and put them away again. I didn't have enough money even for a hot dog; the month simply refused to come to an end. She said that in certain situations in life it was all right to be extravagant. There was not a taxi to be seen; apart from us, no one was waiting.

Two young women, who seemed also to have come from the studio, waved to Martha as they passed and disappeared into the station, the reasonable thing to do. I, too, would have preferred to take the train; it seemed ostentatious to me to be standing there like that. I made allowances for Martha because she had no experience in handling money. She explained where it came from: at the end of each day's shooting, the actors were paid off, as if to minimize their losses if the movie company were to go bankrupt overnight. Once again she showed me the red-and-white bills, as if to point out that movie-making had its good side too.

When a taxi finally turned up, Martha went to the open window and spoke in a low voice to the driver. Was she haggling over the fare? The trip she had in mind was probably so complicated that she first had to obtain the driver's consent. I thought: Forest.

The driver nodded. She signaled to me, and we got in from different sides at the same time. The moment I sat down, a command came from my inner self to close my eyes and not open them again until we arrived. I thought the same thing might happen to me as to the poor boy in the fairy tale whose blindfold is removed after an arduous journey and he suddenly finds himself in the land of happiness.

I asked Martha if the actors got paid even if they had done nothing but stand around all day long.

"Obviously."

I didn't find that obvious at all, but she said that, for an artist, doing nothing was far more stressful than the work itself. I held my face to the wind, could feel when we switched from cobblestones to asphalt, and was careful not to open my eyes.

Martha took my arm, placed it around her shoulders, and tucked my hand into the warm hollow under her arm—I can feel it to this day. It felt so good that it would have been an effort to open my eyes. She whispered into my ear that she could imagine how ghastly this movie business must seem to me; she was only doing it for the money, and surely a student who was chronically short of money couldn't be blamed for that.

I whispered back that she didn't need to apologize, least of all to me, since I was traveling in the lap of luxury at her expense. Anyone who could acquire a fortune that easily, I breathed, would be crazy not to jump at the opportunity.

During the drive—the objective of which was, after all, for us to embrace in private—I could not tell Martha the truth: that it left a bitter taste in my mouth to see a Jewish origin or a Jewish face turned into money. In any case, I was keeping so much from her that this didn't seem the right moment to stress a love of truth. She'll find out soon enough, I thought; don't spoil anything now.

The way in which light and shadow alternated told me that we had left the suburbs behind. I asked Martha if we were driving through forest, and she said we were, but seemed to show no surprise. She snuggled up to me and nibbled my ear. In one way I longed for the drive to end, in another I wanted it to go on like this forever. Once I heard the driver call out "Now, now!" but at that moment we happened to be sitting sedately side by side.

After a curve that blotted out the sun, Martha asked what the quarrel between Father and me was about. I narrowly avoided opening my eyes. I feigned astonishment and claimed the relationship between Father and me was as bad or as good as ever, but that didn't satisfy her. She told me of the following incident: That morning she had phoned our apartment and spoken to Father. After being told by him that I wasn't home, she asked when I would be back, to which he replied that he neither knew nor cared.

Martha said she wasn't complaining about Father's brusqueness—though she didn't know what she had done to provoke it—but I shouldn't try to fool her into thinking there was nothing wrong. She wouldn't believe that even though she had never caught me out in a lie.

Now I wanted to look into her eyes. What was she hinting at? It was out of the question for me to let Martha in on my secret merely because she suspected something and was beginning to sound me out. To reveal it now would be evidence of a lack of trust rather than a sign of love, after keeping it to myself so long.

Instead, I told her the tale of the housekeeping money debacle, in recklessly invented detail. To render Father's anger credible, I told her I had stolen some money from his wallet in order to have at least some bread and butter on the table. Actually I had been considering such a theft, and the only reason I hadn't gone ahead with it was that I was afraid of his reaction, which I now described as if it had taken place.

Martha didn't reproach me, saying only that I could easily have borrowed from her, to which I replied that that would have been the last straw. Subject closed. I asked how far we still had to go. Although I had kept my voice very low, it was the driver who answered, saying we had to turn only one more corner.

When the car came to a stop, Martha whispered that I was on no account to open my eyes yet. I obeyed and thus never found out the amount on the meter. While Martha was paying, I got out and stood waiting for further instructions.

After the taxi between us had driven away, she came over to me, took my arm, and led me off as if I were blind. My hand, which had lain for so long under her arm, felt cold. The air smelled of evergreens. By this time, keeping my eyes closed had become torture. I heard Martha giggle as if she had a surprise for me. I felt firmly trodden earth under my feet, then a hard surface. We stopped. She gave me a little push and said: "Now!"

I opened my eyes and found myself looking at a lake. We were on a boat dock, Martha behind me. She had pushed me so close to the edge that the toes of my shoes were in the air. Immediately I flailed my arms to avoid tipping forward. Martha's little finger would have been enough to push me into the water. We hugged each other and laughed as if this were the joke of the century. I was also happy because my tiny worry that we might have driven to the cottage was now dispelled.

Jutting out from the reeds fringing the shore were other docks, widely spaced, all deserted. The only sailboats in sight were far out on the water, three or four of them moving so slowly that I couldn't make out which way they were heading.

"You don't even know the best part yet," Martha said.

She held out a fist, which I opened finger by finger; in it lay a key I had never seen before. To judge by Martha's expression, I should now have gone into ecstasies, but what about? The key appeared to belong to a padlock.

With a grandiose gesture she told me to pick out the finest

185

of all the boats tied up at the docks. Although I took my time choosing, I ended up pointing at the wrong one.

She had begged her uncle, a dentist, for permission to use his boat. She had to reassure him by claiming that her boyfriend was an experienced motorboat operator, which didn't quite correspond to the truth, since I had never so much as sat in a motorboat. Martha said that shouldn't worry us, she'd been out many times with her uncle and was confident she knew how to handle the boat. All that mattered was to get far enough away from the shore: we were agreed on that.

The first job was to free the boat from its cover, in the middle of which a large rain puddle had accumulated over many days. We bundled up the heavy tarpaulin and threw it into the boat, where it took up a third of the space. Then Martha unlocked a chain with her key, whereupon the little outboard motor, which had been tipped up, could be lowered into the water. I was reassured to see two paddles lying in the bottom of the boat.

Martha advised me to hold my breath and squat on my heels. Several times she pulled violently on a string whose other end disappeared into a hole in the motor housing. To my surprise, a chugging sound was soon heard. Martha looked infinitely relieved. I felt ashamed to be sitting around so idly while she was wearing herself out for us. I asked whether I shouldn't untie the boat from the dock, and she nodded, as if acknowledging a moderately good idea.

When that had been attended to, she managed in some mysterious way to set the boat in motion. We proceeded leisurely and in a straight line toward the middle of the lake, without tumult, without complications, and soon even without fear. Although Martha gripped the stick controlling both direction and speed somewhat tensely, she handled it so impeccably that I wondered how she had acquired such skills behind my back.

About halfway—assuming we were heading for the middle of the lake—I risked standing up. I took off my shoes, then Martha's, and arranged the tarpaulin so we could lie on it. Martha pretended to look shocked, but she lifted her feet so as not to hinder my smoothing of the tarpaulin. The lake was large and empty enough for us to anchor before going as far as the middle, but I didn't interfere with Martha's plans.

I decided to lie down so as to seem, for the rest of the trip, as if ready and waiting for Martha. I clasped my hands under my head and felt wonderfully comfortable. I could look up into the sky, into Martha's face or, if I raised my head a little, under her skirt. Although she had to keep an eye on our course, she didn't miss a thing.

In a few moments, I thought, the terrible days would be over, and I could soon stop thinking about Elle's letter, about Father's coldness, about the stench in the cottage, about my sense of frustration. I could already feel the contentment approaching; it had already begun. I closed my eyes and imagined us later jumping into the water, and how, later still, I would have to push Martha back into the boat from below because the side was too high, and darkness would already have fallen.

In a mood of elation, like someone for whom everything has changed for the better, I arrived home. It must have been before midnight. I felt fresh after my cool swim. We had jumped into the water, just as I had dreamed we would. But I was so tired that on the way from the street entrance up to our apartment door I sat down on the stairs for a brief rest.

After closing the door behind me, I leaned against it and imagined the happiness of walking into my own home with Martha. Just then I heard a voice from Father's room: either the radio was on or he had a visitor. I decided against brushing my teeth; I still had the taste of Martha on my tongue.

My room was above a street lamp; it never got really dark in there. First I lay down on the bed, then I took off my shoes, nothing else. When Martha wanted to get back in the boat after swimming, I really had had to push from below: piece by piece she disappeared over the side until I was holding the last foot in my hand. Instead of letting go, I pulled, and with a scream she flopped into the water and had to be heaved back up again.

Between my father's room and mine was a door that was never used, covered on his side by bookshelves and on mine by a wardrobe. Although I had no intention of listening, I heard voices. They were blurred, and all they told me was that there were people in there. Father's voice was the most distinct, but I couldn't understand what he was saying. Occasionally he had brought someone home from the billiard parlor to play cards, but I couldn't imagine that he would be playing cards these days.

When I was eleven, I once heard a woman give a loud laugh next door, in the middle of the night. At that time the wardrobe wasn't in front of my side of the door, and sounds penetrated more easily. Father told the woman to be quiet, but his own voice was loud. The presence of a woman in our apartment, at night, was so unheard of that there could be no further thought of sleep. They whispered together, but again and again a laugh or a giggle would rise from their murmurs, as if Father was tickling the woman. The keyhole was black, and it became no lighter when I tried to poke a pencil through it. So I had to risk the adventure of going out into the passage to the keyhole of the door to his room. I remember putting on some pants, just in case. There was a light in the passage. After a few steps, something completely unexpected happened: Father's door opened, and a naked woman emerged from the room, probably on her way to the bathroom. In spite of her gray hair, her face seemed very beautiful to me. Since she had been looking back at Father as she opened the door, she didn't notice me until she was well out of the room. Startled, she put her hand to her mouth, but made no sound. Her breasts were indescribably large: I had never seen a woman's breasts before, except in pictures. We stood facing one another for a long time, but I didn't dare drop my eyes from the upper part of her body to the lower. Finally she asked, with a smile and no sign of embarrassment, whether I couldn't sleep. I nodded and ran back into my room. A few moments later Father came to my bedside. He stroked my head and behaved as if he had to comfort me in some grief. He was wearing only his pants

189

and smelled of schnapps. The thought came to me that this woman might in some way be my mother, and that the story of her death had been a lie. I asked Father about that, and he hugged me and whispered that I shouldn't talk such dreadful nonsense.

Now, when I thought I recognized Kwart's voice, I was convinced that a discussion among the kidnappers was going on next door. What kind of a process is that? How can one recognize a voice without understanding a word? Never again was there a woman in our apartment, not at night. Didn't they get bored, discussing for the hundredth time how their captive should be treated, and for the hundredth time not finding the solution? There was a third voice, that of Rotstein, who for me tonight was Turteltaub at a meeting of the camp administrators.

None of them made any effort to lower his voice, not even Father; either they hadn't heard me come in or they saw no necessity to show any consideration for me. They couldn't meet in a bar, in Kwart's home there was Wanda, in Turteltaub's there was doubtless Mrs. Turteltaub. So the only place left was our apartment.

I got up to insist on quiet. Our home the ideal meeting place, our cottage the most suitable prison: suddenly it seemed to me that I was bearing the brunt of the whole operation. On my way to the door, however, I changed my mind. I wanted to listen after all. If there are no problems, I was thinking, why get together at night and confer?

I pushed the wardrobe away from the door. In my memory, this took hours. Since the floorboards to the left of the wardrobe creaked and I had to avoid stepping on them or pushing the wardrobe onto them, I pulled it toward the middle of the room. As I was moving it, the voices became louder, but I didn't listen until I had finished. Whenever there was silence next door, I stopped too.

After pulling the wardrobe far enough from the wall, I lay down on the floor. Between door and threshold was a crack just wide enough to let through some light.

The first words I heard explained why they didn't need to lower their voices: they were speaking Yiddish. It was inconceivable that Father should be able to communicate in that language; I felt there must be a stranger in there with Father's voice. Not only had he always avoided speaking Yiddish in my presence: he had never so much as indicated that he was able to. Without awkwardness, without hesitation, from one moment to the next he had mastered the language. I found that terrifying; I felt betrayed. He was talking louder than the others, so I wondered whether he was counting on my listening and whether this was his way of revealing his secret to me. Never had I felt such hostility toward him.

I had picked up five or ten Yiddish words, I don't know where. Kwart sometimes used the word *tinif*, Father the word *mazel*; somewhere I had heard the word *chutzpa*. It would never have occurred to me to use such words, and, if someone else did, I automatically tried to think which word would normally replace them. To scatter Yiddish words in a conversation seemed to me an ostentatious kind of folklorism. Naturally that only applied to people who could have spoken differently if they had wanted to.

Turteltaub coughed a lot, and the smell of cigarettes reached my nose through the crack. I found the sound of the language unpleasant, not just strange as with ordinary foreign languages. This one moved along the very borderline of the intelligible, and I constantly had the feeling that I would only have to exert myself a little more to grasp the meaning. Perhaps they were talking Yiddish because they thought it especially appropriate for the subject.

After eventually overcoming my resistance to those charmless, distorted sounds, I was surprised by how many of the words were intelligible. At first I ignored the context, letting the words pass by and registering only those that made sense. It was only when the distance between them became shorter and shorter that I began to understand.

The result staggered me: they weren't talking about the kidnapping, they were talking about their past, about war and camp. Each in turn told about his experiences, interrupted by questions from the others and an occasional sigh.

Just when I was beginning to concentrate on the meaning of the sentences, it happened to be Father's turn. He was telling a story I already knew, which helped somewhat: how my sister had survived the war years. Kwart and Turteltaub asked repeatedly for details that to me seemed trivial, but Father was very patient with them. When Elle was three years old, my parents hid her with a farmer's family in Mecklenburg, and for this they had to pay so much that there could be no thought of a hiding place for themselves. After the war—seven years later—Father went to get Elle, but the farmer demanded more money. He maintained that the earlier sum had been calculated to cover three years at most, and that the deal would never have been made if he had known that so many years were involved. Father, who had been released from camp a few days earlier and didn't have a penny, promised to bring him more money. He got Elle back on credit, so to speak, he said. After they reached home, he saw how deeply disturbed she was, and that she began to cry whenever she was asked questions about the last few years. He was seized with rage at that farmer. Turteltaub asked what else could be expected from that German rabble, and he criticized Father for not picking up the first available rock and killing the farmer.

Well, now that I knew what they were talking about in the next room there was no longer anything to keep me at the door; for that subject, I was too tired. I went to bed and wondered why Father, who couldn't bear concentration-camp stories, so willingly shared these experiences.

Even in bed I could hear the voices, those wretched voices: after Father, Kwart, then Rotstein, then Father again, a potpourri of suffering. I fell asleep—but not inadvertently: I opted for the better choice.

I don't know what I can do to stop the days from being so alike. Always the same routine, the same boredom; apart from my sense of frustration, which increases day by day, everything stays the same. In cafés and on the street I smile at all the pretty girls until they turn away. But where am I to find the courage to speak to them? After each failure I lower my standards: useless.

I hardly talk anymore; that, too, is gradually taken for granted. Hugo and Rahel Lepschitz treat me as someone who happens to talk very little. It seems to me that their conversations in my presence are becoming less and less inhibited. Since the matter of the university has been settled, I no longer even expect a letter.

Recently I have been troubled by new misgivings: it might be a waste of time to study philosophy. Of course I have no answer to the question of what I should do instead. From sheer inactivity I have doubts about everything. Like an old-age pensioner I wander around the streets or sit on park benches. Perhaps I am a victim of Fascism after all and refuse to admit it.

Every Monday, Lepschitz comes home from work with his briefcase filled with newspapers, as if he suspected world history to occur preferably at weekends. Then we sit facing each other at the living-room table. He scans the papers in a certain order, so I always know which one I may take without crossing him up. From time to time he reads an article aloud, oblivious to whether anyone is listening.

This morning while we were out shopping, Rahel asked whether I had made any plans for my vacation. There was a chance, she said, for me to join her and Hugo on a trip to the Harz Mountains, in July, staying in a pension near Halberstadt. Martha would be away during that time, with her drama school, and it would be a shame for me to remain alone in the apartment. Rahel Lepschitz could have no idea what pleasure she was giving me with this prospect of three free weeks. I said I had to spend July and August preparing for university. She appreciated that, and I thought that things had to be pretty hopeless if in those three weeks things couldn't pick up a bit.

Lepschitz places his newspaper, *Neues Deutschland*, in front of me, saying: "Take a look at this." He points emphatically at the table, as if I can find the right place without his help. I read headlines: MY AVOWAL—DILIGENT STUDY OF THE LANGUAGE OF LENIN and SOVIET ART SETS STANDARDS FOR OUR CREATIVITY, and FLAME OF FRIENDSHIP BURNS INEXTINGUISHABLY.

When I look up, Lepschitz says: "Now they've gone mad."

I'm no judge of that, though I have to admit that the paper seems even more peculiar than usual. The first five pages deal exclusively with reports on a conference of the Society for German-Soviet Friendship. Turning the pages a second time, it occurs to me that I am a member of this society, have been for years, but I never regarded my membership as important, which it now turns out to be. Lepschitz takes back the paper after we have exchanged a look of complete agreement. At page six he starts reading again. My father didn't like our society, but he was a great admirer of the Russians.

Rahel brings her husband his evening cup of tea. For the first hour after he comes home, until about suppertime, she treats him like a king. At times I think that such a solicitous wife would get on my nerves, and at others I would like to imagine such a wife in my future. She sits down at the table and watches him. Soon I'll be going out, and then he will bring Rahel up to date on the events of the weekend, condensing the overly long articles. I leave just as Lepschitz places the front page before her too.

Out on the street I see a dog run over. Brakes squeal, the little dog lies beside his blood, a woman in house slippers screams. Passers-by quickly form a circle: just like a real accident. Lepschitz's birthday is getting closer and closer; in a few days he will be sixty. I stroll past the stores, my pocket full of money, hoping to find the right gift.

On my own birthday, last October, a big cake was brought in bearing nineteen dripping candles. Lepschitz gave me a shaving kit, which embarrassed me, but it was also useful, because Martha had been teasing me about the fuzz on my chin. Rahel gave me a hand towel and face cloth on which she had embroidered the word "Hans." They take birthdays extremely seriously. Besides, I am the wealthiest person in their family.

Lepschitz is not hard to please, but the store windows give me no inspiration. If the worst comes to the worst, I'll buy him a cut-glass vase; I know where there is one. I mustn't go too far because I've promised to be back for supper. It was easy to find presents for Father: he always wanted books, the main thing being that they had to be old—in other words, secondhand. One day I made a list of all the authors whose books were in his room. Even so, rarely did I have to leave a secondhand-book shop empty-handed. I believe the reason he preferred old books and old objects to unused ones was that he had had to buy everything new when he came out of concentration camp. Lepschitz doesn't care for books.

Walking up the stairs, I meet someone who doesn't know

me, so I pretend not to remember him either, the fellow I met with Martha on the street. Against my will, indignation rises in me: Now she's actually bringing him home! I would never dare show up here with a girlfriend, even if I had one. This time he is wearing a white linen jacket, the most ridiculous garment ever heard of. I still can't rule out that he came uninvited and didn't find Martha at home. And that Rahel said to him: You will excuse us, sir, we are just having supper.

The key having been left on the inside of the door, I have to ring. Rahel opens the door, a bowl of ice cubes in her hand. She hurries to the kitchen the moment she sees me. What's going on? I go into the living room, the table is only half set, no Lepschitz. So I follow her.

My arrival is question enough, there has been an accident, I hear, Martha's hand is broken. But Lepschitz, standing behind us in the doorway, says: "Her hand is only sprained, not broken."

I calculate: the fellow must have been a witness to, or the cause of, her accident, and it was he who had brought poor Martha home. Why didn't he stay? Did I return too soon? Or is it possible that Martha is in the hospital and White Jacket had merely brought the news?

While Rahel maintains that sprains are worse than fractures, I go to Martha's room. Curiosity, just curiosity. I knock so softly that Martha, in case she is there and wants to be left alone, need not hear it. I am annoyed at the way White Jacket looked right through me.

"Yes?" Martha calls.

I enter as if into the room of a dying person: she is reclining on her bed, propped up on pillows that have been assembled from all over the apartment. They have dressed her in her bathrobe. Her right wrist, lying as if dead beside her, is bandaged. Her face looks frail and suffering; I can't figure out why she seems to me to be overdoing things.

"Forgive my curiosity," I say.

"It happened while I was playing tennis. You know how clumsy I am," she says.

I only know how skillful she is, but tennis? This is the first I've heard of it, and I am no less surprised than I was when my father suddenly spoke Yiddish. In my time she didn't play tennis, and I have never seen a tennis racket in this apartment.

"Since when have you been playing tennis?"

"You don't know?" she asks in surprise. "I've been talking about nothing else these last few weeks."

She hasn't noticed how quickly I always leave the room when she comes in. Never mind, what should I have against tennis? I ask whether she is in much pain and whether there's anything I can do for her. The answer is yes, her wrist hurts horribly, and no, what help could I give her? Ron took her to Emergency, she goes on; she fell while playing with him. For heaven's sake, what kind of a name is that? How can she bring herself even to utter such a word? Shall I tell her now that I met him on the stairs, or shall I simply leave? Since this is an emergency, I can't accuse her of dragging her boyfriends into the apartment day after day—I have to admit that.

Martha says it will be at least four weeks before she can use her hand again; that's what they told her at the hospital. What does she care about my sympathy? I've been standing much too long in front of her, I can't think of a single question that wouldn't sound insincere. I take a stab at it and say that, as far as I know, sprains have to be kept warm, for the sake of better circulation. She seems doubtful, although she doesn't contradict me.

Rahel enters the room without knocking; that's how far things have deteriorated. She brings some lemonade with ice in it, and Martha sits up, groaning as if on her deathbed. For

198

the first time I detect a great resemblance between her and Lepschitz. As she drinks, she hesitates when she notices my smile. Truly there is no place for me here.

They can thank their lucky stars, says Rahel, that Mr. Wackernagel took such wonderful care of Martha. Another glance is exchanged between us: Wackernagel! I ask whether that was the person in the natty white jacket. This is confirmed by all present.

Martha has finished her lemonade and is chewing a piece of ice. Mr. Wackernagel is due back at any moment, says Rahel. He has just nipped over to the pharmacy to buy some embrocation. So I was mistaken, for I suppose embrocation is used to cool, not to warm.

I mumble something unintelligible even to myself and leave the room. He now has his foot in the door, and why should he take it away again as long as he finds Martha attractive? I lie down on my bed under the shelter of earphones so as not to hear him come back. Maybe they'll soon give him a key, as they did me. For God's sake, I'm not the first person to lose a father! I'm up to my neck in self-pity and at my wits' end: that will have to change.

Not a single penny before tomorrow, Father said, meaning: not till the end of the month. But when he heard that Elle had asked me to buy some coffee and a Thermos, he gave me twenty marks. Nothing else was mentioned; we scarcely looked at one another. He was haggard from lack of sleep.

Elle showed disappointingly little pleasure over the coffee, although there was still none to be had at the kiosk. With not a word of thanks she put the Thermos away in her cupboard without so much as a sip, and throughout my entire visit, which lasted several hours, she didn't take it out again.

I had made up my mind to have it out with her this time, she must be made to listen to what trouble she had caused me with her blabbing. I intended to explain, without anger, that it is impossible to talk about everything with everybody, that one has no option but to talk to one person about one thing and to the other person about something else. And I wanted to tell her how miserable the relationship between Father and me had become and how she had contributed to that.

By then I was suspicious of Elle's airy assurance in her letter that I needn't worry, that she had lied very cleverly and not mentioned my name to Father. I thought she might be taking advantage of her condition. Many a time I had noticed how people loved her especially for her touching credulity, and it was possible that she was now making the most of this. Of course I couldn't be sure, but many things pointed to that, I felt. First of all, her acute reasoning powers, which occasionally deserted her—but never for long, never for an interval, say, extending from my visit through Father's visit up to the writing of her last letter to me. Was she seriously trying to make me believe that she could tell Father about the kidnapping and at the same time, by not mentioning my name, keep her source a secret? Was she trying to fool me that she believed in this nonsense herself? My mind kept returning to an incident that lay far in the past:

In Elle's section a woman had begun working whom I had never seen but had heard a lot about, Nurse Hermine. Tension developed between Elle and this nurse. Elle complained to the doctor and to the head nurse that Nurse Hermine was harassing her and, when there were no witnesses, treated her so roughly that she was afraid of being beaten. According to what I heard, Nurse Hermine was a large, heavy woman. Elle's complaints met with no success, so she discussed the problem with Father. He started arguing with the doctors, demanding that the nurse be replaced, but got nowhere. Elle's complaints were imaginary, he was told, and where would it lead if the fate of the nurses was dependent on the whims of the patients? He was at liberty, of course, to move his daughter to an institution in whose staff he could have more confidence, they said. There was no such institution to be found far and wide.

One day Elle handed him two pills. For some time she had been feeling strangely tired, she said, and she had noticed that Nurse Hermine was giving her, in addition to her daily medication, some pills that she had never seen before—these

201

very ones. She asked Father to have the pills tested to see whether they had anything to do with her increasing lassitude.

Father had great difficulty finding a laboratory to do the job. I was fourteen at the time and, in taking me into his confidence, he said that keeping my mouth shut would be my "test of maturity." Armed with the results from the lab, Father became suspicious and went to the head of the institution rather than to the doctor in charge of Elle's section. The names and proportions of the active ingredients found by the lab in the pills told Father nothing, but the head of the institution knew how to interpret them. Elle's suspicion was justified, the pills were poison to her: they contained an exceptionally strong tranquilizer that she didn't need and that no doctor had ever prescribed for her. All hell broke loose in the section; Nurse Hermine was dismissed. Father considered filing charges, but a lawyer advised against this—I don't know why. Elle soon recovered from her lassitude, and the affair might have ended there.

Months later, I was with Elle in the park, playing a game she had invented: Tell or demonstrate something to astonish the other person. You could win up to five points, depending on the degree of astonishment. For example, for being able to bend my thumb back to touch my forearm I was given two points. That afternoon Elle suddenly gave a radiant smile and led me to a huge plane tree. After making sure no one had followed us, she thrust her hand into a hole in the trunk, brought out a pillbox, and demanded five points. It contained the very pills she had used to rid herself of innocent Nurse Hermine. I can remember how my heart pounded when I realized what my sister was capable of. She offered no explanation.

Because I considered it likely that Nurse Hermine not only

had lost her job but also would never find another, I told Father what I knew. He accepted the information with surprising calm, as if he had long since considered such a possibility. And he ordered me not to speak to anyone about it.

On her bed lay a doll I had never seen, dressed in a frilly white blouse and green shoes. Elle didn't feel like going outdoors; I stroked her head a few times before starting on my lecture. I told her that Father was angry with me: could she imagine why? She shook her head and opened her eyes wide. I spurred myself on with the thought that she needed nothing so much as to be taken seriously.

"You must have realized the consequences," I said, "when you talked to him about the kidnapping."

Again she shook her head, and I said: "I don't believe you."

Something extraordinary happened: Elle took a few steps back, pressed her hands together in front of her breast, the way opera singers sometimes do, and, her face distorted with anger, said: "I'm afraid I'm feeling dizzy. Maybe we should call the nurse."

There could be no doubt that she meant to shut me up, she was threatening to have an attack.

"I don't know what was behind your betrayal," I said. "Did you want to protect Father from me?"

"You leave me no choice," she said.

She pressed a button beside the night table, and a little green light appeared over the door. Elle lay down on the bed, held her hand to her brow, and presented the very picture of suffering. She had inadvertently lain down on her doll, which was now pressing into her. Elle snatched it out and threw it on the floor before the door opened. A nurse came in.

Elle raised her head, as if by a great effort. But her eyes

were on me, not on the nurse. I knew what that look meant: It was a warning not to betray her when she pretended to be suffering.

"What's the matter?" asked the nurse.

"A good thing you came," I said. "She suddenly felt dizzy."

"He's exaggerating," Elle said quickly. "I'm just thirsty."

"Is that all?"

The nurse went to the washbasin, picked up Elle's plastic mug, rinsed it, and filled it with water, at the same time suggesting that I note the procedure so that at the next attack of thirst I could take over the job of filling the mug myself. She carried the full mug over to Elle, nodded to us with feigned affability, and left the room.

"Why did you want to discredit me with Father?" I asked before Elle could entertain any false hopes. She shrugged and got up. With a smile, she carried the mug back to the washbasin and poured out the water without having drunk any of it.

"I'm furious with you," I said, "and I don't mind your knowing that. I'm not leaving before you explain why you did it."

She sat down with a cigarette, like a lady waiting for a light, and I looked for some matches. Her condition seemed to me to be remarkably good; she was more than usually cheerful and alert. If only I had left well enough alone. Normally everything went the way she wanted; it was a kind of law.

She said she need only have told the nurse that she was feeling ill and I would have had to leave. In the bookcase I found a can full of empty matchboxes. "What difference would that have made?" I said. "Do you think I would understand your behavior better if I were sent away?"

She looked on impatiently, the cigarette between her lips,

while I continued searching. Before opening her cupboard, I asked her permission: she nodded. There were no matches there either, none in the whole room.

"What did I do to deserve this lecture?" Elle asked.

Now her little game no longer seemed cunning but pathetic. For heaven's sake, I thought, when does she ever have a chance to be spiteful and deceitful, and who else can she ever take a swipe at? I changed my tone and said we needn't make a big deal of it; it was just that I had counted on her not telling Father anything about our conversation, hence my annoyance.

Not only was Elle relieved when my expression became brotherly again: I, too, felt more comfortable. I was still hoping for some advice from her, for a suggestion, for the merest hint of what I might do.

She asked me to get a match from outside. I didn't even try asking the nurse but hurried to the kiosk and back so quickly that I had to sit down. Sometimes she smoked in a way that I found unpleasant: she would inhale part of the smoke while the remainder formed a little cloud in front of her mouth. Instead of allowing this little cloud to rise quietly, she would pursue it and suck it into her mouth, like someone after a meal sweeping crumbs from the table into her palm and tossing them greedily down her gullet.

Was it expecting too much, she said, if she asked me to bring her a bassoon or a violin to try out? It was terribly difficult to decide merely on the basis of the radio sound.

"That man is still being kept a prisoner. That guard," I said.

Elle paused in her movements, then went on smoking as if nothing had happened. In an encyclopedia on the book cart, she said, there were pictures of instruments, among them a violin, but how much could a person tell from such illustrations? For instance, she had no idea how big or how heavy violins were. Her words sounded to me like a challenge, like a determined effort to force me into retreat.

"It's not merely a matter of what punishment that man deserves," I went on. "I find that Father looks positively ill. He's sleeping badly, hardly eats a thing, and is tense and wrought up all day long. It's for his sake that we have to try to put an end to the affair."

Even as I spoke I knew she would immediately return to the instruments; I could tell from the way she kept her head lowered, the way she wasn't listening but merely putting up with my talking. A wicked ruse flashed through my mind: tell her I would only bring her a bassoon or a violin if she first gave me some advice. I refrained because I didn't know how difficult it would be to get hold of the instruments. For all I knew, she would accept the deal and I wouldn't be able to deliver.

In fact, when I finished talking, she did ask whether I considered her intelligent and skillful enough to embark on this musical venture. It would have broken my heart not to have answered yes.

She had no illusions, she said, her learning capacity wasn't all that great. Of course I protested. Whether I liked it or not, she made me dance to her tune. She said it would have been smarter if she had had such a crazy notion twenty-five years ago; nobody her age could learn to play a musical instrument just like that, the way a child does.

"How do you know that?" I asked.

"From hearsay. Isn't it true?"

No doubt she believed that the danger was now past, or she wouldn't have dropped the subject. At any rate, she said nothing for a while, as if she no longer had to outtalk me. I shifted my chair so close to her that our knees meshed like two cogwheels. She playfully blew some smoke into my face.

"You don't understand how serious it is," I said. "I'm at my wits' end. There's no one I can talk to about it."

At that she drew my head down onto her lap and said: "Yes, yes, I know that feeling."

I closed my eyes while she stroked me; it made us both feel good. It would have been better if we could have talked things over, but her butterfly fingers were not bad either.

I heard her ask: "Aren't you afraid, then, that I'll tell him everything again?"

On the way home I felt miserable. Elle's small consolation had quickly evaporated, and Martha couldn't be reached because, for the first time, they were filming at night. Father wasn't home. In the larder I found a piece of bread so stale it had cracked. He was in the forest—where else?—sitting in judgment.

The apartment looked as if two old men lived in it. On the stove stood an empty saucepan smelling agreeably of soup. I was furious at the way Father kept me so short of food. I admit I had embezzled some housekeeping money, and for all I cared he might have a hundred reasons for being mad at me, but did that entitle him to let me starve? I threw the bread out the kitchen window, down behind the garbage cans, and began to tidy the apartment. Lying around in my room were piles of stuff that belonged to my schooldays and had become worthless with my graduation.

After my room, I tackled our gloomy green bathroom. The tiny hairs from his electric razor seemed to be stuck permanently to the washbasin; the towels were shamefully dirty. I realized that Father would have changed them days ago if he hadn't been constantly caught up in the great distraction; dirt had always bothered him more than me.

We had run out of toilet paper, and I had no money to

buy more, so I tore some newspapers into postcard-size pieces, threaded a string through them, and hung the sheets conspicuously from the window latch. I hoped he wouldn't take that as a sign that I was now trying to economize.

When I opened a window in his room to shake out a dust-cloth, scraps of paper fluttered from his desk. I gathered them together and put them in a drawer, where I noticed a black wallet. Father's wallet was brown.

It seemed only natural to make the most of such an opportunity. I took the wallet to my room, although Father was due home any minute. As a precaution, I inserted the key in the lock of our front door. I couldn't have said what I was hoping to find.

Meanwhile the wallet has come into my possession; I inherited it from Father. At that time, in spite of my excitement, I opened it carefully and memorized the position of each item in it. One by one I read or examined each of them, and I wrote down every detail in an exercise book as if to collect material for solving a case. *Heppner, Arnold Hermann, born March 4, 1907, in Brandenburg/Havel.* Heavens, he was six years older than Father, but anyone would have taken him for quite a bit younger. *Married, distinguishing marks: none.* I wrote down the address, the identity number, even the expiry date of the identity card.

A punched railroad ticket. On April 4 he had traveled to Leipzig, second class, and returned three days later. In the outer pocket of the wallet, a notebook, photos (the kind to be seen in photographers' windows), slips of paper with figures and dates, money, a receipt for two bags of cement.

In the notebook nothing but names, addresses, telephone numbers. I was surprised that there wasn't a single deviation from alphabetical order, although the notebook was so old that the pages had curled at the edges.

Merkel, H. J.
Mierau, Johanna
Motor Lichtenberg, BSG
Musikladen Frankfurter-Allee
Musikladen Schönhauser-Allee
Mussner, Widukind

There was nothing incriminating in the wallet, but what had I expected to find? His Nazi Party membership card? A photo showing him flailing away at Jews with a whip? His writing was difficult to read because there was hardly any space between the letters, which were strangely elongated, as if every line had been pushed together from both sides after being written. I didn't find the handwriting unpleasant, let alone repulsive, even if I'd had to express an opinion on it. I shuddered at the thought that Father, Kwart, and Rotstein might have checked out all those names in the notebook.

Just as the phone rang, the photos slipped off the table, and I had to pick them all up before hurrying into the passage, by which time whoever it was had hung up. The picture on top had been one of a bridal couple looking out with desperate eyes: I hadn't memorized the sequence of the remaining photos.

I put back the wallet, removed the key from the front door, and vacuumed Father's room. He had never been able to part with a faded, threadbare rug because Mother had once spilled some red wine on it. Perhaps he didn't care what kind of rug he had in his room; in any case the wine stains were my mother's doing. When I finished vacuuming, I took the loose pieces of paper and spread them out on the desk again.

The kitchen remained to be done, and it was getting late. We had never argued much about cleaning up the kitchen, but this time I felt that, if I did it, I would be capitulating. I took one of the many dirty cups and threw it against the wall. Not that it was a habit of mine to vent my rage on crockery, but my fingers were itching to smash the whole squalid pile of dishes. I was hungry.

I ran around my room like a trapped marten, dreaming up impossible things to say to Father. *You're confusing me with your Nazi—why else won't you give me any food?* Or: *Do you believe that every Jew should go miserably hungry at least once in his life?*

Then I did something that inexplicably came to mind, not piece by piece, but suddenly, as a whole: I took out Heppner's wallet again and pulled a photo at random from the middle. From the wardrobe I took a cardboard box in which Father kept his own photographs, not in any particular order, chronological order. I slipped Heppner's picture in among our family photos, put wallet and cardboard box back where they belonged, and for a few seconds felt satisfied. To this day I don't know whether I meant to lay a trail as evidence that I was in on the secret or whether I had simply gone out of my mind.

Fragments of the cup were lying all over the kitchen. I swept them up and kept finding more. Before leaving Elle, I had had to promise her to see whether it was possible to borrow a violin somewhere for half a day. It was sad to think of what would follow: She would draw the bow across the strings, hear those ugly sounds, and there would be nobody around to teach her. She would try it a few more times, and that would be the end, forever. There was even a chip lying in the sink.

While I was filling the sink with water to wash the dishes, Father looked into the kitchen. I turned off the tap and pretended I had merely been washing my hands. He said this was the pleasantest sight he'd had for a long time, seeing me work like that, and he didn't wish to disturb me. Before I could get a word out in reply, he disappeared again. I took the few pieces of crockery I had already placed in the sink and piled them back on the others.

He had gone to his room. With a little money in my pocket I would have left the apartment at once. The realization that he couldn't stand the sight of me was an important by-product of the kidnapping; from that point of view, the affair had its good side too. Or is it normal for parents to get tired of their children one day? For only a limited quantity of concern and kindness to be available, and when this supply is exhausted, for annoyance and hostility take over, just as they do with other people who have to live at close quarters?

Father came back and opened the refrigerator door behind me. Then I heard him rinse out something. I was standing at the window, reluctant to turn around. He said that, if I decide to clean up once every five years, I should do so not only where it showed but also in the corners. Contrary to all reason I had expected him to say something conciliatory. I whirled around and cried out so violently that it seemed overdone even to myself: "I'm hungry!"

He calmly answered that he had brought home some meat and intended to cook it later, then wiped a glass and poured himself a beer. When I tried to leave, he grabbed me by the sleeve and pointed to a chair. His peaceable expression led me to believe that he would make some conciliatory remark after all, but I remained standing.

He sat down, asked whether I'd been to see Elle, and drank up his beer while waiting for my answer. I tried to imagine what he was leading up to; whether, for instance, he intended to ask for an accounting of the money he had given me for the Thermos. "Well?" he asked.

"You know I've been to see her," I said.

"I know it from you," he said, as if information from such a source was of little value. "But what I'd like to know is: did you discuss this case with her again?"

"What else?" I answered. We looked at each other for a long time, and I could observe the rage mounting in him.

Countless times since then I have reproached myself for having had nothing in my head but my sense of injury, for not realizing that I was merely a peripheral figure. Countless times I have asked myself why I regarded Father as a Hercules of whom each and every effort could be expected. But my eyes were narrower than his; I was trembling with indignation even more than he was. However, because I was the greater coward I left the kitchen and then the apartment. I fled down the stairs and headed for Alexander-Platz.

That was a time when Martha had to cope with a triple burden: her film work, her studies, and me. If she had had more leisure, she would have noticed that my behavior was different from usual, that I talked suspiciously little, and that I was constantly absent-minded. But maybe she did notice and explained it by my being jealous of her activities.

She was sitting at the table, two shoulder blades with a valley in between, working on an essay that had to be handed in at the beginning of the new semester, more than a month away. She was afraid we might not have enough time for a little of the Baltic Sea. I sat in her rocking chair, unable to get beyond the first two pages of a book she had pushed into my hands the way one sticks a pacifier in a baby's mouth.

On going into our filthy kitchen that morning, I had found the housekeeping money for August spread out on the table like a fan. Father must have put it there the evening before, or during the night; he was still asleep. To show him how well it paid off to treat me right, I promptly washed the dishes and mopped the kitchen floor. Then I went downstairs to the nearest Konditorei and stuffed myself with five or six pieces of cake. As a result I felt ill all day long, including the afternoon spent sitting behind Martha as she bent over her work.

That evening she had to go to the studio again, for the last time. So there I was, sitting behind her, not only bored but also knowing with certainty that there was nothing pleasant to look forward to. Nevertheless, I preferred to feel deserted while close to her rather than far away from her. She wrote page after page, so hurriedly that it seemed as if she knew the text by heart and was afraid of forgetting it.

Her mother came in with a lame excuse; immediately after knocking she opened the door, and Martha looked in annoyance first at me, then at her. This was the second time she had come to check up on us; the first time she had wanted to know whether I was staying for supper. Without consulting me, Martha had replied: "We don't know yet."

This time her mother wanted to know whether Martha had seen the kitchen scissors anywhere, and Martha said impatiently: "Everything's okay, Mama. You needn't worry."

No sooner did Rahel leave the room than Martha locked the door. The scene had embarrassed me, and my hopes were not raised by her locking the door. On the way back from the door to her desk, Martha passed the rocking chair and gave me a little kiss so that at least I'd have something to go on with.

I forced myself to read, a detective story whose thread I couldn't find. After several attempts to pick it up, I lost all interest.

I asked how much longer she would be busy. Martha replied: Until it was time to leave. I had no right to be hurt— what did I know of the commitments of a student? I put the book down on her desk and proceeded to rock so violently that the tips of the rockers touched the floor, but Martha was not to be distracted. She was so immersed in her writing that I envied her.

I couldn't listen to music since Martha had no earphones. In the midst of all this misery I began an account of what had happened that Sunday in the forest. Perhaps I was thinking that this story would provide the only interruption Martha would be forced to acknowledge. Could she remember the suspicion, I asked, that had come to her the last time we had met in the forest?

After an interval, which she doubtless needed to finish writing a sentence, she asked what I had said. I repeated: "Do you remember how we were going to meet at the cottage and then couldn't?"

Only now did she give me a brief, surprised look and say: "Why should I have forgotten that?"

She resumed her work, and I thought: You'll not go on writing for long. I said that at the time she had told me straight out that something was wrong, and she'd been perfectly right: I'd been beside myself. I had just come from an experience that it was now time I talked to her about.

At that moment there was another knock at the door. I could see the door handle being pressed down a few times. Martha turned around and gave me a sign to leave it to her. She called out: "Just a moment!"

I realized that she hadn't been listening to me, or rather, that she wasn't aware of having heard the beginning of something important. She went to the bed, pulled down the covers, threw them back onto the bed, and made two dips in the pillow with the palm of her hand. Then, grinning at me as if she had acted in both our names, she unlocked the door.

Mrs. Lepschitz's eyes immediately darted to the bed. I wished Martha had taught her mother this lesson when I wasn't around, although I realized that I was part of it. "What's the matter, Mama?" Martha asked when the pause went on too long for her liking.

Mrs. Lepschitz had a hard time remembering her reason for coming, and I wouldn't have been surprised if she had left again without a word. But she managed to overcome her confusion; perhaps she even saw through Martha's little ploy.

216

Tearing her eyes away from the bed, she asked whether we had been listening to the radio the last few minutes.

In an exchange of glances, Martha and I agreed not to burst out laughing; then we simultaneously shook our heads. Mrs. Lepschitz said it had just been announced on the radio that Walter Ulbricht had died. For a moment she stood there, apparently wondering whether she could leave us alone with such news; then she left.

Martha picked up the pillow from the bed, put it on her chair, sat down, and resumed her work without a word. To me it seemed heartless. Not that I was an admirer of Ulbricht, but surely the news deserved a few moments' reflection. I felt strangely affected, as if someone in my circle had disappeared. Of all the country's leaders he was the most familiar to me, even though recently he had hardly ever been mentioned. At one time his portrait had hung in every room in my school, even in the gym and on the staircase.

There was no sound of writing, only Martha's elbow moved slowly along. I recalled a sentence I had written in a school essay for his seventy-fifth birthday: *And that is why we shall always love and revere him.* I asked Martha whether the World Festival would now have to be called off.

"Is it your World Festival?" she said.

At that point her sheet of paper was full, and she opened the drawer to take out another. Because she often got her material and notes mixed up, I had once asked her why she always wrote on loose sheets and not in notebooks. She had replied that university students didn't write in such books; those were for school kids. She said I had begun to talk about the cottage; she must rest her hand a bit and could listen to me now.

I saw that she wasn't really curious and hadn't become suspicious either: she was digging around in the drawer. So I said that these damn visitors were taking over the place

217

more and more and for the time being had no intention whatever of leaving our cottage. That was all.

She found what she was looking for and tossed me an envelope containing some movie stills. Martha appeared in each of them: with an old gentleman on the street (perhaps Mr. Turteltaub); in a train compartment reading a magazine; standing in front of a policeman who was checking her identity card, she rigid with fear. Her eyebrows seemed bushier to me, her lips rounder or fuller. I asked her about this, and she said that before every take she had to go to a make-up artist, who painted her face any way she wanted; this was how things were done in the movies.

"Why didn't you destroy the pictures immediately?" I said. "Someone might see them."

Martha pursed her lips, as though for a chirp or a kiss, and gave me a long, surprised look. For a joke, my remark had turned out much too rude, but I hadn't meant it only as a joke. The long wait had made me crabby; I felt rejected. So I returned her gaze like someone who has nothing to take back.

She took the envelope and pictures away from me; I managed to salvage one photo and held it out of her reach. After a few unsuccessful grabs at it, she sat bolt upright and merely held out her hand, looking so fierce that I placed the picture on it.

"I'd be delighted to quarrel with you if you like," she said, stuffing the pictures into the envelope.

I annoyed her even more by taking her offer seriously and nodding; in my present mood, a quarrel that I didn't expect to get totally out of hand seemed preferable to sitting behind her until it suited her to leave. But she didn't stick by her offer; instead, she turned back to her work as if she were wasting her time with me.

"Let me tell you something, my friend."

So here it came: I hadn't been hoping in vain. She crumpled up a sheet of paper, threw it into the wastebasket, and proceeded to keep her promise after all.

"I've known for a long time that there is a certain subject one cannot discuss with you," she said. "The moment there's a word starting with J, you break out in a sweat. The real victims are forever wanting to celebrate memorial days and organize vigils, and you want silence to be kept. Maybe you imagine that to be the opposite, but let me tell you: it's the same hang-up. Where does that hang-up come from? I don't know your father well enough, but I do know the other influences you've been exposed to: are they so feeble? And haven't you always told me how he survived concentration camp so wonderfully intact?" That's roughly what Martha said.

Hardly had she finished when the ball-point was in her hand and she was busy again. Apparently I had not been criticized but scolded. Had it been criticism, I would have had the right of rejoinder. Her elbow was already moving forward again.

I got up to leave. What had I done but wrinkle my nose at Martha's involvement in an unsavory business? Wasn't I allowed to protest this constant lewd pawing over the same piece of the past, and by people, what's more, who reminded me of looters? Did one have to praise this garbage just because one's parents had been in a concentration camp?

On my way to the door I heard Martha ask whether I was serious about leaving. When I put my hand on the door handle, her eyebrows shot all the way up. I said that I would only let her attack me if she wasn't too busy to listen to my defense. She laid down her ball-point, turned around, and assumed an expression of wide-eyed expectation.

She had to reach out a hand to hold me back. I needed to walk only two or three steps to be within her reach. She pulled me down onto her lap, where at first I felt somewhat uncomfortable because I'd never sat there before. She whispered into my ear: "Go ahead—defend yourself!"

At last, time started passing again; there was nothing pleasanter than being held by her. The first sensible thought I could muster was that there was no one in the world who deserved my forbearance more than Martha. She would never be kissing me, I thought, to divert attention from the fact that she was in the wrong; it could only be explained by love, I thought, sheer love.

When there was another knock at the door, Martha wouldn't let me get up. This time the door wasn't locked, this time Rahel Lepschitz was waiting for a reply. Martha held me so tightly that we would both have fallen over if I had tried to use force to get up. She called out: "Why don't you come in?"

The scene took place behind my back, and I would rather have died than turn my head. One of my legs was clamped between Martha's knees as if in a vise. I heard a silence that seemed never-ending. Then Martha whispered something to me, which I believe was: *Keep your cool.*

Whether I care to admit it or not, I am a docile fellow. My discontent is generally expressed by no more than a lousy mood, rarely by action. Yet I have always preferred rebellious people to meek and never doubted that I would turn out to be one of them. The whole trouble is that there is nothing in my surroundings for me to rebel against.

The idea of doing battle with the Lepschitz family is absurd; I would die of pity, quite apart from the fact that there would be nothing to gain. And who should I confront about finding a place to live? An enemy must have something hostile about him, and he has to be visible; otherwise one is just flailing blindly about. At university things may improve; with any luck I will find someone there who is worth resisting.

Although a new room is nowhere on the horizon, I have collected some cardboard boxes. Even now I enjoy thinking about the process of moving; it allows me to breathe a little of the air of moving. And I don't have to worry about being found out; either Martha has already told her parents, or I shall do it myself when the occasion arises.

I prefer cardboard boxes to trunks or crates because they make it so much easier to sort things out, although I have to admit I've only moved once in my life. Ideally, each object would have its own box.

On that earlier occasion I didn't do most of my own packing: Martha, Hugo Lepschitz, and an ash-blond stranger I never saw again crammed everything into the movers' containers. Lepschitz kept asking me whether such and such an object was to be included, and each time I shook my head, until Martha asked him to stop pestering me. So a lot depended on chance, although so far I haven't missed anything. In our basement they found an empty coal bin on wheels, which they brought upstairs and filled with all our papers. After the move it was put in the basement here because there was no space for it in my new room. The bin stood in the Lepschitz basement until this morning, when I trundled it across the courtyard and lugged it upstairs.

I am sorting its contents into four boxes: Father's papers, photos, my papers, miscellaneous. My papers consist of school reports, certificates, and a few letters, especially Elle's. And when I come to my school things—the dog-eared books and used notebooks—a new category begins: garbage.

Fleetingly, I consider the question of whether my new life shouldn't start off by classifying the entire bin plus contents as garbage. No, I decide; in that way my old life would continue. Nevertheless I don't begin to read Father's mail now, or become engrossed in his photographs; not for a long time yet.

Suddenly I find in my hands the notebook into which I copied the camp guard's notes, a few days before Father's death. There is no explanation for what prompted me to open this particular notebook; from the outside it looks exactly like the others. *Heppner, Arnold Hermann, color of eyes: blue-gray.*

I remember the wallet—of course, it's in the wardrobe, hidden under shelf paper. In this apartment I have held it only once: the time I hid it. Like a sleepwalker, I had taken it from Father's drawer, the only item of my legacy that I didn't want my helpers to see. I had forgotten it—to think that during my pending move I would have left it where it was!

He lives in the district of Lichtenberg, on a street called Weitling-Strasse, so what? The notebook undergoes the strangest transformations: first it is consigned to the garbage, then I put it with Father's papers, then with mine, and finally in the box for miscellaneous. But that's not the right place for it either. I pick it up for the last time and go on tearing it up until there isn't a piece left larger than a postage stamp. Yet I still remember street and house number.

I try to shake off the notion of going to see him, but it is irresistible. Although there isn't a single good reason for the visit, I look at my watch and think: The afternoon would be the best time.

I go into the living room because there is a city map in one of the drawers there. At the window, Martha is reading. Like an invalid, she sits there in her bathrobe, on her lap a book and the sprained hand. Like a snail sensing danger, her knee withdraws into its bathrobe shell.

When I spread out the map, Rahel, who is also in the room, starts asking: Am I looking for a street; if so, which street; what takes me to that street? I always answer her, I always answer something.

From Lichtenberg station it is just around the corner. The building is run-down. Half of its façade has lost its stucco; there are small holes in it, the kind often seen in the city, made by shell fragments. The entrance hall smells of cats and cooking.

A great many tenants' names are listed on the board, but not his, although the board looks as if it hadn't been added to since the place was built. I walk up the stairs and examine every nameplate, two or three on almost every door, but no luck.

In the courtyard, propped against the wall, is a lady's bicycle, minus saddle. I try my luck in the building across the courtyard too. The name that comes closest to the one I am looking for reads *Hübner*.

I am back in the courtyard again; my futile enterprise seems to have come to an end. A workman comes plodding across, I ask him about Heppner. Even before I have finished speaking he shakes his head. But isn't it a fact that the camp guard was living here a year ago? Someone must have known him.

In the front building I ring in vain at three doors; the fourth is opened by a man holding a cup. I apologize for the intrusion and repeat my question. He looks good-natured, thinks it over amiably, but arrives at no answer. He beckons me into the apartment. I follow him into a room of which half is a kitchen; I always feel uncomfortable in other people's homes.

Sitting at a table is a woman who looks like the man's sister; I have interrupted their game of Halma: the same dark brown hair, two thin, narrow faces. With his cup he gestures to me to repeat my question.

So: "I am looking for a Mr. Heppner who lives in this building or did until recently."

She has to think about it too. Then she says something to the man, but, for God's sake, in sign language! I have landed in the home of some deaf-mutes—he has to put down the cup before answering her. Then they both look at me.

The woman starts moving her hands for my benefit, then to my relief breaks off. She gets paper and pencil, writes something, and hands me the slip: *Were you asking about Heppner?* If I'd known that my words must be lip-read, I would of course have spoken more distinctly. I nod. The woman knows something; she hesitates, not as if wondering how best to enlighten me, but like someone who doesn't want to get into trouble. She is about thirty and has the most observant eyes I have ever seen.

A conversation starts up between them; he seems to treat the matter more lightly than she. I figure out that what I had taken for a bell push by the door is actually a light switch; somewhere in the room must be the corresponding light, which I can't immediately locate. Instead, I see a radio; perhaps they're not the only people living in the apartment.

While they go on exchanging signs, I give way to a temptation and make a loud grunting sound behind my hand. They don't react. What did I expect? They seem to be arguing; why else would they have to carry on such an endless palaver after a clear-cut question like mine? They move hands and fingers with extraordinary speed, and they constantly interrupt each other, exchanging impatient looks, the way people do who don't agree on something.

At last they turn back to me. The woman asks me a question that for safety's sake I repeat: Do I know Heppner? The man confirms that I have understood her correctly; the woman is waiting for a reply. I decide not to know Heppner and shake my head, but that doesn't get me any farther. Now they are both looking at me suspiciously: why am I asking about someone I don't know?

I explain, pronouncing each word slowly and exaggeratedly, underlined by such gestures as happen to occur to me: that my father had known Heppner; that now he was dead—with my thumb and middle finger I close my eyelids; that among his things I had found a letter from Heppner; that I would like to talk to Heppner about my father. My father, I add craftily, hadn't had many friends.

They understand me; the woman's skepticism turns into sympathy. She points to the piece of paper already written on—from now on it stands for *Heppner*. Then she holds up a stiff hand like a hurdle and, in a wavelike motion, jumps over it with the other. Another jump and another: then I grasp what obstacle Heppner has overcome—the Wall. The thing is so obvious that I can't imagine why I didn't think of this possibility long ago.

The man writes the word "pensioner" on our slip of paper: recently, old-age pensioners have been allowed to travel abroad, and obviously Heppner hasn't returned from a trip. Perhaps no stranger ever stumbles into this apartment: they are incredibly helpful.

I am made to sit down, am pressed into a chair by the man while he remains standing. The woman cups a hand around her dead ear and turns her head this way and that: All she knows is what people are talking about in the building. Neither Heppner nor his wife, also a pensioner, returned last year from behind the stiff hand. Hadn't my father known about that?

Heppner had lived in the front building, first floor left. I enjoy deciphering this foreign language. The apartment was empty for a long time, sealed and all that, until new tenants moved in, quite nice people, he was a truck driver, she a hairdresser.

Besides being helpful, the woman also loves to chatter. I have no idea what other questions to ask in connection with Heppner: he doesn't interest me. The notebook is responsible for this conversation, not I. If his name had been on one of the doors, I would have disappeared anyway. What would have been the point of ringing? *Yes? What can I do for you? Good afternoon, Mr. Heppner, I am the son of the man in whose house you were kept a prisoner. I set you free. Don't you remember? But of course, do come in!*

I get up and point to my watch. I still have a lot of questions, not about the camp guard but about what life is like for a deaf-mute, but I don't dare make use of this unexpected opportunity. When I read in their eyes that no one is forcing me to leave, I ask at least one question: How do they know when someone rings the bell?

The man is delighted by my curiosity; he beams and nods, as if wishing to exclaim: I bet you'd like to know that! He signals to me to watch the ceiling light, then goes out of the room. I hear the front door, and immediately the light goes on-off, on-off. He comes back and smiles, so I switch on the light myself and ask: "What happens now?"

He nods and again hurries to the door. I can already foresee: The light goes off-on, off-on. We shake hands in parting: I am sincerely sorry to have to go. They are relieved because I don't seem too deeply affected by Heppner's flight.

Once again I am in my room sorting. The box that fills up quickest is for miscellaneous, the slowest is the one for my papers. If I had destroyed Heppner's wallet, would he then have vanished even more completely? I have never succeeded in hating him wholeheartedly; all I wanted was to be thoroughly separated from him. So that has now been accomplished, with him beyond the Wall and myself inside. When I move, I will destroy the wallet; not now.

A few sheets of paper lie rolled up in the coal bin; I pull off the rubber band to see where they belong. Letters to Father, written before I was born. *I regret to have to inform you that your application of March 3, 1952, cannot be approved.* They had been sent to him by a magistrate, from a Department of Licenses.

Out of curiosity to see what Father had applied for, I read the letters. Needless to say, his own are missing; the roll contains only replies. He intended to open a photography business—Father a shopkeeper! He must have pursued the plan stubbornly, for between the first reply and the last (the eighth) there is a space of a year and a half. With increasing impatience the department explains why his application cannot be approved; a plethora of paragraphs and regulations state the reasons. *In the law relating to the Five-Year Plan of*

October 31, 1951 (Folio No. 128, page 991), binding rules are laid down or prescribed which also govern the Dept. of Licenses. This decision is final.

I am surprised that someone like Father didn't succeed in realizing such a modest plan. Standing behind the counter would have killed him, for he was no longer the prewar photographer who only needed a bare living to be happy. For this kind of career he had become much too demanding.

When I come to the photographs, I begin to look for one in particular: the picture of Heppner that I had slipped in among our family photos. I can't find it, but then there are a great many pictures scattered throughout the coal bin, like grains of sand in a suitcase that has been brought back from a trip to the beach. I wish I knew whether Father ever discovered the one that didn't fit in with the others.

After supper, during which for the first time I saw Hugo Lepschitz crumble matzos while he was staring at the TV, Martha and I left the apartment. She was heading for her last night of filming; I was going home. As far as Ostkreuz station our routes were the same. There she kissed me behind my ear. We intended to meet again the following evening; it was too soon to look forward to it now.

By this time Father's frequent absences seemed to me more of a relief than a drawback. In a few days Martha and I planned to take a trip to the coast somewhere; I could hardly wait. We were afraid of not finding a place to stay, but I thought that no vacation could be as bad as it would be good to get away from here. I still had to face negotiating with Father for the money.

For the first time in a long while the larder was full, so I had a second supper. Wanda phoned and asked agitatedly about Gordon Kwart: Did I have any idea where she might find him? She went on about some life-and-death orchestra affair, and extracted from me the advice to try phoning a certain Rotstein, although I didn't have his number.

After hanging up I looked in the directory myself. Unable to give her either his address or first name, I had assumed that innumerable Rotsteins would make the search more difficult, for the name seemed to me a fairly common one. There wasn't a single Rotstein in the book. I ran my finger a few times down the column of names thinking I had made a mistake; there was a Rotsch, and a Rott, with nothing in between.

I went to bed early like a child, intending to fall asleep quickly and if possible not wake up until it was time to meet Martha. There were clean sheets on the bed—a wonder that he had found time for this. I hoped he had been seized by a desire for reconciliation: in the morning the fan of money, and now crisp sheets. It was more likely, however, that cleanliness at home, in contrast to the daily stench in the cottage, meant more to him than to me.

In the middle of the night I was woken by the racket he was making. I thought he would never stop walking about, slamming doors, dropping forks, and coughing. The noise sounded intentional. I wondered why he didn't simply knock on my door if he needed company. I got up, pulled on my trousers, and went out to complain. One look was enough to see that he was drunk.

He was standing at the stove, swaying as he broke eggs into the frying pan. Eggshells littered the floor. The fat was much too hot so the moment the eggs dropped into the pan they turned white and bubbled. He blithely let them go on frying. I picked up the eggshells before he could step on them. That was when he noticed me. He was not startled: he looked at me with vacant eyes, and there was already a smell of burning.

A schnapps bottle stuck out of the garbage pail. I sat down. A shapeless slice of white bread lay on the table, more broken off than cut, and covered with half an inch of butter. I was worried and also disgusted; he seldom drank, and, when he did, it was only in company and moderately. In any case he wasn't a drinker; I had never seen him in this state. I would have left the kitchen if I hadn't been afraid he might need help.

At his first attempt to turn off the stove, he missed the switch. I was ready to leap into action. He put the piping-hot pan on the table and sat down across from me, his eyelids drooping. When I lifted the pan, the scorch mark was already there. I put it down again, and he began to eat.

I went to get myself some milk and, as I stood at the refrigerator, Father laboriously got up and staggered out of the kitchen. It was enough to break your heart. Obviously he would be back—maybe a sudden wave of nausea. I wanted to find out whether he had got drunk for a definite reason or had simply gone out and got drunk. I took a knife and scraped at the hardened fried eggs in the pan, cutting the yolk out of one and putting it in my mouth. He would never be able to finish even what was left.

He came back carrying a bathrobe and threw it onto my lap, a red-and-green-striped object weighing half a ton that he had already owned when I was born. He waited until I put it on. Then he collapsed onto his chair, shook vast amounts of salt onto the eggs, and took a bite of the bread, which he could hardly manage to get into his mouth, smearing his chin with butter in the process. Once again he tried to get up, but instead indicated the door and said: "D'you mind? In my room, right there on the table."

I went in and found two hip flasks of cognac or brandy; it cost me an effort to bring him one. I cut the plastic cap that sealed the cork; he might have killed himself doing that. The sleeves of his bathrobe were much too short for me.

He pushed the frying pan to the other end of the table and looked at me as if he had forgotten something extremely important. His mouth was dry, his face looked bloated. He glanced toward the cupboard containing the glasses and then drank from the bottle. Screwing up his eyes he shook himself so violently that his teeth rattled. Before putting the bottle back on the table, he looked at it balefully.

I took a glass and poured myself a schnapps; he made no objection. On the contrary, he nodded, as if I should have done that long ago. "What do you say about Ulbricht?" he asked.

"I find it sad," I said.

So did he. I downed my schnapps, which was a fairly hefty one, and made an effort to keep my expression under control. I rejected the idea that there was some connection between Father's condition and Ulbricht's death.

"D'you know what I liked best about him?" he said.

But instead of continuing, he bit off some more bread. Speaking was making him more alert. I passed him a napkin so he could wipe his chin, and in return he poured me another schnapps. Then he lifted the bottle to his lips, but waited until I had picked up my glass. Only three days earlier, at dinner with Kwart, I wasn't even supposed to drink champagne.

He stood up, more easily than before, took two hesitant steps as if to test his legs, and gestured for me to follow. We went to his room, to the second hip flask, and sat down. He said the bathrobe suited me splendidly; his grieving for Ulbricht had evaporated. He pushed the flask across to me to open. I didn't want to drink another drop, those two glasses were already causing me some trouble. Perhaps he was afraid of losing the peace that had broken out between us, perhaps that was why he had invited me from our kitchen to his bedroom.

"I'm a bit drunk," he said, "but I know what I'm saying."

The dryness in his mouth impeded him; he kept passing his tongue between his upper lip and his teeth. But he didn't

232

forget to drink. Each time he took a tremendous gulp, as if the bottle contained water. Since then I have learned that alcoholics usually work their way in tiny sips down to the bottom of a bottle or glass, especially when they are already drunk. That evening Father drank like a man dying of thirst. And if I say he became livelier as he talked, this effect was in turn undone by his steady drinking.

His claim that he knew what he was saying was not followed by words that I could have doubted: he remained silent. His head propped in both hands, he stared with unfocused eyes at the table and groaned to himself; then he looked at me again and seemed surprised, as if I had materialized out of thin air. In order to keep his eyes open he had to raise his eyebrows. Behind him I could see the big double bed, clean sheets on one of the twin mattresses, the other side empty like the sleeve of an amputee.

He asked how things were going with Martha, and I nodded contentedly and said: "Not bad." To my surprise he spoke of Martha as a nice person, pretty too; slowly, he said, he was getting used to the idea that we were serious about each other. Then he placed a hand on my arm, gave a cunning grin, and said: "I can imagine how much it inconveniences you two that our cottage is occupied. I may be dumb but I'm not blind."

Today I imagine that the hand on my arm was trembling. At the time, I grinned back and thought that I didn't need to be embarrassed, that it was a good thing my secret had been mentioned in this manner. It was different when he asked: "But you don't happen to have a key, do you?"

I made a face like someone who has been asked a tiresome question for the hundredth time. If there was ever a favorable moment for admitting possession of the key, this was it: in his condition and in our peaceful mood, my confession would

233

have found a soft landing. But my fear won out: how was he ever to trust me again if I confessed to having deceived him for so long?

He didn't pursue his suspicion; with the hand he removed from my arm, he wiped the subject aside. He took another huge gulp, shook himself, and said: "Today was a good day."

He must be referring to the cottage. What had happened there to make him feel so pleased? Was it no longer a prison? Had an amnesty been declared? Again and again he paused to moisten his lips, to keep me on tenterhooks, to give himself a rest. He certainly was a long-winded storyteller.

In a theatrical voice he said: "He has confessed."

After more of his drinking, shaking, and groaning, I learned that the prisoner no longer denied having witnessed executions. He still wasn't admitting to having been one of the firing squad, but that was completely ridiculous, like a mother of seven children claiming never to have touched a man. With his version that there had been bad and good camp guards, said Father, Heppner couldn't have picked himself a worse audience.

I must have sat there looking disappointingly unimpressed: no applause, no joyous surprise, no congratulations, nothing. Wasn't it inconsistent of Father first to say that camp guards were camp guards, but then to go after details? So the fact that for the first time he had been the one to bring up the subject of the kidnapping seemed more important to me than what he was actually saying.

"What's supposed to be so good about the confession, then?" I asked.

He meant to laugh, but it turned into a cough, an attack that lasted long enough for him to forget my question. When it was over, he was panting with exhaustion; I had never seen him look so old. I pushed the flask, which was still a third full, toward him so he would go on drinking and talking. I can't forgive myself for that.

Father stumbled into my trap; he drank and started on a new episode: The camp guard had clutched his chest and claimed to be suffering from a weak heart and that as soon as the pain began he had to take certain medication. He had said to them: *Just imagine your situation if I die under your very noses!* They had answered that he needn't worry about that; they would manage all right.

For a few moments there was silence. Then Father erupted into uncontrollable laughter such as overwhelms only the drunk. Each time he got his breath back, he would shout: "Our situation!" with the tears running down his cheeks. To me he seemed to look more tormented than happy. If he had been photographed while laughing like that, anyone looking at the picture would have said he was crying.

When he had finished laughing he laid his head on his arms and fell asleep.

It was hard work carrying Father to bed. I made every effort to lay him down gently, but he dropped from my arms onto the bed, and I fell on top of him. This didn't wake him up, although our heads collided; his condition was a blend of sleep and unconsciousness. I took off his shoes.

What Father had so grandiloquently called the camp guard's confession was in my eyes a puffed-up triviality: a confession is meaningless if nothing depends on it. I could only see Father deteriorating, see our relationship wasting away, see new lines in his face every day. For the first time I thought of the possibility that the affair could never end well, that no one was in a position to help, that everything had to happen the way it was happening.

Ever since childhood I had adored the smell of my father's bathrobe; I now placed it at the head of my bed. When I put out the light the room began to sway, and I felt nauseated. Outside, some boisterous drunks were passing by. I dressed and crept downstairs without putting on the light on the stairs. Out on the street I breathed long and deep, my mouth wide open, until the nausea subsided.

I don't know what made me think of Elle—perhaps because I felt such pity for Father. Suddenly I found myself wondering whether our father was mentally ill and might have to be put in a home. And since one couldn't help thinking it might be some kind of genetic disorder, I started looking for oddities in my own behavior. I didn't have to try very hard.

At Königstor I was attracted by the confusion of voices coming from the open door of a bar. Most of the customers were exotic-looking foreigners shouting remarks and jokes to each other across the big room. The few Germans sat among them, silent and smiling, like spectators. I went to the counter and asked for a glass of beer. Normally the bar would have been closed hours ago, but during the festival the city had given orders that as little as possible was to be prohibited. It was already past three o'clock.

The bartender didn't let go of the handle of my beer glass until I had put a mark down on the counter. I watched the shouting, happy foreigners and thought: So this is the World Festival. Whenever one of them, the life and soul of the party, shouted something, the others would laugh louder than ever: they were ready to laugh as soon as he opened his mouth. I was envious of their carefree mood and consoled myself with the thought that they didn't always have as easy a time as during these few days. They looked like South Americans.

Someone tapped me in passing and pointed to a table where there was an empty chair. I drank the beer, then went out onto the street again, as aimlessly as I had come in. Father had quite seriously claimed that this had been a good day; he could no longer distinguish between good and bad, between useful and disastrous. Three more such good days, I thought, and he's a goner.

Since the streets leading to Alexander-Platz were becoming more and more crowded, I was drawn in that direction; after all, I hadn't left the apartment in order to be by myself. Most of the people still up were couples, couples with nowhere to go. In each case it seemed to me that the young man was a foreigner and the girl German, never the other way around. And I came upon armies of street sweepers, some of them shining flashlights onto the sidewalks to make sure they didn't miss a single grain of dust. Inside the buildings all was dark.

I had never seen Alexander-Platz at night, yet the square seemed to me completely different from other nights. On a stage at one side, young people were dancing to their own music, and in the center of the square was a small crowd standing around some people arguing. I stepped closer and could hear angry voices, but it was impossible to get through to the core; I couldn't even get close enough to understand what it was all about.

After fighting my way out again, I saw a suburban train crossing the bridge, which gave me the idea of picking Martha up from her last night of filming. I got on the next train for Köpenick. The World Festival was going on at the station too, even on the train. I looked forward to Martha's surprise and to coming back with her.

A few years ago, Father came to my room one night somewhat the worse for drink. It was winter, his galoshes were covered with snow, and he had rambled on incoherently. I soon fell asleep and would not have remembered the incident if Father hadn't apologized next morning and explained how tempting it is to start drinking when you dislike the company you find yourself in. "Don't be angry with me, Hansi," he said. I was surprised that he made so much of such a trivial matter.

At the theater in Köpenick, a new disaster: no one was shooting a movie here. Hadn't Martha said she was going to Köpenick that night? For a few seconds I suspected betrayal, then I came to my senses again; I must have misunderstood her, some damn mistake that could only be cleared up when it was too late to do anyone any good. And why should they be shooting at night in premises where they could have night whenever they wanted it? I hammered so violently on the

238

door that I would have died of shame if anyone had opened it. On the other side of the street a large dog was strolling by.

I sat down on the steps of the movie theater, closed my eyes, and tried to fall asleep, since that required the least effort. My thoughts quietly petered out; I recall the last thing that went through my head: It could be a bit warmer. I was on the way to a pleasant dream when a car stopped right in front of me. A policeman got out and waited for me to approach him. When I stood up, he asked for my identity card. Somehow he had recognized that I wasn't part of the festival.

As I moved toward the edge of the sidewalk, a sense of great relief: I had my identity card on me. After a thorough scrutiny, it turned out that everything was in order. Because the policeman seemed to be a helpful sort, I risked asking him whether a movie was being shot somewhere nearby. I could hardly believe it when he told me the street, and even how to get there. A miracle had happened: the right antidote.

First light had long given way to dawn. A phrase from one of Elle's letters: *The dawn fears that have seized me.* . . . I was sure Martha wouldn't think I was spying on her. Back into town with Martha, I thought, to her front door, hugs, kisses, to see us through the day, then back to wretchedness. The police car slowly overtook me, as if the policeman was checking to see whether I was keeping to the suggested route.

Once I saw a movie in which someone got lost in the desert and was found because vultures were circling above him. In a similar way I could tell that I was approaching my goal: spectators were standing on balconies or leaning out of windows, pillows under their elbows, looking down onto the street.

As I arrived, the movie crew was busy packing up its stuff. They made a great deal of noise, and I was surprised that none of the residents told them to be quiet. Scrawled across

239

a big store window were the words GERMANS! DON'T BUY FROM JEWS! A man with a pail and cloth went up to remove the slogan. There weren't so many people on the street that I could have failed to see Martha. Obviously she was no longer there.

But then, when I stopped looking for her and was merely getting in the way of the movie crew, she came dashing up. She had got out of a car with its motor running and someone waiting in it. Her mouth gaping in surprise, she could utter only disjointed words, "Well!" and "What a . . . " I didn't know whether she was pleased or resentful, until she hugged me. Even as we embraced I was ashamed of my doubts.

She took me by the hand and hurried off, to the car. Before we reached it, she stopped once more and asked whether I was planning to do anything other than drive into town with her. I said I wasn't. In the car sat a middle-aged man, an actor, who lit a cigarette when he saw Martha approaching with me. When she asked him whether he minded taking me along, he replied: "Don't be silly." We both got into the back, and he stepped on the gas so violently that the tires squealed.

On the first curve I was pulled or pressed over to Martha's side. I didn't resist, just put my head in her lap. A hollow opened up that exactly fitted my head, like a velvet case. Martha went on folding over my ear until it was obvious that it wouldn't stay like that. This was exactly what I had spent half the night looking for.

She bent down to me and whispered that I had been drinking. I said I knew that. She sniffed, as if that would enable her to determine the amount. Maybe the man at the wheel was Mr. Turteltaub himself, I thought as I was falling asleep, maybe even an SS man; I hadn't looked at him that closely. He was a terrible driver, continually stepping on the brake and taking corners so sharply that I had to hold on although I was lying down.

The car was divinely motionless when Martha started shaking me like mad. Even before opening my eyes I heard her apologizing for my condition, and the actor asking whether I wasn't a bit young for such capers. Then we were out on the street, the car had driven off. To be on the safe side, Martha took my arm. She wasn't overdoing it; I was swaying and felt drunker than before my sleep. I asked where she was taking me, and she patted my hand soothingly.

We were walking through her entrance hall, no doubt about that: there was a red coconut runner in the Lepschitz building, not in ours. I remembered that we had left the building together in the evening; now we were returning in the morning like a married couple. As we walked up the stairs, Martha said we must be as quiet as mice, although apart from her no one was talking.

The moment was so extraordinary, and I was in no shape to appreciate it. For the first time I was allowed into Martha's room at night—in terms of visiting, the night was far from over—and here I was, dazedly climbing the stairs beside Martha and thinking: If only I were up there already and could lie down!

She unlocked the apartment door so stealthily that my eyelids drooped again; then she led me along the passage as if I were blind, one hand gripping my arm, the other ready to cover my mouth as soon as it threatened to open. We didn't bump into anything, we made no sound, we advanced by means of that most silent of all forms of motion, floating. When at last we stood in her room she looked at me, as relieved as if she had piloted us through a minefield.

I lay down on the bed and with my last ounce of strength managed to pull off my shoes. I remember Martha looking down at me, surprised or annoyed, and how I intended to explain everything to her later, after I had slept. The pillow was more comfortable than my own; even under my head it remained both thick and soft. I closed my eyes and wanted to make some nice parting remark. I said: "Oh God, how comfortable this is!"

She lay down on top of me and pushed up my eyelids, forcing me to look at her. I would have resisted if I hadn't been so battle-weary. In any case, it was a great nuisance, and when she let go a little while later I preferred to keep my eyes open rather than give her a chance to start tormenting me again. She asked me what kind of trouble I was in. Since getting into the car we hadn't exchanged ten words, and I put my arms around her. But she would have none of that, she was waiting for an answer. If her questions could have been answered by a shake of the head or a nod, she would have learned something, but there was no way of getting me to talk.

A little later I heard her ask: "You're having a problem with your father?"

That was better; I nodded. She took plenty of time over her next question; I almost fell asleep under her hands. Today I am convinced that I was not only tired but also playing the role of a tired man. She asked whether the problem had only just begun, and I shook my head and thought: Good question. Then she asked whether she had had anything to do with this problem. I shook my head and had to smile.

Martha either took pity on me or lost the thread: the questions stopped. She pushed one arm under my head and kissed me. It wasn't her intention to drive away my tiredness; she just gave me a few consolation kisses, and I was content with that. As it was, it seemed miraculous how well the night had turned out after all. I was looking forward to waking up in a few hours and gazing at the sleeping Martha.

242

She whispered that she'd be back in a minute, then rolled off me and stood up. I didn't hear her walk across the room, or open and close the door, but then I heard voices in the passage. Oh my God, her parents; I had to rely on Martha to take care of everything. Suddenly I felt chilly, and I barely had the strength to crawl under the covers.

I was awakened by street noises. The sun was shining brightly, as I could tell from the sharpness of the window's shadow on the curtain. Since Martha was lying on my arm I couldn't look at my watch. I made use of the opportunity and scrutinized Martha's face so thoroughly that I could have described each little crease in it.

She lay on her back with her mouth half open, the position in which ordinary people snore. She was wearing a night-gown, the first nightgown that had ever been worn in my presence, lavender, with a low neckline bordered in green. It cost me an effort not to touch her. My hand with the wristwatch was hanging over the edge of the bed so Martha had had no choice but to lie on my arm. I carefully bent over her and breathed in her breath. Her long hair lay on the pillow like a brown scarf.

What was I to do? I couldn't fall asleep again and then get up and leave the room with Martha—Mrs. Lepschitz, Mr. Lepschitz, that would have been too much. I withdrew my arm from under her head; I believe that no arm has ever been so slowly withdrawn from under a head. It was eleven-thirty.

I could feel my heart beating as I climbed out of bed over Martha and her nightgown. Not for a moment was she in any danger of waking up. I had only my shoes to put on; they stood toe to toe with Martha's shoes. Although I could rely on Hugo Lepschitz being at work, I still had to get past his wife—unless a merciful God has sent her out of the apartment, I thought. The idea of her seeing me slink out of Martha's room was appalling. At first it seemed smart not to put my shoes on until the maneuver had been successfully completed: then I caught sight of myself in Martha's full-length mirror, with my shoes in my hand, and I put them on.

I opened the door; our heartbeats were moving farther and farther apart. The passage was empty; to this day I don't know where Martha's mother could have been. And the apartment door was unlocked. I walked for a while, then took the streetcar. On our street I bought some flowers with the housekeeping money. There were two letters in the box, an official one for Father and a letter for me, from Elle.

Dear Hans
it is sad how adviceless you had to go away
but can it Not also be
that you overestimate me . . .
When someone has lived so long in retirement
as I have now
then you must No longer
expect so much of that person mydear
for where should he find his wisdom . . .
It is night now
but I still have you sitting here withme
with your much too great power of understanding
for my little ignorance
so you ask in vain
so you are annoyed
and I am supposed to have betrayed you too . . .
The whole problem is a mistake
to which you cling
with what is to me incomprehensible dog gedness
I mean
what makes you think I am so reasonable
and helpful and sharp witted and shrewd
I am None of those things
you can ask anybody . . .

No one expects you
to help him our father
on the contrary in what he is doing
he has trouble enough without your help
he is no longer a youngman
and then this war . . .
Don't you know
that Not Everyone can always do only
what Everyone considers right
therefore finally and for the last time
leave him alone please leave him alone . . .
This stranger this nonman or our father
there is no third choice
so it can Not be difficult for you to decide . . .
The moment is still ahead of you
when you do what you must do
but only then will it be seen
whether you are blue or yellow
and until that time comes
you can think about it allyoulike
at the crucial moment everything looks different
I know this from myself . . .
Just now at suppertime something funny happened
in the dining room how shall I tell you
Gertrude a dreadfully crazy person
fell her full length onto the floor
with all the food and drink
of which the tea flowed over my hand
which didn't stop anyone laughing except me
my hand was bandaged with ointment
at first it hurt then No more but now
the hand with which I am writing toyou is hurting
    again . . .
The good thing about the night is

you hear objects more clearly than during the day
when everything is a jumble of voices
so I was already in bed
when this letter whispered quite clearly to me
write me write me
now I am rather tired and hope
that it will Not occur to a second letter
to want to be written
for you are wakened here at six-thirty sharp
whether you were busy during
the night or Not . . .
Suddenly an alarming thought comes to my mind
that this may be the very moment
when you are doing what you must do
and that therefore you intend
to stay Father's hand
I hope this is only a fantasy
it would be too sad
if your destinies
were to confront each other in such hostility
then you could Not belong together
and I simply can hardly believe that . . .
I haven't thanked you properly yet
for the coffee it tastes good and pungent
each day I will
drink only a mouthful
that way it will last halfway to eternity . . .
And about the instruments
I must ask your forgiveness
it was Not a good idea
for I am sure a bassoon will cause a lot of trouble
you will run yourself ragged searching for it
and might find one for a lot of money
then it or the violin will lie around here

will Not be learned and Not played
and it was all in vain . . .
So let us Rather wait
until I am more sure of myself
I have quite forgotten what it is like
to be asked to do a favor
so I often ask unthinkingly
don't be angry with me
did you ever know that it was I
who thought of the name Hans for you
Yoursister

Lepschitz has brought a carp home from work; he tells us that a colleague, a keen amateur fisherman, has given rather than sold the fish to him. It is still alive, which is evident from the tail as it flaps in mortal weakness from side to side. To transport it, they have wrapped it in damp paper, as if it were a bunch of flowers. We fill the bathtub with water to allow the fish to regain its strength.

Rahel is unhappy. She shudders at the thought of the blood bath facing us and announces that she will have no part in either cooking or eating the fish. Her husband cannot understand that. He asks her to explain why she prefers a commercial fish from the store to a freshly caught one. For Rahel has cooked, fried, and eaten fish a hundred times, including carp. She says: "If you can't understand that, it's no use my explaining."

"For such logic one can only love you," says Lepschitz.

I gently lower the carp into the water. It must be a marvelous moment for the fish. It sinks to the bottom, musters strength for a few seconds, then slowly starts swimming, from one end of the bathtub to the other. Rahel asks me to get a piece of bread. Of course Lepschitz will be expecting me to butcher the fish, perhaps as soon as tomorrow; I will do so and reap Rahel's contempt.

Day by day my stay in this apartment seems more unbearable. I take this as a good sign, a sign that my mental apparatus is beginning to function again. As long as it stood still, I couldn't be dissatisfied, merely unhappy. Day by day the situation is changing in my favor. Six months ago it would never have occurred to me to refuse a request by Lepschitz; now the notion is flitting around in my head.

When we move from the bathroom to the living room, Rahel leaves all the doors wide open, as if afraid she won't hear the carp's cries for help. Now the evening's relaxation really begins: the newspaper, the tea. I steal away when Rahel's forefinger reaches out for the button of the TV set. Back in the bathroom I watch the carp for a while. If it were a bird, I would open the window for it.

My mind is made up: I will not do Lepschitz the favor, because of my dissatisfaction. If he finds enough courage to pick up the hammer himself, I won't even hold the carp for him. When Rahel buys a carp, she has it filleted on the spot and gives the woman two marks extra; I have seen it myself.

In the passage, Martha, silently beckoning me into her room; she has come in from outdoors. I follow her. Probably she now needs the money to buy a gift for Lepschitz. I have had it ready for days. I point to her bandage and ask how her hand is coming along; she seems to consider, then waves the question away with the other hand.

"I've found something for you," she says.

That's the most important information I have had in a year. My God, she is my savior. Martha is breathing new life into my affairs. *I've found something for you!* I don't know the correct way to behave at such a moment. Should I calmly wait for details—address, floor, rent? Or would it be appropriate to fall on her neck right now?

My inertia is such that I sit down and wait. The important part of the news has already been given: if Martha says she has found me a room, that's good enough for me. I don't believe there is any room in the entire city that I would refuse—except, perhaps, if she were to offer me a room where that blond person lives, that White Jacket. But Martha wouldn't do that to me. She smiles before telling me what has happened:

The parents of a certain Bernhard from the drama school are going abroad next month, for several years. Overnight they have been appointed to the diplomatic service and are now being sent to an embassy in Asia or Africa—our country is being recognized in more and more places all the time. The apartment is a real stroke of luck, in the suburb of Weissensee. Bernhard has made a sketch since Martha doesn't know the place. I would have a room with a balcony: my head's in a whirl. In addition to Bernhard there is also a grandmother, says Martha, which, since there are five rooms, isn't likely to be a problem. And a pleasant young man would be acceptable, she says, though unfortunately the decision isn't up to Bernhard but to the parents, whom she knows only by phone. She has arranged for a visit next weekend.

"Am I a pleasant young man?" I ask.

"I would think so," says Martha, "all in all."

She looks in her handbag, on her desk—what do I care about the sketch? She holds the bandaged hand behind her back so as not to use it inadvertently. I would like to say something that sounds infinitely grateful, but I can't think of the words. I am touched at how dependable Martha is, even if her help might seem somewhat patronizing. She understood my desperate need and has done something about it. I will never forget that.

"You seem to be in a hurry to get rid of me," I say.

My God, what am I saying? Is that the way to express one's gratitude? Not being able to find the right words is no excuse for using the wrong ones. I shall say that the sillier of my two halves took the liberty of making a joke that I as

251

a complete entity do not approve of. Martha stares at me like someone still hovering between surprise and indignation.

"That was a rather stupid joke," I say.

She nods but is not mollified. She decides on being moderately offended; that's how it looks, with the aid of a facial expression that comes from the drama school. She crumples up the sketch, which has meanwhile turned up, throws it in the wastebasket, and says: "So much for that."

"Oh, come on, I'm sorry!"

The main thing is a room, what do I care about her reasons? Besides, I would have to be an idiot not to see that my move would be to her advantage too. And never has she let me feel that it would be better without me in the apartment, not by a hint, not by a look.

I bend down over the wastebasket, which is empty except for the crumpled sketch. I retrieve it and smooth it out on the desk, but before looking at it I do something about Martha's mood. I punch her in the arm, light as a feather of course—it's a long time since I have touched her—and I say: "Now there, Martha, remember your good heart."

For another ten seconds she leaves me in suspense; then my worries are over. She sits down at the desk and explains the drawing: my room has a window, a door, sloping walls, and, there it is, a balcony. I shall plant the most beautiful flowers on it, and Bernhard and his grandmother can be my guests as often as they want.

The memory of my only move to date is hideous. It overwhelms me every other day, and, needless to say, it doesn't waste this opportunity either. At the time, people helped me as best they could: *Do you really want to keep this picture? Excuse me—but six chairs? Which rug do you like best—you only need one of them.* Father had been dead for only a week. Martha had been watching me as I answered so she could intervene if necessary; she looked at me like a boxing referee who studies the eyes of a groggy boxer to see whether he's still capable of fighting back. What can there be so terrible about a minor move like the one I am facing?

I ask Martha for the address of the apartment. I promise not to spoil things; I'd just like to see the building from the outside and walk around a bit in that unfamiliar area. She smiles at so much impatience. Then with one hand she tries to leaf through her notebook, but it keeps shutting until I hold down the front cover. She points to the last entry for me to read. The name sounds enticing, Amalien-Strasse. I picture a short, fat street, with shrubs in front of every building.

There is now no further reason for me to remain in Martha's room; probably she doesn't want me there any longer either. I present her with my most charming farewell smile. Amalien-Strasse, how delightful! Once again I reassure her that I won't bother those people; I don't even know their name.

"Kubisch," Martha says, "they're called Kubisch."

"When did you say we'd be coming?" I ask.

She would have to clarify that with Bernhard, Martha says.

This is not the moment to ask her whether she needs any money; I go to my room. The carp has taken up time, or Rahel would have already called us to supper. I sit down by the window and enjoy my new prospects. Only an hour ago nothing had changed. Ought I to phone Gordon Kwart now and tell him he need no longer ask around in the orchestra? The weather is just right for a little foray, a few innocent clouds in the sky, no problem getting to Weissensee before dark. I'll call him next week; the room isn't mine yet.

A knock, Martha again. She offers to go with me to Amalien-Strasse.

"Right now?" I ask.

"When else?"

253

I'm not really all that pleased. I would rather be alone with my expectations. What does she have in mind? We slip out of the apartment. On the landing Martha remarks that there seems to be a smell of fish, and I tell her the story. As we cross the street I catch a glimpse of Hugo and Rahel Lepschitz standing by the open window. I would never have had the courage to suggest that I go with her. What on earth are we going to talk about?

Martha says she knows the way, and we head for the streetcar; Number 74, she says, a bit beyond Anton-Platz. I can feel my embarrassment at having to walk beside her, feel myself becoming stiffer with every step. It is as if I had to pass a tricky test. Yet I can see no prospect of anything ever starting up again between us. I wouldn't agree to it, quite apart from Martha's wishes. Maybe my embarrassment can be explained by the fact that I am still not used to not loving her.

While we wait for the streetcar Martha says: "By the way, I wouldn't have tried so hard to find a room if I weren't convinced that it's better for you to move out."

What she says is no different from what I have been thinking for a long time, yet I have to force myself not to feel offended. She is wearing a necklace for which I committed my first noteworthy theft: it represents the housekeeping money of some half-month or other. I say that my only worry is how her parents will react to my move.

"They'll kick up a fuss," Martha says. "Don't take it too seriously, most of it is put on."

"You know more about it than I do," I say.

On the streetcar we have to stand, there being no two empty seats together. We look out of different windows and don't talk. Although I don't want to hear or say anything, the silence seems oppressive. Maybe she's already regretting her offer to come along; she could easily have found some other opportunity to let me know that she, too, was in favor of my moving out.

When I finally say that, with that hand, she really should be sitting down, she answers that we're almost there. The area, which is not familiar to me, is pleasant; we seem to be going through a little town without any four-story buildings. My father once knew a woman from Weissensee who swore that she would never move to any other part of the city.

We get off, and Martha asks an elderly couple the way to Amalien-Strasse; then she says we should have gone one stop farther. I don't mind walking a bit, although this will prolong the outing. Only Martha knows the way, she takes my arm; I can't believe it. What kind of test has she in mind for me?

We walk and walk; I have ceased to notice the streets. I hold my arm away from me at a stiff angle. I stop trying to figure out what Martha is plotting by taking my arm. There's nothing to figure out, I suddenly realize; she has nothing particular in mind. I alone take everything to heart, I alone suspect something important behind every petty occurrence, I alone perceive every insignificant trifle as mysterious and ambiguous.

We owned neither a wire cutter nor a file.

I couldn't forget the sight of my drunk father: over and over again I was dragging him across the room, over and over again I was laying him down on the bed. In the afternoon, when he left the apartment, his face was gray: that trace of affability of the previous night was long forgotten.

I imagined him soon sitting across from the camp guard and saying: *Once more, from the beginning!* How bored he was by what Heppner was saying, how the sight of him became less and less bearable, how from one interrogation to the next he longed more and more fervently for an end to it all, without admitting it. The only person who could force that end was myself: everything depended on my boldness.

I checked our toolbox. Wasn't there also a chance that one day Father would be grateful to me if I relieved him of the prisoner? After all my hesitation I was now firmly convinced that he and the camp guard could only be saved together. In the toolbox only screwdrivers, two hammers, and a pair of child's pliers, but I was determined not to give up at the first setback.

The biggest hardware store I knew was at the Oranienburg Gate, so that's where I went. The salesman offered me a choice of three files, two of which I bought, the finest and the coarsest. There was no wire cutter. Seeing my disappointment, the young man asked what I needed it for. To cut through a half-inch-thick piece of steel, I said, which made him smile. First of all, the tool I needed was called a bolt cutter, he said, and secondly, bolt cutters were even more impossible to get.

I went from store to store until closing time, without success. I didn't think there was much chance of filing through the handcuffs with the two files. As a last resort I could file through the bedpost, though in that case the camp guard would disappear with manacled hands, and it would be up to him to find a way to get rid of the handcuffs. The object, after all, was not to help him but to get him out of the cottage.

I shuddered at the idea that, while I was engrossed in the filing, one of the kidnappers might suddenly appear at the door. But I could see no point in preparing myself for such a moment: I simply had to prevent it happening. A tightrope walker doesn't prepare himself for a fall. The only precaution I could take was to choose the right moment. Sometime after midnight, it seemed to me, the risk would be lowest. If, nevertheless, I were discovered, I would simply say: "I have only been doing what was necessary." Apologies and pleas for understanding wouldn't get me anywhere.

I took the streetcar home to wait for nightfall. Since then I have often wondered why my choice fell on that particular night rather than on one of the thirteen preceding nights. Merely because of Father's drunkenness? I don't know whether I had a premonition; one does hear that there are people whose sixth sense warns them of a danger threatening someone close to them. Most likely it was coincidence, damn coincidence. I could just as easily have gone to the cottage a day or a week earlier, when there was still time to prevent the disaster.

I phoned Martha and told her that once again we wouldn't be able to meet. She asked what it was this time, and because

I was too worked up to invent a sensible excuse I replied that I would tell her tomorrow. I hung up as quickly as possible and thought how much easier everything would be if I had Martha as an accomplice.

There were four hours to get through. Because I was short of sleep I didn't dare lie down. Although I could have set the alarm, there was a chance Father might come home early and hear it ring. I took a nail, the thickest I could find, and tried out the files on it. A useless test—yet it was reassuring to see how easy it was to cut a notch in the nail and break it. I had never filed metal before; I still have the two halves of the nail.

The filing took care of only a few minutes. I heard someone coming up the stairs and was relieved when the footsteps passed our door. I didn't want to see Father again that evening. So I left the apartment and went out to our forest, to wait there.

Because by nature I tend to hesitate, reasons kept occurring to me, until the very last moment, for calling off the plan. I sat in the train and thought: Some rescue, when the person being rescued curses the rescuer! I waited for the bus and thought: The son a family policeman. I walked about in the forest and thought: After it's done, we will be irrevocably on opposite sides.

But I fought off all scruples by telling myself that one couldn't be forever eliminating the same doubts. Only one of them was new, and it made me even more uncertain: what would happen if I released Heppner—if he went home, and they kidnapped him again?

The bus stopped only for me. As far as the forest, my path was laid out for me; then the loitering in the forest began. If I wanted to keep to my plan of not starting anything before midnight, I still had two hours to kill. First I walked along the well-trodden path; then, when I had become used to the darkness, I struck off through the forest. I had to be careful to avoid the trees; the files were clinking in my pocket, and I couldn't shake off a certain uneasiness, aroused perhaps by the dark forest or by what lay ahead of me.

I walked in a wide curve toward the pond, guided by the North Star. In every clearing I took my bearings. Once at the pond, I found the waiting became easier. Nevertheless, I was torn by contradictory desires: for the time till midnight to pass in a second, and for it to last forever. It was hardly to be supposed that Heppner was still counting on my help; he might well believe that the sum he had offered hadn't been tempting enough. I didn't want to get too close to any of the other cottages, whose whereabouts I more or less knew. It is well known that dogs are quick to bark when a stranger passes in the night.

On a little rise by the shore I found the right place to wait; the pond looked like a dish full of gold and silver coins. I sat down on the dry ground, with a tree to lean against. There were no mosquitoes to annoy me—the wind kept them away—and it was pleasant, warm and cool at the same time. As I sat there, my mind grew easier. I looked out over the water, and one thought after another died away. For three nights suddenly I'd been on the go: the first night for love, the next from restlessness, and now with a job to do.

I wasn't bothered by something tiny crawling along my hand; as long as it didn't hurt me, it was welcome to crawl on. My eyes gradually closed. I still remember that as I dozed I would have liked to put my hands into my warm pockets, and that I thought or dreamed that in such a situation one couldn't possibly put one's hands in one's pockets.

When I woke up, it was not too late. For a few minutes I lived only with my eyes and ears, but there was no sign of any change. Only the reflection of the moon, which had divided the pond into two halves, had now moved slightly toward the shore on the right. I stood up, made sure I had the files, and started on my way. Every step was an effort, and I yearned for some external event to prevent me from carrying out my plan. How thankful I would have been, for instance, if I hadn't found our cottage in the dark.

I arrived at the time I had planned and stepped through the gap in the hedge, which was gradually becoming overgrown. This year Father hadn't asked me yet to cut back the hornbeam hedge, and it would never have occurred to me to do it on my own. Before I dared approach the door, I walked around the cottage: it was a shock to see a light burning behind the sheet draping the window of the prisoner's room.

But at the same instant came new hope: if one of the kidnappers was in the cottage, I had my excuse to disappear. I listened, I pressed my ear to the window, not a sound to be heard. Then from some distance away I threw a few little clods of earth against the windowpane, but nothing moved. No further caution was possible. Either the prison rules required that a light be left on at night or it was sheer forgetfulness.

On my way around the cottage to the door I felt like an adventurer who disregards all warning signs—so little did I trust my own checking and calculating. The wind had grown stronger and was tearing the needles off the trees. If I'd been Father, I would have changed the lock long ago. I opened the door, took a deep breath, as if about to dive, and went in.

I found myself in almost complete darkness. A thin yellow line at the lower edge of the door to the room was the only light. I knew every distance—to the stairs, to the bathroom, to the kitchen, to the cellar door. I didn't need any light. When my supply of air ran out, I was once again assailed by the stench; I had feared it so greatly that it now seemed bearable.

With five medium steps I was in the kitchen, where I switched on the light. They had cleaned up, there were no dirty dishes lying around, there were no food remains—that was progress. On the table a scribbled note: *I gave him the last pill today. Someone should get some more, or perhaps not. I'll be back day after tomorrow. Gordon.*

As I approached the room, I was hoping that the whole business would be taken care of quickly and with not much being said. Today it seems to me that the moments before I opened the door were the final seconds of another life.

The camp guard was not asleep. He had turned his head to one side and was looking toward the door as if expecting nothing good. He had no strength and didn't even raise himself as far as his handcuffs allowed. At the sight of me, a sight that should have pleased him, he showed no sign of relief. His face was covered by a gray beard that grew remarkably straight and looked as if it had been combed; across his right cheek ran a streak, the width of a finger and scabby.

I left the door wide open in order to dilute the smell, which was much stronger in the room than in the hallway. To save myself explanations and to forestall his questions, I immediately took out one of the files. I looked at the handcuffs, my idea being to find their weakest point and begin work on them right away. It was all I could do to hide my outrage at his wound; all doubt had left me as to whether I was doing the right thing. As I came closer, Heppner jerked his head around to the other side to draw my attention to something.

Between the wall and the bed lay Father, strangely contorted. At first I recognized him only by his clothing, since he was lying facedown. I heard an unbearable sound, as if someone were scratching a slate with fingernails: the sound

261

came from the center of my head and escaped through my ears. I knelt beside the body, but for a long time I didn't dare touch it. Perhaps I believed that as long as I didn't turn it over it might be someone else. Yes, that's how it was; I was still kneeling motionless long after I had recognized the scar on his neck.

A few weeks after the funeral, I happened to be sitting one day with Martha in a meadow, crying. To comfort me she said she didn't want to make my pain seem less than it was, but she suspected that I was missing my father beyond anything his presence had ever meant to me. I didn't respond— I hardly spoke at all in those days—but I found that she was right only in a limited sense. Essentially she was wrong. She couldn't seriously have meant that grieving was no more than the sum of various ingredients that can be checked off one by one.

A cowardly thought shot through my mind: Run outside for help. When I jumped up, the prisoner screamed, afraid I'd fling myself on him. He wasn't to blame, he said; it wasn't his fault. After a few steps, I turned back and knelt again beside Father's body. If I had gone for help, it would have been for myself alone, for no one else. I pushed one hand under his head so that, when I turned him over, the floor wouldn't hurt him. Then I saw Father's eyes, looking past me, as if at seeing something that no one would have believed possible.

I found myself unable to lift him; the night before, when he was drunk, I had managed to do so, but suddenly I didn't have the strength. I tugged at him, grabbed him from behind under his arms, and finally raised him enough to drag him along as I walked backward. Perhaps the reason I was so weak was that my exertions were so useless. The prisoner said again that none of it was his fault.

I dragged my father to the armchair by the window and sat him in it. I had to shift him around so he wouldn't tip over; that needed a lot of adjusting. Then I turned to Heppner, about to yell at him, but he nodded quickly, like someone who acknowledges his mistake.

In movies I had been shown often enough how to close the eyes of a dead person: by passing the palm of one's hand down over the face. I could not bring my hand to make such a movement, although the open eyes were terrible. For a while I considered what the next step should be, it being obvious that something had to be done.

Then I remembered why I had come. It would be best to release the camp guard first and then call someone—fire brigade, police, or Red Cross, not the other way around. Just as well that a few minutes either way no longer made any difference. So I stepped up to the bed with my tools.

Heppner had closed his eyes; a few tears ran down his face, toward his ears. His breath smelled so vile that it was even distinguishable from the pervading stench in the room. I had to bend over him to get at the handcuffs, but it was unbearable. So I pulled the bed farther away from the wall and stood behind it to get to work.

The two steel cuffs around his wrists looked indestructible. The chain connecting them was much thinner, so I started filing one of the links. The thought occurred to me that I could take revenge on Kwart and Rotstein by going away and leaving the dead man and the prisoner to them. After a while, I examined the place I'd been filing and found hardly a scratch.

"May I say something?" Heppner asked.

I didn't answer. Picking up the other file, I thought: One more word! The bedpost was thicker than I remembered, although certainly of softer material. First I had another go at the chain.

After a hundred sawing movements, when I was inspecting the result, Heppner said: "He has the key on him."

Since my second attempt was also unsuccessful, I started working on the iron bedpost. I stopped counting and went on filing until my fingers were numb. Then I went over to Father and put my hand in his pocket, first in the wrong one, then in the right one.